SMUGGLER'S COVE

Books by Fern Michaels

Fight or Flight
The Wild Side
On the Line
Fear Thy Neighbor
No Way Out
Fearless
Deep Harbor
Fate & Fortune
Sweet Vengeance
Fancy Dancer
No Safe Secret
About Face
Perfect Match
A Family Affair
Forget Me Not
The Blossom Sisters
Balancing Act
Tuesday's Child
Betrayal
Southern Comfort
To Taste the Wine
Sins of the Flesh
Sins of Omission
Return to Sender
Mr. and Miss Anonymous
Up Close and Personal
Fool Me Once
Picture Perfect
The Future Scrolls
Kentucky Sunrise
Kentucky Heat
Kentucky Rich
Plain Jane
Charming Lily
What You Wish For

The Guest List
Listen to Your Heart
Celebration
Yesterday
Finders Keepers
Annie's Rainbow
Sara's Song
Vegas Sunrise
Vegas Heat
Vegas Rich
Whitefire
Wish List
Dear Emily
Smuggler's Cove

The Lost and Found Novels:
Secrets
Hidden
Liar!
Proof

The Sisterhood Novels:
Rock Bottom
Tick Tock
19 Yellow Moon Road
Bitter Pill
Truth and Justice
Cut and Run
Safe and Sound
Need to Know
Crash and Burn
Point Blank
In Plain Sight
Eyes Only
Kiss and Tell

Books by Fern Michaels (cont.)

Blindsided
Gotcha!
Home Free
Déjà Vu
Cross Roads
Game Over
Deadly Deals
Vanishing Act
Razor Sharp
Under the Radar
Final Justice
Collateral Damage
Fast Track
Hokus Pokus
Hide and Seek
Free Fall
Lethal Justice
Sweet Revenge
The Jury
Vendetta
Payback
Weekend Warriors

The Men of the Sisterhood Novels:
Hot Shot
Truth or Dare
High Stakes
Fast and Loose
Double Down

The Godmothers Series:
Far and Away
Classified
Breaking News

Deadline
Late Edition
Exclusive
The Scoop

E-Book Exclusives:
Desperate Measures
Seasons of Her Life
To Have and To Hold
Serendipity
Captive Innocence
Captive Embraces
Captive Passions
Captive Secrets
Captive Splendors
Cinders to Satin
For All Their Lives
Texas Heat
Texas Rich
Texas Fury
Texas Sunrise

Anthologies:
Lilac Time
Tiny Blessings
In Bloom
Home Sweet Home

Holiday Novels:
Santa's Secret
Santa & Company
Santa Cruise
The Brightest Star
Spirit of the Season
Holly and Ivy

Books by Fern Michaels (cont.)

Wishes for Christmas
Christmas at Timberwoods

Christmas Anthologies:
A Snowy Little Christmas
Coming Home for Christmas
A Season to Celebrate
Mistletoe Magic
Winter Wishes
The Most Wonderful Time
When the Snow Falls
Secret Santa
A Winter Wonderland

I'll Be Home for Christmas
Making Spirits Bright
Holiday Magic
Snow Angels
Silver Bells
Comfort and Joy
Sugar and Spice
Let it Snow
A Gift of Joy
Five Golden Rings
Deck the Halls
Jingle All the Way

Published by Kensington Publishing Corp.

FERN MICHAELS

SMUGGLER'S COVE

KENSINGTON
PUBLISHING CORP.
kensingtonbooks.com

KENSINGTON BOOKS are published by

Kensington Publishing Corp.
900 Third Avenue
New York, NY 10022

Copyright © 2025 by Fern Michaels
Fern Michaels is a registered trademark of KAP5, Inc.

All rights reserved. No part of this book may be reproduced in any form or by any means without the prior written consent of the Publisher, excepting brief quotes used in reviews.

Without limiting the author's and publisher's exclusive rights, any unauthorized use of this publication to train generative artificial intelligence (AI) technologies is expressly prohibited.

This book is a work of fiction. Names, characters, businesses, organizations, places, events, and incidents either are the product of the author's imagination or are used fictitiously. Any resemblance to actual persons, living or dead, events, or locales is entirely coincidental.

All Kensington titles, imprints, and distributed lines are available at special quantity discounts for bulk purchases for sales promotion, premiums, fund-raising, and educational or institutional use. Special book excerpts or customized printings can also be created to fit specific needs. For details, write or phone the office of the Kensington Sales Manager: Kensington Publishing Corp., 900 Third Avenue, New York, NY 10022. Attn. Sales Department. Phone: 1-800-221-2647.

KENSINGTON and the K with book logo Reg US Pat. & TM Off.

Library of Congress Control Number: 2025930732

ISBN: 978-1-4967-4131-8
First Hardcover Edition: September 2025

ISBN: 978-1-4967-4788-4 (e-book)

10 9 8 7 6 5 4 3 2 1

Printed in the United States of America

The authorized representative in the EU for product safety and compliance
is eucomply OU, Parnu mnt 139b-14, Apt 123
Tallinn, Berlin 11317, hello@eucompliancepartner.com

Prologue

Smuggler's Cove

Hidden along the banks of the Navesink River, a hamlet is nestled among the trees and winding waterways. Mansions line the riverbanks that date back to the nineteenth century, when the area served as a summer colony to bankers and industrialists. The legacy of wealth continues into the twenty-first century, with the bedroom community, Smuggler's Cove, boasting the second-highest per capita income in the state of New Jersey. The land, originally purchased from the Lenape Indians, became a safe haven for Dutch traders in the 1600s. One of Henry Hudson's ships, the *Half Moon*, came ashore along the Sandy Hook Bay and discovered it was rich in plants, flowers, and trees. But more importantly, it was refuge from storms blowing in from the Atlantic Ocean, and their competition. They discovered they could navigate the waterways unnoticed and began their expansion.

However, the Dutch traders also faced other dangers. Pirates learned of this new network of goods and began their raids along the shore. The marauders would intentionally cause shipwrecks and then loot the ships once they wrecked ashore. In the late 1600s, a New York ship captain named William Kidd was hired to hunt the pirates and put a stop to the attacks. Ironically, Captain Kidd himself was arrested for piracy in 1699. Legend has it that he, and other pirates, buried their treasure along the Jersey Shore.

PART I

Chapter One

Gwendolyn

Gwendolyn Wainwright was born into a middle-class family in a small town in Connecticut. She was one of the millions to become the baby boomer generation. Her father was a World War II veteran; her mother, a homemaker. Like most American families, at the time people were readjusting to a postwar culture and society. Hollywood was launching movies by the hundreds, with blockbusters like *Around the World in Eighty Days*, *Singin' in the Rain*, and *Ben-Hur*. And television was becoming a common source of entertainment, bringing shows like *I Love Lucy*, *The Honeymooners*, and *Leave It to Beaver* into households across the country, while Frank Sinatra, Sam Cooke, and a gyrating young man from Memphis named Elvis Presley filled the airwaves.

Gwendolyn's childhood was well-adjusted, and everything seemed alright in the world. Even as the '50s turned into the turbulent 1960s, Gwen remained sheltered in the suburbs of Connecticut. Despite protests over U.S. involvement in Vietnam, civil rights, and women's rights going on in the country, she preferred not to engage in politics. Instead, she was interested in books—literary fiction and poetry.

In 1968, Gwendolyn turned eighteen years old and headed off to college to major in English at Western Connecticut State University. It was far enough away from home for her to feel independent, but close enough to get back in under two hours. The school was small enough so she wouldn't get lost in a huge student body, but large enough to feel that she really left home and was out of high school.

Gwen was good-natured, and a good student. The combination gave her a measure of popularity, and she would often take day trips into New York City with some of her female classmates. Regardless of what the plans for the day entailed, Gwen would insist they stop at Rizzoli Bookstore on Fifth Avenue.

After several treks into the posh bookstore, she began to imagine herself working under the chandeliers among the beautifully illustrated books and gliding across the marble floors as she ran her hand along the polished oak paneling, or gazing down from the second-floor balcony that flanked the sides of the store, while customers perused the vast collection of titles.

Gwen had no solid plans for what she would do after she graduated. She thought maybe she'd pursue a career in publishing, but mainly she assumed her life would go on as most others: she would meet someone, get married, have a kid, and then figure it out. Although many of her contemporaries had bigger visions for themselves, Gwen willingly went with the flow. There was enough turmoil brewing around the world. She didn't need to feed her head with more by worrying about the future.

1972

In a snap of a finger, before she knew it, four years were behind her, and she was about to graduate. But there was no future husband in sight. Not yet. She weighed her options. She could move back in with her parents. And do what? No. Gwen knew there was more, and like many young women of the early 1970s, she wanted to see the world. Experience life. And what better place than New York City? It wasn't the brightest time for the Big Apple. Cities were in decline, and New York was not immune. But Gwen couldn't let that deter her. Things would *have* to improve at some point. Didn't they always?

Two months before graduation, Gwen made a list of employment agencies in Manhattan and lined up as many appointments she could cover in one day. She was determined to accomplish her goal of finding a job and a place to live. She wasn't sure which would be more difficult, but she wasn't going to stop. It took several interviews until she finally landed a job as a receptionist at a small bank near Wall Street. It was a few miles from Rizzoli, and a twenty-minute subway ride could get her there. In the meantime, she would gain some experience and eventually find an entry-level job in the book business.

But first she had to find a place to live. Her new job started in six weeks, after the current receptionist was due to retire.

She combed *Backstage* newspaper every week. She wasn't interested in show business, but the classified section was a good place to look for roommates. She found a three-month sublet by a dancer who was going on tour. It was temporary, but it bought her a little time, and she could live there while she looked for something permanent. She had enough money to cover the rent, pizza, and Chinese takeout until she started her job. If she got hungry, she could hop on a train and visit her parents before they turned her bedroom into a home gym.

Gwen was new to the city, single, and scraping by with her receptionist position. But there she was. Living in New York. With a grown-up job.

She was very efficient and was constantly asking if there was something she could do for the loan managers. She wasn't deliberately sucking up. She was bored and she knew she had to make the most of her situation. She could learn a new skill.

One afternoon, another young woman followed her into the women's bathroom. She blocked the door, cornered Gwen, and sneered at her. "You're making us look bad!"

"I disagree," Gwen said as she turned to look at herself in the mirror, with the woman's reflection staring back at her. "I'm making myself look good."

Unruffled, Gwen pulled out two paper towels, dried her hands, and then turned around. She spoke calmly. "It's a man's world out there, regardless of how many bras we burned. Women must work harder to make the same amount of money, so might as well start now." She shrugged, turned, walked past the woman, and out the door.

The young woman followed Gwen, and gently touched her arm. "Want to have lunch?" The woman's name was Sandra, and the two became good friends. Gwen had a maturity about her approach to life, where Sandra easily let her emotions hang on her sleeve. They made a good pair.

One of Sandra's roommates was getting married in September, and they needed a replacement if they hoped to keep splitting the 1600-dollars-a-month rent four ways. Again, timing was on Gwen's side, and she moved from the sublet to her new, barely larger space.

It was an old prewar building with high ceilings. The four roommates occupied one of the few three-bedroom, two-bathroom apartments around. Sandra had one bedroom; Gwen had another. Fran and Paul inhabited the third bedroom with the adjoining bathroom.

The apartment had been in Paul's family for two generations; therefore, he was the happy recipient of a rent-controlled dwelling. As long as a family member occupied the apartment, the landlord was limited as to the amount of rent he could charge and how much he could increase it. If Paul moved out, the rent could go up to three thousand a month.

Gwen considered herself lucky. She shared a bathroom, and all four had access to the kitchen. The apartment was conveniently located in Chelsea, a few blocks from the subway.

Within a couple of years, Gwen was promoted to a position assisting one of the managers. A woman. It was very unusual at the time for there to be a female manager, but again Gwen was lucky, because the manager took a liking to Gwen and became her mentor.

1974

One afternoon, her boss approached her. There was an event later that night for one of the symphony orchestras where one of the bank's directors sat on the board. Her boss explained that her husband could not attend the gala and asked if Gwen would like to be her "plus-one." It was an opportunity Gwen could not resist.

Gwen raced home at five p.m. to get ready for the evening. On her way, she stopped at a vintage clothing shop in Greenwich Village. It was known for carrying previously owned designer clothes. The rich did not typically wear the same thing twice, especially to a gala, and often donated the clothes after just one wear. Gwen found a little black dress by Halston, a pair of elbow-length gloves, and several strings of imitation pearls.

With her outfit secured, she hopped onto the subway and made her way to her apartment building. She didn't have time to wait for the old, clunky elevator, so she took the stairs to the fifth floor. She also didn't have time to shower and wash her hair, so she gave herself a good wipe down, freshened her makeup, pulled her shoulder-length dark blond hair into a chignon, tossed several long strings of fake pearls around her neck, and donned a pair of clip-on earrings. She easily looked the part of a young socialite blending in at the spectacular Cipriani Wall Street event. For that, she was going to splurge on a taxi.

Little did Gwen know that evening would change her life. It was at the gala that she met Jackson Taylor, and her life took a turn for the posh and privileged. Jackson was an up-and-coming hedge fund manager, a scrappy young man, determined to be rich. Wealthy. Powerful. He had jumped into the growing and mystifying segment of the "gunslinging" part of the market, where it was totally possible for someone who came from nothing to become something, especially on Wall Street. Your lineage wasn't relevant, even though Jackson had a well-crafted revisionist history of himself; it was far more important to have a talent and a thirst for making money—and Jackson had both in abundance.

While Gwen stood alone with a glass of champagne in her hand, a rambunctious young man bumped into her, causing her to spill her bubbly. He apologized profusely and begged her to give him the opportunity to make it up to her with dinner. Gwen thought he was cocky by assuming she was available and could be interested. "That's rather presumptuous of you, isn't it?"

Her confidence was startling, which piqued Jackson's interest. He smiled and made a slight bow. "Pardon my insolence."

"Apology accepted." She handed her glass to him as she dabbed the wet champagne from her breast. "And only if you get me a refill. It's the least you can do." Gwen may have been somewhat of a country girl, but she was learning the ropes. Quickly. It was the only way to survive in the city.

Jackson snapped his fingers at a waiter and held up the empty glass. In less than a minute, Gwen's champagne was reinstated. She could get used to that kind of service.

Jackson introduced himself and turned up the charm, setting his sights on winning over this gorgeous woman. He had his life planned. His sights were set on climbing his way up. He was on a lightning-speed track, and this new acquaintance could fit in. She had "the look": tall, thin, willowy, and all-American. The girl young men want to marry. He was sold on the idea that she would be good for his image.

Jackson pursued and wooed Gwen, something Gwen became accustomed to. Her backup plan for marriage, children, and whatever, was beginning to unfold.

In just over a year, they were married, and Gwen moved into his Upper East Side apartment. It was a luxe lifestyle. Jackson was making a lot of money—too much for a twenty-six-year-old. But he was determined and seemed invincible. Even the downturn of the market in the mid-1970s didn't stop Jackson from boosting his finances and his social status. Where there's a will, there's a way. There was no stopping him. He was intent on being successful, even if it meant coloring outside the lines.

The stock market continued to be on rocky ground when Jackson decided it was time to start his own financial advisory firm. He partnered with two other individuals who shared Jackson's appetite for wealth.

Gwen quit her job a year after they were married, and she immersed herself in the spoils of her husband's success and demands. That was when Jackson informed her it was time to have a baby. He was twenty-eight. She was twenty-six. He reminded her about the ticking of her biological clock and told her he wanted two children, so they should start now. He believed a family would give him his full credentials as an upwardly mobile, solid citizen.

It wasn't until Jackson introduced the idea of becoming pregnant that Gwen questioned if she wanted to be a mother. It required a level of responsibility that she wasn't sure she was prepared for. When she approached Jackson with her concerns, he admonished her. He ticked off all the reasons why she shouldn't complain. He provided her with everything she wanted, underscoring that it was due to his hard work and success. The least she could do was bear his children. Case closed.

1976

Madison Taylor was born in an exclusive pediatric suite at New York Hospital, a place where the rich and famous completed the last few hours of pregnancy. Heaven forbid someone would see you or hear you go through labor, let alone without your hair and makeup done professionally. The suite consisted of a large bedroom, a sitting room, and an adjoining sleeping area should a family member choose to stay overnight. A private nurse was always within reach, as well as a private catering menu. Gwen demanded only the best if she was required to bear her children.

Just after Madison turned one, Jackson informed Gwen that it was time to have their second child. Gwen had barely bounced back from pregnancy and the demands of having a newborn, but when Jackson wanted something, he got it. Soon she was pregnant with baby number two, and their two-bedroom apartment wasn't large enough or grand enough for Jackson and his growing family. As soon as Lincoln entered the world, Jackson investigated available co-ops in Sutton Place.

It was one of the oldest, richest residential areas of Manhattan, and you had to be vetted to be "allowed" to live there. The stodgy old-money residents were not only leery of the nouveau riche, but they were also interested in one's pedigree. Unlike condominiums, where an association's main purpose is to maintain the exterior of the property, co-ops had a board that made all the decisions, including how one could renovate their interior, and exactly who could or could not move in. It was a type of discrimination that defied the law.

Jackson knew these people were elitists, and he was intent on having them believe he was one of them. When he met with the co-op board, he wore a simple Cartier tank watch, French cuffs with unobtrusive cufflinks, and his Brooks Brothers suit and vest. He dared not show up in something by Gucci or Versace. Gwen donned a Halston dress, her hair in a chignon, with simple clip-on earrings. If nothing else, they looked the part.

During the interview/interrogation, Jackson implied that he was an ancestor to the one-year, 197-day serving president, Zachary Taylor. He cited a little-known fact that President Taylor had terrible handwriting that made it difficult to read. He also noted that his daughter's name was Madison, and his son was Lincoln, both named after presidents. That much was true.

The co-op board believed they had a proper couple with ancestry at hand and agreed to allow Jackson and Gwendolyn Taylor to purchase a two-story co-op on Sutton Place. They also couldn't afford to have empty real estate with the climbing costs of maintenance. The housing market in New York was still reeling from the economic fluctuations, and it was imperative to keep all the apartments occupied.

Within a few months, Jackson, Gwen, Madison, and Lincoln moved into a building of the privileged and notable. Jackson could boast that Henry Kissinger was his neighbor.

With a toddler and an infant, they hired an au pair from

Belgium, who lived in the maid's quarters on the premises. She eventually became one of Jackson's "hobbies" while Gwen dealt with her baby weight and hormonal mood swings. Postpartum depression was something people did not discuss, and at the urging of her physician, Gwen insisted they hire a second nanny, so the children would have one each. The young au pair didn't seem to have the wherewithal to handle two children, and neither did Gwen at the time. Neither could barely handle one. This time, Gwen conducted the interviews and hired a middle-aged German woman. Under no uncertain terms was she going to provide more entertainment for her husband.

1976–1996

As the economy slowed even further, Jackson and his partners became desperate to continue their cash flow. They started trading in junk bonds and cleaning out many retirement accounts of unsuspecting investors. They were laundering money and dabbling in Ponzi schemes and offshore accounts. They rode the '80s like Al Unser at the Indy 500.

It went on for two decades until 1996, when the intercom house phone rang. It was Phoebe, their long-time housekeeper, calling from the main living area. Her voice was shaking. She began to explain that men from the U.S. Marshal's office were at the door, and they had a warrant. Gwen didn't know why, but she knew it couldn't be good.

Ten years earlier, the Ivan Boesky scandal had rocked Wall Street. It was widely known that the government was cracking down on insider trading and other shenanigans in the financial arena, but Gwen made a conscious effort to ignore it. And then came the great reckoning.

"Keep them occupied downstairs. Show them all the cupboards. Whatever. Just keep them busy," she whispered into the phone. Gwen frantically opened the safe where she kept her jewelry and stashed as much of it as she could into her undergarments. She pulled out a wad of cash and stuck it into her bra. She smirked, remembering the time when bras were incendiary items. She shoved diamond earrings into her socks and pulled on a pair of riding boots. Then she began to stuff a few items of clothing in an overnight bag. The Louis Vuitton. She stopped abruptly as an officer climbed the stairs to the master suite. He gently knocked on the doorjamb. "I'm sorry, Mrs. Taylor, but you cannot take anything with you."

Gwen was almost paralyzed. "But I am going to need clothes."

The officer motioned for her to open the bag, where he thoroughly searched.

"What are you looking for?" she asked.

No answer.

"Can you please tell me what it is going on?" Her hands were shaking, and she was close to weeping.

The officer showed her a copy of the warrant that allowed them to seize anything that could be perceived as of value.

Over the years, she'd grown to appreciate the lap of luxury. Her marriage left a lot to be desired, but shopping, high tea, spa treatments, and lavish vacations more than made up for Jackson and his "hobbies," which were mostly young women, cocaine, and alcohol. She was also aware that he would often take a new street drug called Ecstasy. He never did it at home, but one evening, she overheard him on the phone asking the person on the line if he could hook him up with some "X." After a few subtle inquiries among friends, she learned it was supposed to make you high and increase sexual pleasure. She didn't know which came first, the floozies or the drugs. In either case, they were turning Jackson into an arrogant, nasty individual.

Throughout their financial climb, she never asked where

the money came from. Her instincts told her to look the other way; now it was blowing up in her face.

"Jewelry?" the marshal asked patiently.

Jogged from her thoughts, Gwen opened the safe again. She removed all of Jackson's watches, which ran the gambit of luxury brands, including Breitling, Montblanc, Patek Philippe, and Rolex. They had to be worth a few hundred thousand dollars in total, and Gwen had no trouble handing them over to the marshal. If her life was going to be disrupted, she wasn't going to leave anything behind. At least nothing of value to her.

"Give me a moment." Gwen rifled through the rest of the contents of the safe and handed over three diamond pinky rings and a dozen sets of gold cufflinks. She also gave the officer a wad of cash that she couldn't fit into her waistband. Then she went into Jackson's dressing room and grabbed one of Jackson's Tumi travel bags. "You can put everything in here." She passed it to the marshal.

The officer seemed surprised at how accommodating the woman was, until he saw the fire in her eyes.

"May I call my children?" she asked politely.

"Yes." He cleared his throat. "Mrs. Taylor, you should know that your husband has been placed under arrest."

"Well, zip-a-dee-do-da," she huffed, zipped her bag, and headed downstairs. "Tell him I don't have bail money," she called over her shoulder. She apologized to her housekeeper and walked out the door. Her mind was racing as she rode the elevator to the lobby. *Were they going to come after her next? Where could she go? Could she leave the country?* She quickly added up the value of the jewelry she had stashed under her clothes and in her boots. It had to be close to a quarter million dollars. Plus, the wad of bills. She hadn't counted it, but she knew Jackson kept twenty or thirty thousand dollars within reach. She figured she'd swiped at least ten of it.

When the elevator doors opened, she took a deep breath and held her head high. People had already gathered in front of the door attendant, whispering and speculating about the fuss. It wouldn't take long for them to learn that one of the posh residences was soon to become the property of the State of New York.

The door attendant wiggled past the onlookers and gave Gwen a perplexed look as he hailed a cab for her. He was aware of the U.S. Marshal's presence in the building, and that they were in the Taylor's residence, but he dared not to ask why. She nodded at the chattering gawkers and left her lavish co-op on Sutton Place for the last time.

When the yellow cab pulled up, she didn't wait for the doorman to open the taxi door for her, as he was normally obliged to do. Instead, she yanked it open and tossed her small travel bag into the back seat. She turned to the man, whose mouth was agape. " 'Bye, Reggie. It's been real." He continued to stare as the car drove away.

Gwen kept looking in the side mirror, expecting a police car would be following them. But it was traffic as usual, with no one bearing down on her. The driver turned left onto Fifth Avenue, and Gwen made her final pass at the Rizzoli Bookstore. She had come full circle and realized it had been a dead end.

Chapter Two

Jackson

Jackson Taylor was born two years after his father came back from World War II. He was too young to notice his father's sullen moods, but by the time Jackson was three, he became aware of the loud arguments, the tears, and the slamming doors. It was a regular occurrence. For Jackson, he had no way of knowing it wasn't normal. A year later, when his younger brother Kirby was born, the noise got louder, the tears more like a river, and the slamming turned into holes being punched in the walls. It took a few more years before Mrs. Rita Taylor packed her bags and left town.

Six-year-old Jackson sat near the window on the bus. His mother was next to him, with his two-year-old brother on her lap. He watched the scenery change from paved sidewalks to trees and more trees. The bus made occasional stops, and travelers got off and on. He didn't know how long they had been on the bus, but he knew he had to go to the bathroom. He squirmed in his seat as his mother patted his hand and asked him to hold it for just a little longer. She got up from where she was sitting, with her infant in her arms, and approached the driver. "Will we be stopping at a restroom area soon? My son needs to use the facilities."

The driver pulled over to the side of the road. "This is the closest thing." He pointed to a mound of brush along the highway.

Rita blinked in horror. "But I can't let him do that."

"Sorry, but there isn't a gas station for another half hour or so."

Rita was stunned and embarrassed. She looked around at the rest of the passengers. There were only two left. An older woman got up from her seat and offered, "Here. I'll hold onto the little one while you take the boy outside." Rita had to put her trust in a total stranger. She was grateful that Kirby was a happy toddler, and that people were kind.

"Thank you so much." She gave Kirby's hand to the compassionate lady and motioned for Jackson to come with her. The two stepped off the bus, and Rita brought Jackson to the other side of the bush for some scant privacy.

Jackson began to whine. "But I don't want to go pee-pee here!"

"Sweetheart, it's the only place you can go now." But before Jackson could complete the process, he wet his pants and began to wail.

"Jackson, honey. Please. Mommy will get you a dry pair of pants." She waved toward the driver. "Can you please bring my suitcase out here?"

The driver was willing to oblige. It was clear this wasn't his first kid-who-peed-his-pants rodeo, and he brought the luggage to the woman who was standing behind a bush with her distressed child. Rita was mortified. She really hadn't planned her escape very well, but at the time, she didn't think there were any other options. Get out or get punched. She thanked the driver profusely, opened the valise, and pulled out a fresh pair of underwear and pants for Jackson. A few minutes later, they were back on the bus. Kirby was back on his mother's lap, and they were on their way.

Jackson was still red-faced from the embarrassment, and suspected everyone knew what had happened. That was one memory that stayed with him for the rest of his life.

About half an hour later, the bus pulled in front of a country store. Behind it were fields of corn. The driver opened the door and addressed the disquieted family: "Here you go." He got up from his seat and helped Rita with her suitcase and carry-on. "Good luck to you, ma'am." The driver had been around enough people to know when someone was not going on a fun family vacation.

A lady who resembled Rita hurried toward them. "Rita! Are you okay?" she said in huffs.

"Better now." Rita turned to her sister, Betty, and gave her a quick hug. Then she placed her hands on her son's shoulders. "Betty, you remember Jackson. And this here is Kirby."

"Jackson, you have gotten so tall since the last time I saw you!" Considering she hadn't seen her nephew since he was three, it wasn't an exaggeration.

Jackson didn't know what to make of this situation. One thing was for certain, it would be an exceptionally long walk home.

The sprawling fields and almost deserted highway were vastly different from the concrete and rows of houses he was used to. His mother let him play in their backyard, which was surrounded by a chain-link fence. That was all he knew of the outdoors. This place was very different.

Aunt Betty lifted the suitcase, took Jackson's hand, and walked them to her shiny green Oldsmobile sedan. Jackson was astute enough to realize it was much nicer than the car they had at home. Jackson climbed into the back seat with

Kirby, his mother in front with Aunt Betty. They drove past more fields and groves of trees for several minutes until they came upon a long gravel driveway. Jackson had his face pressed to the window. "Where are we?" he said, half in awe and half in doubt.

"We're at my house," Aunt Betty said, as she glanced into the rearview mirror.

"Is that a cow?" Jackson asked, recalling a picture of one in a book.

"It sure is," Betty replied. "We live on a farm."

"With chickens?" Jackson became more interested.

"Yes, chickens. We even have a small pond in the back where you can fish."

"Fish?" Jackson asked.

"Yes, fish. Has your father ever taken you fishing?" Betty asked innocently.

Jackson shook his head, then said, "No." His father barely did anything with him. His father would go to work in the morning and come home smelling stinky just before dinner. Jackson didn't know what the odor was until he heard his mother complain that he "stunk of booze." Jackson didn't know what booze was, but he knew it made his father mean, and his mother sad.

Aunt Betty seemed like a nice lady. She showed Jackson to a room down the hall. "This is where you and Kirby will be staying. Your mom will be right across the way."

Jackson looked around the sparse room. There was a trundle bed, a small dresser, and a rocking chair. Betty showed Jackson how the bed worked. "You pull the bottom out, and now you have two beds. One for you, and one for your brother."

Rita's room had a little more flair with twin beds, a double dresser, an armoire, and a vanity. "This is the official guest room," Betty said as she switched on the overhead light.

"Thank you, Betty. You are a life saver." Rita wasn't far from wrong.

"Uncle George and I stay upstairs, so you will have some privacy," Betty announced. "I'll let you freshen up before dinner. Uncle George should be back soon."

"Aunt Betty?" Jackson got her attention. "What kind of farm is this?"

"Chickens and corn." She smiled. "You can help Uncle George get some fresh eggs for breakfast. How does that sound?"

Jackson shrugged. He had no idea how to get eggs from a chicken.

Rita took a deep breath and commented, "Something smells delicious."

"It's freshly baked chicken pot pie. It has become one of my favorites. I finally figured out how to make a flaky crust." Betty chuckled.

Jackson was beginning to think that everything was going to be okay.

Rita and Betty were raised in Paterson, New Jersey. Rita met Jackson's father after the war. Enlistees were praised and lauded as they arrived back in the States. She saw him celebrating in a pub with some of his fellow military comrades. He was charming and nice-looking. And he was in uniform.

Within three months, he was discharged and got a job working for the railroad. After a year of dating, he decided it was time he took a wife, and time for Rita to marry. And so, they did. Two years later their first child, Jackson, Jr., was born.

Rita had no idea the man had a temper. A bad one. Even though they dated for a year, it was casual. No long vacations or weekends. If it were Saturday night, Rita and Jackson would go to a dance or a movie. There were no deep conversations. Ever. In retrospect, they barely knew each other before they got married.

It didn't take long for the Mr. Hyde version of the charming Jackson Taylor to show his hideous side after consuming copious amounts of liquor. There was also a problem of some backroom gambling at the pub. Money was a constant issue.

Known as "J.T." to his friends, Jackson Taylor was digging himself deeper into a hole that seemed almost impossible to get out of. You didn't have to be a psychic to see that the future was not looking good for any of them.

Now Rita was on the lam with her two boys. She knew she was taking a substantial risk leaving her husband and running away, but her safety and the safety of her children was paramount.

By the second day, the family began to settle in at the farm. There was plenty of outdoor space for Jackson to kick a ball around, and Uncle George put together a makeshift fence so the kids wouldn't wander off.

There had been no communication between J.T. and Rita. He hadn't called looking for her, and she didn't want him to know where she was. It wasn't until noon on the third day when the heavy black phone in the dining area rang. It was the police. They were looking for Mrs. Jackson Taylor. The man explained they got Betty's name from one of Rita's neighbors, Lydia Foster. Betty handed the phone to her sister.

"Mrs. Taylor, I'm afraid I have some bad news. Your husband was in a wreck last night, more like the wee hours of the morning. He is in the hospital."

Rita began to shake. "What happened?"

Betty scurried to her side.

"He was intoxicated and slammed into a bulkhead."

Rita didn't know what to say or do. "How is he?" creaked out of her mouth.

"He's unconscious. From what we can tell, he was pitched from his seat, smashed into the windshield, and then got thrown from the car after it hit the concrete. He's still unconscious. Lucky to be alive."

Horrifying images raced through her mind. *What if he is incapacitated indefinitely? Would she, could she care for him?*

"Which hospital is he in?" she asked.

"St. Joseph's in Paterson," the officer replied.

"I'm in Barnegat. I don't know how I am going to get up there." She looked at Betty.

"I'll give you the phone number of the hospital. You can try to call them in a few hours," the officer said. "Maybe there will be a change in his condition."

Rita's hands trembled as she scratched out the numbers. Again, her mind was racing. *How would she get there? What about the children?* She thanked the officer and ended the call.

"What happened?" Betty gasped.

"J.T. was in an accident. He was drunk and ran off the road. Into some kind of concrete thing."

"How is he?"

"Unconscious," Rita replied. "Betty, I don't know what to do." She began to weep.

"If he's unconscious, there is nothing you *can* do." Betty looked out the kitchen window.

Rita dried her eyes. "This might put the kids in a tizzy. They're just beginning to get used to being in the country."

Betty put a kettle on the stove. "Come. Sit down. Let's talk this through."

Betty convinced Rita to wait a few hours. Then she could call the hospital and see what the prognosis was.

"They're going to think I am a terrible wife if I don't go right away," Rita said, sniffling.

Betty let out a raspberry. "You are worried what total

strangers will think of you when they don't even know what you've been through?" The kettle began to whistle. Betty began to fix tea.

"I often wondered why the Brits make tea during a crisis," Rita mused.

"Gives them something to do." Betty chuckled. "Come on, sis. This is clearly a sign from above. Imagine if you were home? The police coming to your door in the middle of the night? You missed out on a ruckus."

"What am I going to tell Jackson? And Kirby?" Rita asked, as she watched her son enjoy the sunshine.

"Don't tell them anything until you have some real information." Betty brought the teacups to the table. "If you want, I will drive you to Paterson."

"I can't ask you to do that," Rita protested.

"You didn't ask me. I am offering. Now drink your tea."

Even before the news of the accident, Rita had no plan of action. She was using the time as a vacation from reality. She hoped and prayed an idea or a solution would come to her. Going back to that environment was not an option. Even if the man was unconscious. It was no atmosphere to raise children. Such a quandary. If her husband survived but was in a vegetative state, would that be better than if he were in a raging alcoholic state? Once again, she thought of the children. It would be horrible for them in either case.

George came in for lunch. "Why the long faces, ladies?"

Betty explained the situation to him.

"We can drive you up there, Rita. If that's what you want to do." He was as confounded as Rita.

"I say we wait." Betty folded her arms. She was always the more willful of the two sisters.

Jackson bounced into the kitchen with Kirby in tow. "Hey, Uncle George."

"Hey yourself, kiddo." Uncle George tussled Jackson's hair.

"Ready for some lunch?" Betty asked, before any further conversation about the accident occurred.

"Grilled cheese, please?" George asked.

"With bacon." Betty knew it was George's favorite. "What about you, Jackson? Kirby?"

Jackson said, "Yes, please." Kirby bobbed his head up and down enthusiastically. "Yes, please," he parroted his brother. Jackson had heard them whispering when he walked into the kitchen. He wondered what was going on. He looked at his mother. He could tell she had been crying. The wadded-up tissue in her clenched fist was a big hint. But the quietness. There was no conversation, unlike all the other meals over the past two and a half days. He wondered if he had done something wrong. But if he had, would Aunt Betty offer him bacon?

Jackson's thoughts were interrupted by the ringing on the telephone. Everyone jumped. Rita began to shake. George got up and picked up the receiver.

"Hel-lo," George said in a pleasant tone. He looked over at Rita. "One moment." He put his hand over the mouthpiece and then looked toward Jackson and Kirby.

Rita just didn't bother shooing them out of earshot. The kids were going to find out eventually. She scraped the chair away from the table and walked over to where George was holding the phone.

Rita took the receiver from him. "Hello. This is Mrs. Taylor." She listened. "I see. Yes. Yes, that will be fine." She listened again. "Thank you." She turned to the curious eyes that were carefully watching her. "No change, but they are moving him to a special unit."

"Who's moving, mother?" Jackson asked.

Rita crouched in front of her son. "It's Daddy. He was in an accident. He's in the hospital."

"Oh." Jackson's response was succinct.

Kirby wanted to know what an "axel-dent" was.

Rita looked at Betty and George. *Should she tell them more?*

"It's called an accident," she corrected him. "It's when someone gets hurt."

"Daddy is hurt?" Kirby asked.

"Yes. They think he might be in the hospital for a while. They are going to call again later." Rita spoke slowly, carefully, looking for any signs of distress from her sons.

"Okay," Jackson replied, and finished his grilled cheese and bacon sandwich. He couldn't remember when he ever tasted something so delicious. Kirby pulled the cheese from the sandwich in ignorant bliss. After lunch, they went back outside to play while the adults pondered what might happen next.

By dinnertime, there was still no news as they sat down for meatloaf and mashed potatoes. Once they finished dinner and brought their plates to the sink, Rita asked if the children could watch a little television as a diversion. A favorite at the time was *The Jackie Gleason Show* with musical and comedy skits. The kids were enthralled by the magic of television and didn't seem to care what was on. Even though they had a small TV at home, they were rarely allowed to watch it.

After an hour of entertainment and distraction, Jackson and Kirby were tucked in their beds, with Kirby on the lower part of the trundle. George, Rita, and Betty sat in the living room when the phone stirred everyone's nerves again. George answered. He nodded to Rita. "Yes, one moment, please."

Rita put the phone to her ear, not knowing what news she was hoping to hear. "This is Mrs. Taylor." She listened. This time, whatever she was being told took a little longer. "Yes, I understand. Just give me a moment." She put her hand over the receiver. "They said I should go up there. Paperwork, and such."

George immediately offered to drive her. "We can leave first thing in the morning. Should take about two hours."

Rita returned her attention to the caller. "Yes, I can be there by eleven." She reached for the pad and pencil that were sitting on the table where the phone was perched. She began to write something down. "Yes. Thank you." She hung up and read the address to George and Betty. "They're taking him to the VA hospital tomorrow afternoon, but I have to bring his discharge papers before they can transfer him."

"Did they give you any indication of his condition? Has anything changed?" Betty asked.

Rita was staring off into the distance. "Sorry, what did you say?"

"How is he doing?"

"Not well. That's why they are transferring him. They don't have the capabilities for someone who is in a coma."

"A coma?" Betty let out a long puff of air.

"Well, that's what the doctor alluded to. He needs to be accurately diagnosed." Tears dripped down her face. "I don't know if I can handle any of this."

"I have an idea. Why don't you let Jackson and Kirby stay here until you can sort things out? You can't be toting two little boys around."

"I can't ask you to do that," Rita said.

"May I remind you again? You didn't ask. I offered."

"I think I should bring Jackson with me. He'll want to see his father."

"I wouldn't be so sure about that," George cut in. "He didn't seem too upset by the news."

Rita hung her head. "There's been too much drama in our lives. Jackson's father can be extremely aggressive."

"Has he ever struck the children? Or you?" Betty asked in dread.

"No. No. That's why I had to leave. It was just a matter of

time." Rita sat down at the kitchen table. "I figured if I left and took the children, he'd either decide to be less of a bully, or divorce me. But things could not stay the way they were."

George sat across from his sister-in-law. "People don't really change. You didn't know a whole lot about him before you married him. Don't get me wrong. I'm not trying to make you feel bad. A lot of people did the same thing. If you weren't married before the war, then time was a-wastin', and you had to beat feet and get to it." He reached over to Betty and patted her hand. "We were lucky. We grew up together. All three of us, but Betty was the fortunate one, and she got to marry *me*." He chuckled.

"You're the lucky one, buster." Betty gave him an elbow.

Rita took a deep breath. "This is what I am going to do: George, you will drive me and Jackson to the hospital. Kirby will stay here with Betty. George, I don't know what condition our car is in. Would you mind phoning the police station for me? If it's okay to be on the road, I'll use it for transportation."

George picked up the phone and asked the operator to put him through to the Paterson Police Department. Several minutes later, he had the answer. The windshield needed to be replaced, and the front-end bumper and fender took a beating. "You can pick it up at the impound lot. They want a hundred-dollar bond to secure fines against J.T. He's going to have to go to court at some point. Unless he can't. But one foot in front of the other."

"I can't thank you both enough. I invaded your privacy and brought a whole lot of commotion with me."

"Now, you hush." Betty frowned. "We're family, and we will figure this out like family." She put her arm around her sister. "I'll fix us a cup of tea." Then the two women burst out laughing.

"What's so funny?" George asked.

"Tea."

George shrugged. Understanding women required a skill he did not possess.

The next morning, Rita told Jackson they were going to visit his father, and Kirby would be staying with Aunt Betty and Uncle George. Jackson was puzzled. He didn't know what it meant to be in the hospital, but he guessed he was going to find out. And why wasn't his mother bringing Kirby with them? She gave him a vague explanation.

"Your father was in an accident, and we must visit him. Children Kirby's age aren't allowed, so he's going to stay here until we get back." She didn't say how long it would be, because she really had no idea. She simply hoped it wouldn't be indefinite.

George carried Rita's suitcase to the car, and then Rita positioned Jackson in the back seat. Betty handed Rita a basket of sandwiches and waved them off.

It was eerily quiet the first half hour of their drive. Finally, Uncle George broke the silence.

"Jackson, when we get back, I'm going to take you fishing like I promised."

"Okay," was his response. Nothing more. His world had been turned upside down. One day they were home; the next, they were on a bus and ended up at his aunt and uncle's house. A couple days later, his uncle was driving him and his mother to a hospital to see his father. Why hadn't his father come along with them in the first place? His emotions were unidentifiable. He wasn't unhappy that his father hadn't gone with them. Was that wrong? Now they were going to visit him, and he felt a little uneasy. Was that wrong, too? He didn't want to burden his fretting mother with questions, so he remained silent until she offered him a sandwich. He took it, thanked her, and went back to his pensive mood.

He could tell they were getting close by the appearance of a few more cars on the road, buildings rising in the distance, and trees becoming fewer and more scattered.

Uncle George pulled in front of a police station, and Jackson asked, "Are we there?" It was the first he had spoken since his sandwich.

"Not yet, honey. Mommy must get our car first."

"Where is it?" Jackson asked.

"I am going to find out. I'll be right back."

George offered to go in. "Let me handle this. You wait here."

Before Rita could protest, George got out of the car and up the short stone steps. Several minutes later, he reappeared, holding up a set of keys.

Rita let the oxygen out of her lungs. "What about the bond?" she asked.

"Let's not worry about that now. Let's get the car. It's just around the corner," George explained, and drove them to the impound.

Once again George left Rita and Jackson in his car until he could square things with the guard and reclaim the vehicle. Rita looked on as the guard pointed to their mangled auto. She gasped when she saw the front end and the shattered windshield. She got out of the vehicle, and her hands flew up to her face.

"Oh, George. I can't drive this thing."

"You'll take my car, and I'll find someone who can fix this. I'm sure the guard can recommend a place."

Tears started rolling down her face for the third time in the past twenty-four hours. *Why was this happening to her? She should have stayed at her sister's. Now Jackson will see the smashup his father caused.*

"Mommy? Why does the car look like that?"

"Oh, honey. That was from the accident your father had."

Jackson's eyes went wide. "Wow." That was the closest thing to an emotion he expressed. Then he went back to brooding.

Rita turned to face him as she blotted the tears.

"Why do you keep crying?" he asked, pouting.

"Because, well, a lot of things have happened, and I'm a little upset. I don't want you to worry. Everything is going to be alright."

Jackson shrugged. He wasn't convinced. Before they left for Aunt Betty's, things didn't seem alright at home. Now they were back.

George returned to his automobile. "The guy has someone who he thinks can patch this up in a day or two. Drive this to the hospital. As soon as I get some information, I'll look for you there."

The hospital was several blocks away, and Rita drove as slowly as possible without coming to a complete halt. There was a sign for visitor parking in the front. She asked Jackson to roll up the windows, and then she opened the rear door. She took his hand, and they walked to the main entrance. A woman in a nun's habit greeted them.

"Hello. I'm Sister Theresa. How can I help you?"

"Hello. Ny name is Rita Taylor. My husband was admitted two nights ago."

The sister pushed up her reading glasses that hung at the tip of her nose and began to check the patient information log. She frowned. "He is in a special ward."

"What kind of a special ward?"

The nun looked hesitant and eyed the little boy.

"Does that mean we don't get to see him? I drove all the way from Barnegat. The doctor told me I had to come." Rita tried valiantly to remain calm. "Something about paperwork." She took a huge breath and let it out.

"Give me a minute, please." The nun walked from behind

the desk and disappeared down a hallway as Jackson looked on with curiosity.

"Is she going to get Dad?" he asked.

"I don't think so. Maybe a doctor."

Several minutes later, and man in a white coat walked briskly with nun in tow.

"Mrs. Taylor?" he asked.

"Yes. And this is my son, Jackson." She placed her hand on one of his shoulders.

"I'm afraid your son will not be able to visit him."

"Why not?" Rita asked.

"It's a special ward," the doctor offered.

"Yes, I understand that, but why can't my son visit his father?"

"Perhaps you should have him sit here with Sister Theresa while you go in."

Rita turned to her boy. "You sit with the nice lady. I'll be back shortly."

Sister Theresa had experienced similar situations before. No child should encounter a parent who was in the state Jackson Taylor was in. "Come. You can sit here." She patted a chair along the wall. She opened a drawer and pulled out a coloring book and a few well-worn crayons. "You can pull your chair up to my desk if you'd like."

Jackson followed her instructions. He opened the book and tried to find a page that wasn't covered in markings from previous visitors.

"Thank you," Rita said, and followed the doctor down a long hall.

"Mrs. Taylor, I must warn you. Your husband is in bad condition. He's lucky to be alive."

There's that sentence again, she thought. "How bad is it?" She wanted to brace herself as best she could.

"With the exception of his left eye, nostrils, and part of his mouth, his head and face are completely covered in bandages."

Rita was getting nauseous. She grabbed the doctor's arm.

"Do you need to sit down?" he asked kindly.

"No. No. Let's get this over with." She hoped she didn't sound cold, but there was no need to delay this excruciating situation.

The doctor guided her to a room that had a dozen beds, approximately six feet apart. One patient looked worse than the next. It was like being in the middle of a horror show.

"There was a fire last week. Most of these are burn victims," he whispered.

Rita felt bile burn the back of her throat as she suppressed a gag. It was horrible. No wonder they wouldn't let Jackson in. The sight would haunt him forever, as she knew it would haunt *her* for the rest of her life.

The doctor guided her to the side of her husband's bed. He looked worse than she imagined. She touched his unbandaged hand. "Jackson? J.T., it's me, Rita."

He didn't respond. She looked at the doctor.

"He hasn't spoken since he was brought in. He was unconscious for the first two days, and finally opened one eye this morning."

"J.T. If you can hear me, blink twice," the doctor requested.

Nothing. J.T. continued to stare at the ceiling.

"What do we do now?" Rita fought back her instinct to scream.

"He should be transferred to the VA hospital. We don't have the capacity to treat him."

"Treat him for . . . ?" Rita was still looking for some sort of diagnosis.

"His mental state, for one thing. We don't know what kind of condition he will be in when his bones heal."

If he wakes up was what the doctor didn't say, but was understood, nonetheless.

"Can you explain the process? What do I need to do?"

"You'll fill out paperwork. Do you have his discharge papers from the military?"

"Yes, somewhere at home. How did you know he was in the service?"

"The tattoo."

"Oh, of course." Rita remembered the star and bars on his forearm.

"The sooner you can get that to us, the better. He may recover much faster at the VA hospital." The doctor tried to be encouraging, but by the looks of it, the outcome seemed bleak.

The doctor walked Rita back to the reception area where her son was doodling. She spied George entering the building. The minute she saw him, Rita began to sob.

George put his arms around her, and Jackson just stared.

Rita managed to compose herself. The kind nun handed her a hankie. Then Rita turned to Jackson.

"Sweetie, I'm sorry, but you're not going to be able to see your father today."

"Is he dead?"

Shock waves bounced off everyone. George and Rita swapped startled glances. "Dead? No. No, he didn't die. But he's got a whole lot of bandages, and the people around him are very sick."

"But why are you crying?" Jackson was more engaged than he had been all day.

"Because he's sick, and that makes me sad." Rita wasn't sure if she was lying to herself or her son.

Jackson shrugged. It was becoming his go-to response lately.

"George, I have to go home and find J.T.'s discharge papers. What about the car?"

"The mechanic said he can fix it in two days. I'll phone

Betty when we get to your house and let her know I'll be up here for another day or two."

"Are you sure, George?" Rita asked.

"Of course. I can't leave you with all this. Besides, Betty will be happy to have me out from under her feet."

Rita knew that was a fib. Betty and George had a solid relationship. They were best friends. George knew there was nothing Betty wouldn't do for her sister, and nothing he wouldn't do for her, either. Besides, someone had to mind Jackson while Rita was handling the details.

By the time they got back to the Taylor house, it was dinnertime. Rita rummaged through the refrigerator to find something to cook. It was sparse. There was a slab of Velveeta, a quart of milk, and a half loaf of Wonder Bread. She checked the cupboards. Rice. Beans. Macaroni. She couldn't top Betty's grilled cheese and bacon, so she decided on macaroni and cheese. It was the best she could do with what she had.

Rita began cooking, George went to call Betty, and Jackson went to his room to play with his toys. She sliced the cheese and slowly melted it in a small saucepan with some milk. As she stirred the cheese, she thought of how Jackson didn't seem to be reacting to everything that was going on. He was too stoic for a six-year-old. He didn't cry once—not when she uprooted him and his brother, not when they had to return here and leave Kirby behind, and not when he heard about his father's accident. Rita was concerned about him.

George walked into the kitchen saying, "Betty sends her regards and said to tell you that Kirby is being an absolute angel."

"I can't thank you both enough for all that you are doing for us," Rita said.

"We're family, Rita, and we'll always be here for you."

"Well, since you're here"—Rita smiled—"do you mind keeping an eye on this cheese? I want to check on Jackson."

* * *

In his room, Jackson was playing with two Cootie bugs, simulating they were in a fight. She watched her son smack the plastic bugs together, then rip their legs out. It was startling. "Jackson, honey? Why are you beating up your bugs?"

"Cause one is the good guy, and one isn't." He said it as if she should know. "Like the bad guys in the war."

It occurred to her there had been a lot of talk about war during the past decade. J.T. rarely spoke about his experiences in World War II, but sometimes, when he had been drinking, he would rant about the horrors he'd witnessed. And then came the Korean War and daily reports of the fighting, bombing, and loss of lives. Rita never thought about the impact this was having on her. She promised herself she would be more aware and more engaged with her children.

"We're having mac and cheese for dinner," she announced.

"Goody!" He whooshed the bug as if it were in flight. "I like mac and cheese!" He smiled up at his mother and waved one of the bugs at her. "This one is the good guy."

Rita felt a sense of relief. Jackson was behaving like a kid—playful, imaginative, full of joy. He wasn't sullen or unhappy.

"I'll call you for dinner as soon as it's ready." Rita moved toward her bedroom.

"Okay!" Jackson sang out.

Rita rummaged through the dresser drawers where her husband kept his personal papers. She was taken aback when she found a disciplinary letter from the railroad among his things. She slumped on the bed and read it. He had been caught drinking on the job and put on probation. The letter was dated a year ago. The probation was for a period of one year. She checked the calendar. The year was up this week. She wondered if that had anything to do with the accident. She thought she may never know.

She continued to sift through the papers and found his military discharge. At least it was "Honorable." She slipped the paper into her purse and returned to the kitchen, where George was dutifully stirring the cheese with one hand and the boiling macaroni with the other.

"You are a man of many talents," Rita quipped.

"At your service, madam." George bowed with a flourish.

Rita smiled but quickly turned serious. "I found the discharge papers, but there was also something among his things."

George noticed the corners of her mouth turned down. George furrowed his brow.

Rita continued, "There was a disciplinary letter from the railroad. He was caught drinking on the job."

George stopped stirring. "When was this?"

Rita looked down the hall to be sure Jackson wasn't within earshot. "A year ago. He was on probation for a year, and the year expired this past week."

"Hmm. Do you think it was a night of celebration that got him into this?"

"Possibly." Rita sighed. "But I can't let his behavior have a negative influence on the children. I have to come up with a plan. Regardless of what happens at the hospital, I must find a way to be more in control. You saw Jackson's mood swings?"

"I thought it was the change in scenery. Being away from home. But when the call from the hospital came, I dunno, the kid acted strange. No offense."

"None taken. But you are correct. I don't think we realize how much our moods affect others, no matter how hard you try to pretend things are alright." Rita was nodding to herself. "I think I should speak to a lawyer."

"About?" George thought he knew the answer.

"A divorce." Rita pulled out the colander and handed it to George. "I can't keep living this way, and now I see how much it's influenced my son. Kirby is still young, but in a couple of years, he'll be Jackson's age, and Jackson will be older and much more aware."

"Whatever you need, Rita. Betty and I will back you up." He rinsed the macaroni and then dumped it into the pot of melted cheese.

"Look at you! A regular Chef Boyardee," Rita joked. "I'll get Jackson." She went down the hall and found Jackson lying on his bed, staring at the ceiling.

"Sweetie? Are you okay?"

"Yep. Is dinner ready?"

"Yep," she replied. "Come on."

They returned to the kitchen, where George was scooping the saucy mac into bowls. The three sat at the kitchen table and ate. Uncle George was encouraging conversation with Jackson. "Your mom tells me you like Cootie bugs?"

"I like to smash 'em up," Jackson said gleefully.

George shot a glance at Rita, who nodded imperceptibly with a worried look in her eyes.

The following day, George drove them to the hospital. "I'm going to check on your car. Jackson can ride with me while you take care of business."

Rita was trembling as she walked into the waiting room. She had no idea what lay ahead. A few minutes after she checked in with the nurses' station, she saw a doctor walk her way. She smiled at him. Why not? Good news or bad, she had to remain in control. If nothing else, her emotions. *It's not about what life hands you, it's how you handle it.*

The doctor was gentle in his approach. "Good morning, Mrs. Taylor," he said, then paused. She knew that wasn't a good sign. "I'm sorry to say there hasn't been any change in his condition."

Rita nodded. She assumed they would have phoned if

there was. "I brought the paperwork you requested." She handed him an envelope.

"Come with me." He motioned to a room to the side of the waiting area. The doctor introduced her to a woman who looked very efficient. Her desk was neat as a pin. The walls were bare. A single photograph was propped next to her official hospital pen holder.

It took about an hour for the woman to explain the papers Rita signed. "Mr. Taylor will be transferred to the VA hospital in a few hours. You'll be able to visit him after they get him processed and assigned a room."

"How long do you think that will take?" Rita asked.

The woman checked the watch pendant around her neck. "Most likely dinnertime, but I suggest you phone ahead." She wrote the number on a piece of paper and handed it to Rita.

"Thank you for all your help," Rita said as she rose from her chair.

"Mrs. Taylor?" The woman stood. "I don't want to alarm you, but the VA hospital can be overwhelming."

"Thank you." Rita wondered if she could be any more overwhelmed than she was. She walked outside, where George and Jackson were waiting.

"Everything okay?" George asked, as he opened the passenger door for her.

"Yes. They said I can visit him later this afternoon, but I must call first."

Jackson remained silent.

Rita turned to her son. "Sweetie, I'm not sure if they'll let you visit."

"I'll drive us over there. Jackson and I can wait in the reception area for you."

"You don't have to do that, George."

"Yes, I do. Your car isn't ready, and I don't want you driving there by yourself. End of debate." He grinned. "How about we go to Howard Johnson's for lunch?"

"Really, Uncle George?" Jackson became animated. "Ice cream! Ice cream!"

"After you had your lunch. That is, if your mother says it's okay," George replied.

"Only if you eat your whole lunch," Rita added.

Jackson continued his chant for the next block. "Ice cream! Ice cream!"

When they arrived at the orange-roofed diner, the server showed them to a booth complete with paper placemats, a napkin dispenser, and salt-and-pepper shakers. Jackson thought he was special. They had never eaten inside before. The only time they had been there was to get ice cream, and Jackson always waited in the car.

"What'll you have?" George asked.

Jackson made a face and shrugged.

"How about a hot dog?" Rita suggested.

"Yeah!" Jackson was finally acting like a little boy again.

Later that afternoon, George drove them to the hospital, where Rita was directed to a ward. He and Jackson waited in a gray and green room, with an ugly linoleum floor and a few chairs that looked like they, too, had been through a war. Jackson whispered in his uncle's ear, "This place isn't as nice as the other one." Jackson scrunched up his nose. "It smells funny."

George nodded. After World War II, there were fifteen million vets returning to the country, with a quarter million of them requiring hospitalization. VA hospitals were packed to the brim, filled beyond their capacity. George knew this was not going to be a pleasant situation.

About a half hour later, Rita returned, looking as if she had seen a ghost. George stood right away. "How is he?"

She couldn't speak; otherwise, she might scream. George ushered her out the door, with Jackson clinging to his mother's hand. He was happy to be out of that creepy place.

When they got back to the car, she explained the situation. She wasn't going to mince words in front of Jackson. "J.T. is going to be in this hospital for an exceedingly long time. We don't know how long, either. Jackson, honey, this is not a nice place to visit your father, so until he gets better, we'll just have to pray for him. Can you do that for me?"

Jackson nodded, but he wasn't quite sure what he was supposed to be praying for.

"According to the administrator, the VA will pay for J.T.'s medical expenses, but I must cover the rest." She thought for a moment. "When Jackson starts school in the fall, maybe I can get a job at the factory where I worked before I got married." She let out a huge sigh. "There doesn't seem to be any reason for me to visit every day." She continued to think out loud. "I'll have to find someone to care for Kirby while I'm at work."

"He can stay with us," George offered. "At least until you find your sea legs." George served in the Navy and often used nautical expressions.

"What about the captain?" Rita was referring to Betty.

"She'd be thrilled." He knew Betty would be happy to help.

The following day, the repair shop phoned to let them know the car was ready. Then Rita phoned her old boss, who was delighted to have her back. She was a hard worker, and they were always in need of conscientious employees. He was happy to take any hours Rita could put in. That was one thing she could check off her list. Next was to see if there was someone who could babysit until school started. She didn't want to wait two months before she began to earn money.

There was a phone number on the card the administrator gave her. It was for family assistance. She hoped they could help.

George drove her to the repair shop where her car was waiting. The mechanic did as much as he could to fix the mangled mess. There were still lots of scratches and dents, but it was drivable.

Now that Rita had transportation and had secured a job, she insisted that George return home. He was reluctant to go and suggested he stay one more night, just in case. Just in case of what, he didn't know, but he felt uneasy leaving Rita alone. However, Rita knew she *was* on her own, and she needed to start taking care of herself and her children, so she sent George on his way.

The next morning, a neighbor knocked on Rita's door. The news of J.T.'s accident had spread up and down the street. "Hi, Rita. I just wanted to see how your husband is and if there is anything you need." It was Lydia Foster, the woman who lived next door.

Rita's first impulse was to say, "No, but thank you." Instead, she asked, "Can you recommend a babysitter to look after my son while I go to work?"

"For both boys?"

"Just Jackson for now. Kirby will be staying with my sister and her husband for the rest of the summer."

"How many hours a day?" Lydia asked.

"As many as I can get. I'm going back to my old job, and they'll let me work whenever I can." Then Rita realized she hadn't answered Lydia's question about her husband. "Unfortunately, J.T. will probably be in the hospital for a long time."

"Sorry to hear that," Lydia said with a grain of sympathy. She wasn't a major fan of J.T. He could go from charming to nasty in the blink of an eye.

"We're going to have to manage, which is why I need to go back to work."

"I babysit for my grandson Monday through Friday. My daughter is studying to be a nurse, so I look after him. Once school starts, I watch him from two to five every day during the week. The school bus drops him off right in front. The boys may be in the same class, and they can play in the yard together after school. I can watch your younger boy, too, when he gets back."

Rita thought about it for a moment. She didn't know how to ask about money, but Lydia chimed in, "And don't worry about paying me. I have to mind Rickie anyway, and Jackson will be a good distraction for him."

"That is very generous of you, Lydia."

"Us gals have to help each other out."

Rita realized Lydia made a good point. Women had to look after each other, regardless of any difference in their age or marital status.

"I promise I will make it up to you somehow."

"I am sure you will, dear. When do you want to start?"

"I'll call my boss and see when he wants me back."

"Okay. Just give me a holler when you know." Lydia turned to walk away, then stopped. "You're gonna be alright, Rita. There are a lot of people on this block who think very highly of you. You are always there with a pound cake, or an apple pie whenever someone has a birthday, or isn't well. You're a good neighbor, dear."

Rita watched as the woman walked to the end of the sidewalk. She didn't remember anyone ever saying she was a good neighbor. If they did, she didn't believe it. She had to admit her self-esteem was nonexistent. But now? Now she had to pick up the pieces, and she found strength in the challenge.

* * *

Jackson had acclimated to the new circumstances rather quickly. He was excited to have a friend, and Mrs. Foster made the best chocolate-chip cookies. His mother would bring him to the Fosters' house in the morning, then she'd go to work. He stayed with Mrs. Foster until his mother got home in time to make dinner. Aunt Betty and Uncle George brought Kirby home every weekend to keep the family unit as close as possible. Betty and Rita slept in Rita's room, and Uncle George slept on the sofa. Kirby and Jackson were in their usual twin beds, playing like brothers should. Rita loved seeing her sons together, and she missed Kirby so much, but Betty and George convinced her that it would be no trouble for them to keep the boy with them during the week—at least until he was old enough to go to school.

Rita visited J.T. at the hospital at least once a week. And once a week, she was reminded that this was the way life was going to be for a while. Maybe forever.

This arrangement went on for the next two years. During the summers, both boys stayed with Betty and George. It gave Rita an opportunity to put more hours in and make more money. It was throughout that time when Jackson began to understand the importance of money. Rita made sure he did. Everything she did was for the sake of money. Money for food. Money for house payments. Money for electricity. Money for gas for the car. And with careful planning, money for schooling when the boys got older.

By the time Jackson was in high school, he learned the art of finesse. If you said pleasant things to people, you could get them to do things for you, even if you didn't mean it. He was fascinated by the Eddie Haskell character on *Leave It to Beaver*. Eddie always complimented Beaver's mother, June Cleaver. He would have a line that would be akin to "That's a lovely dress you're wearing, Mrs. Cleaver." She would respond with a "Thank you, Eddie," and give Mr. Cleaver an eye roll. Everyone knew Eddie was disingenuous. He just didn't know that everyone else knew. So Jackson decided he would have to be better; he honed his skill at compliments and made them sound more sincere than they were. He got particularly good at it and charmed his teachers. If he didn't do well on a test, he'd pluck at their heartstrings explaining how his father, "a war hero," was in the hospital, and his mother didn't have time to help him with homework. That excuse worked for a while. His father never regained consciousness and passed away from kidney failure, and he milked that excuse until he graduated.

Jackson also learned that dressing well got you further, and he offered to help his mother with the laundry. By now he was able to fit into his father's clothes. Even though they had been sitting in the closet for eight years, with a little TLC, he could convert some of them into his own wardrobe. He ironed his own shirts and pressed creases into his trousers. He used Vitalis Hair Tonic, advertised as popular with upscale gents. After ridding his face of any peach fuzz, he'd splash a few drops of English Leather in his hands, rub them together, and pat his jawline. He believed if you were well groomed, you could talk your way in or out of anything.

Jackson was physically fit and played on the school's baseball team. Most of his classmates weren't as confident as he was, and Jackson had no trouble finding dates. He just never fell in love. That was one emotion he strategically put in a vault. The only loving relationship he observed was between his aunt and uncle. But they were a different sort. As far as he was concerned, love was for losers. He was never sure if his parents loved each other. It was doubtful.

When he turned eighteen, he got accepted to a local community college. He wanted to go into finance. The business of money. From there, he chose a four-year school where no one knew him or his family. That was his opportunity to reinvent himself. He was Jackson Taylor, descendant of Zachary Taylor, twelfth president of the United States. No one was going to check. His father was a decorated hero and died of injuries from the war. No one was going to check. His family owned farm country in the south. Not entirely a lie, but no one was going to check on that, either.

Jackson got his degree in finance and moved to New York. He took a job at a small banking firm and brown-nosed his way into management. He fashioned himself as a member of the *haut monde*. One of the gentry. Cream of the crop. He would charm himself into the high life, no matter what it took.

Jackson Taylor reinvented his life, yet the harder he tried to be less like his father, the more he emulated him. He had no empathy. He was a cheat. A substance abuser. An emotional wasteland. But none of that mattered. Not to him, anyway.

It was obvious that Kirby was the opposite of his brother. He was meant to be outdoors. He enjoyed hiking in the woods and fishing with Uncle George. As Kirby got older, his uncle taught him how to handle a small motorboat. They'd hitch the craft to Uncle George's truck and tow it to the boat launch on the bay, where they would spend the good part of the morning clamming. Kirby also learned how to set a crab trap, clean, and filet fish. When fluke, also known as "summer flounder," were running, they would catch dozens of the popular fish. Kirby was intrigued that flounder had two eyes on one side of its head. Uncle George explained that the fish live at the bottom, and one eye eventually migrates to meet up with the other one on top. He also pointed out that the summer flounder's head faced left, and the winter flounder faced right, and was slightly darker. It was nature's mysteries that interested Kirby, and the way nature and wildlife adapted. Neither George nor Kirby had any interest in hunting. They saw no reason to kill animals when you could go to the grocery store.

Kirby had no interest in college or working in an office, but his mother urged him to get a degree in something. It was the typical "something you can fall back on" advice. To satisfy himself and his mother, he enrolled at the Maritime College in New York State. It was either that or risk being drafted into the army. Not that he wasn't patriotic, but he didn't want to serve in a fruitless war. His brother escaped it by a year.

After Kirby got his degree, he was still not the least bit interested in a desk job and went to work on a deep-sea fishing rig. It took him out for weeks at a time, but it paid good money. After five years of hazards on the high seas, and near-death experiences during life-threatening storms, he decided he'd tempted fate too many times. He was able to save enough to put a down payment on a small bait and tackle shop along the shore, and that's where he stayed.

Kirby and Jackson led two separate lives, only seeing each other on holidays and other family events. Jackson and Gwen only lived fifty miles away in Manhattan, but it might as well have been another world. Kirby enjoyed spending time with his niece and nephew when they were young, but visiting was always a challenge. His brother had become a big financial honcho and was very particular about inviting Kirby to any events. Only family gatherings were acceptable to Jackson until their mother passed away. That's when the brothers became estranged.

Kirby made a life for himself doing something he thoroughly enjoyed. It saddened him that he had no real family, but he always remembered Madison and Lincoln's birthdays, and Gwen made sure her children remembered his, even if Gwen hid it from her husband.

Kirby was well-liked by his friends and his water-loving colleagues, and they were crestfallen when he died at the age of seventy-five from a heart attack. The year was 2025. His mates held a simple memorial at Bahr's Landing, but it wasn't until several weeks later when Madison, now forty-eight, and Lincoln, forty-six, got word of his passing. Both felt pangs of guilt, realizing their only contact with their uncle had been through the mail and infrequent phone calls over the years. They never understood why their father wasn't close to his brother. Madison and Lincoln were thick as thieves. Had there been irreconcilable differences? Over what? Uncle Kirby was a gentle soul. Kind. Generous. What was it that their father disdained? Eventually Madison and Lincoln would discover the secrets her father had buried.

Chapter Three

Madison

Madison Taylor grew up surrounded by wealth and had little idea about the world outside of her safe and privileged orbit. Her friends were hand-picked by her parents, as were her clothes, her school, and her activities. She was to learn how to play the piano, take ballet lessons, and when old enough, tennis and skiing were on her list.

Madison was a happy child, and she enjoyed the many luxuries that were afforded to her. Her father enrolled her in a preschool when she was three. She made friends, but her favorite playmate was Olivia Martinez. She was the daughter of Sandra, Gwen's best friend. Jackson wasn't thrilled with the idea that his daughter was keeping company with someone whose mother married "the guy from the mailroom." Gwen suggested Jackson could help the Martinez family with a retirement fund. "There's a one-hundred-thousand-dollar buy-in to be a client," he scoffed. "I doubt he has that kind of money."

"But they're our friends," Gwen persisted.

"They're *your* friends, Gwen." For Jackson, everything was a transaction, including friendship. He saw no value unless it elevated him financially or socially. As far as he was concerned, Sandra's family offered neither, forcing Gwen to do a work-around so she and her daughter could keep their best friends in their life. Gwen was not going to allow Jackson to interfere in her relationship with Sandra, or Madison's with Olivia. Gwen would plan outings in places where running into her husband was remote. Gwen and Madison had their own little secret they promised each other in a pinky-swear. Gwen may have surrendered to the trappings of the rich, but she still had integrity and loyalty, something that had faded from her husband. She wondered if he had either at any point in time.

In a few short years, Jackson had turned into an elitist snob, determined to insinuate himself into the old-money crowd. But the façade wore thin. After a year, most of the neighbors realized he was too slick for their style. He loved to flash his money around. Jackson never missed an opportunity to quote the price of something he recently purchased. As far as they were concerned, he was the personification of the word *gauche*. They had no qualms regarding Gwen. She was a good sort, and a good mother, but Jackson Taylor was insufferable. It was equally tedious for Gwen, and she began to distance herself from him as much as she could.

When Madison completed kindergarten, her father planned a lavish party at the Waldorf Astoria. He invited all of Madison's schoolmates and their parents. It was over the top, with an invitation list hovering around one hundred guests. Gwen wanted to have a simple gathering at their house, but Jackson needed a grand excuse to garner more clients, so he created an opportunity. He had his assistant make the necessary arrangements and left Gwen out of all the decisions. Jackson insisted it was to keep the details off her plate, but Gwen knew he was disingenuous. He simply wanted control, and no feedback from her.

It cost tens of thousands of dollars, complete with a basketball arcade game, a scavenger hunt, ring-toss, and clowns. But when the men with the painted faces, goofy hair, and red noses arrived, Madison freaked out. She ran from the grand ballroom, shrieking in fear. Gwen ran after her. Madison was hysterical. She could barely get the words out between sobs: "Mommy! Mommy! I'm scared! I'm scared! Please make them go away!" Gwen did her best to calm her child as Jackson stood in the doorway with a look of contempt, spun on his heel, and returned to his guests. Had he known his daughter better, he could have avoided the scene, yet he chose to be angry at his wife and child instead.

Gwen assured Madison that the clowns were nothing to be afraid of and coaxed her back into the room. But Madison did not leave her mother's side for the rest of the afternoon. She clung to Gwen's Chanel suit while dozens of children played games, the adults drank champagne, and Jackson ingratiated himself to the other wealthy parents.

Madison showed no interest in the pile of blue boxes from Tiffany, given by her father's business associates. That was another thing that irked Jackson. He expected his daughter to squeal with delight, not scream at the top of her lungs.

When the party was over, and they returned to their apartment, Jackson announced that Madison would be going to the Hackley School in Tarrytown the following year. As soon as Lincoln was old enough, he would join her.

Madison wasn't sure what all of it meant. "What's boarding school, Mommy?" she asked.

"It's a school where you live." Gwen's eyes darted at her husband, who remained mute. She was baffled. This was the first time she'd heard of Jackson's educational plans for her children.

"Are we going to move?" Madison asked innocently.

"No, sweetheart. We will still be here."

"But will you be coming with me?"

"No, honey. Daddy, Lincoln, and I will be staying home."

"But why?" The child was totally confused.

"Because your daddy wants you to get the best education."

"But Mrs. Crowder said I was really good. I can even read books!" From the time Madison was two, Gwen shared her interest in books with her daughter, and Madison was light years ahead of her peers.

"And you are really good, but this new school will make you even better. And they have drawing classes, too. You love to draw." She gave her daughter a reassuring hug and glared at Jackson. "You are going to have a wonderful adventure. I promise."

The sound of Lincoln chattering in the hallway broke the mood. Mrs. Braun was walking the four-year old into the grand living room. He yelped and ran toward his mother and sister as if his father weren't there, which was usually the case.

Madison loved her little brother and fawned over him. She wasn't sure what this boarding school thing was, but if Lincoln was going to be attending, then it would not be too bad. She wasn't sure why her father was sending her away. Regardless of her mother's words of comfort, it really appeared that way.

It wasn't as if she felt unloved, but when it came to her father, her young perception made it seem she was more of an accessory than a darling daughter.

* * *

The summer before she was sent off to school, Madison began piano, ballet, and tennis lessons. She wished she could play with her friends, but her father insisted she be ready for school. He explained there would be a lot of other children who have talent, and she had to be the best. "You want me to be proud of you, don't you?" Jackson asked, but Madison knew it was more for himself than for her benefit. Madison proved to be a very astute six-year-old. It was a talent that would serve her later on in life.

When Madison wasn't practicing, she would look through the piles of her mother's fashion magazines. She would occasionally ask her mother if she could play dress-up. Gwen would find something from her vast wardrobe that she no longer wore so that it wouldn't be a disaster if Madison ruined it. But Madison showed an appreciation for the workmanship, fancy buttons, and piping. She also had a closet full of dolls, each with their own wardrobe. Madison would often change outfits, creating her own fashion show.

One afternoon Gwen came home with a shopping bag from New York Central Art Supplies. She called Madison into the kitchen. "I have a new project for you," she said, and smiled at her daughter. Madison wasn't sure if it was good news or bad news. She barely had time for all her lessons and tutoring. Jackson was adamant that Madison be ahead of the other students at the new private school and scheduled her from the minute she finished her breakfast until dinner. She knitted her eyebrows and looked up at her mother.

"Go get some of the magazines you like. The ones with the clothes and pocketbooks."

Madison didn't ask why and went into the area that had been designated as their playroom. She picked three of her favorites—*Vogue, Town & Country,* and *Harper's Bazaar*—and skipped back to the kitchen. On the table were scissors, paste, and cardboard. "We're going to make what is called a collage. It's when you get a bunch of pictures with a similar theme, like clothes, and you paste them to make a poster." Gwen pulled out a chair. "Come. Let's make one together." Madison was captivated with this new craft, and the word. "Colarge?"

"It's *collage*. No 'r'." She winked at Madison.

The two began sifting through the pages. "When you see something you like, tear out the page," Gwen instructed her.

"Are you sure it's okay?" Madison was leery about ruining anything that belonged to an adult.

"Of course. They're my magazines, and I'm sharing them with you." She handed Madison a pair of safety scissors.

They sat quietly while Madison carefully went through the glossy photos. "I like this one, Mommy." She pointed to a hot pink and black color-block dress with black and gold buttons. "But I don't like her earrings."

"If you're careful, you can cut them out of the picture."

"Really?" Madison's eyes went wide.

"Yes. You can do whatever you want."

Madison rubbed her hands together and went to work. The next thing she picked was an apricot bow-blouse with a matching pleated skirt. Then she came upon a photo of Princess Diana wearing a sweatshirt, jeans, boots, and a baseball cap. "Look, Mommy. You have the same hair!" It was true. Every woman in their neighborhood donned the style and the color. Next, she found a cherry-red jacket with shoulder pads, which went to mid-thigh, over a short, tight black skirt. The outfit included a wide black belt and red patent leather pumps. But what stopped Madison was a photo of Iman, a stunning Black woman wearing a thigh-length white satin jacket, and a matching long white skirt. Several strings of pearls finished the outfit. "Ooh. She is beautiful." Madison stared at the Somali-born supermodel.

"Yes, she is. It's been said that she inspired Calvin Klein and Yves Saint Laurent. You have one of his outfits there." She pointed to a blue peplum jacket over a black pencil skirt.

"So do men make clothes for ladies?" Madison asked.

"Lots of men. I think there are more men than women. In fact, I am almost certain of it."

"But why?" Madison asked innocently.

Gwen remembered her first chat with Sandra in the ladies' room a decade before. *"It's a man's world."* But she was not about to feed that information to her daughter. She wanted Madison to approach life with an "I can do anything" attitude.

"Maybe they can sew better?" Gwen offered. Madison giggled, and the two continued to cut out slacks, dresses, shoes, and accessories.

Gwen continued the conversation. "There are a few very influential female designers, though. Coco Chanel for one. She was a pioneer for women in fashion." She pointed to one of Madison's choices. "This is one of her classic suits."

"You have a bunch of them," Madison said as a matter of fact.

Gwen chuckled. "I suppose I do." She could count over a dozen in her head.

Once they finished cutting up the magazines, Gwen helped Madison begin to glue the pieces on the board. The first one was the photo of Iman, all in white. Then she began to place a pair of jeans with a peplum jacket. She then went on to create her own combination of tops, bottoms, shoes, scarves, and dresses.

When they finished, Gwen spotted another talent in her daughter. She had a good eye for color and style. Gwen checked the time. Jackson would be home soon. "Why don't you go practice piano for a little bit while I clean up here?" Gwen didn't want Jackson to think they had been dawdling and wasting time while Madison could be honing her skills on the subjects he was most concerned about. Madison was long past "Twinkle, Twinkle, Little Star" and "The Itsy Bitsy Spider." She was determined to master "Für Elise" before she left for school. Maybe then her father would be proud of her. But more importantly, she could be proud of herself.

A month before the school term began, Gwen and Madison took a quick trip to Tarrytown. It took about an hour along the scenic route of the Henry Hudson Parkway. Gwen explained that Madison would come home on the weekends, which eased some of Madison's angst. Gwen's, as well.

The car turned into the long, beautifully landscaped driveway of the three-hundred-acre campus. Madison smushed her face against the window. "It looks like a castle!" Gwen could tell Madison's mood was a little more promising than it had been most of the summer. Ever since her father's announcement, Madison had become pensive. Reticent. The unknown filled her with fear, but she dared not complain or pout.

When they arrived at the school, the headmaster, Nelson Bridwell, took them on a tour of the sprawling compound. They were shown the lower-grade classrooms, the physical education center, art classrooms, and the performing arts center. Madison was in awe. "I can play the piano, but will I be able to take art?" she asked, looking up at Mr. Bridwell.

He leaned over and said, "Yes, of course. And there is an art show at the end of the year. It's all part of the curriculum."

Madison nodded and repeated the word *curriculum*.

"Do you know what that means?" Mr. Bridwell asked kindly.

Madison was not sure how to answer. If she said she didn't, would they not allow her into the school? She decided honesty was the best avenue. "No, sir. I do not."

He smiled. "It's a combination of all the classes you will be taking. Math, science, art, music, and physical education."

"All at once?" Her eyes grew wide.

"Not exactly," he explained. "You'll have a few different classes every day with different teachers."

Madison bit her lower lip. "I only had one teacher every day."

"Yes, and now you'll have a bunch," Gwen chimed in. She placed her hands on Madison's shoulders. "Won't that be fun?"

Again, Madison wasn't sure how to answer. Instead, she simply nodded, not necessarily in agreement, but in understanding.

"You'll also have a 'Buddy'," Mr. Bridwell explained. "Someone from the fourth grade will be your friend. A partner. This way, if you need any help with anything, they'll be someone you can talk to besides a grown-up, because we know sometimes grown-ups don't understand."

Madison became increasingly more interested in this new way of life. "Where will we live?"

"Come. I'll show you."

The three meandered through the garden-lined walkways and past the tennis courts. "I was learning this summer," Madison said, looking at the court, "but my father told me I need to do better." She grimaced.

"Well, that's something we can work on." He gave Mrs. Taylor a quizzical glance. "You have a lot of activities, Madison. We'll introduce you to the tennis coach and the music teachers. They will be able to suggest the appropriate lessons for you. How does that sound?" He chuckled. "We don't want to wear you out."

Madison slipped her hand through her mother's. "Sounds okay to me." She wanted to skip but thought better of it. Her mother was right. This was going to be an adventure.

They continued to the building where Madison would live during the week. "This is the residence building," he explained as he pressed the bell. A disembodied voice responded through a speaker. "Good morning. How can I assist you?"

"Good morning, Gladys. Mr. Bridwell, here." A buzzer sounded, and the door unlocked. He turned to Gwen and Madison. "I have my own key, but I wanted you to experience our level of security for anyone who intends to enter the building."

Bridwell noticed a look of relief and concern on Gwen's face.

"We are quite resolute when it comes to safety, and I am pleased and proud to report that we have never had an incident." He held the door open for them.

"That's very reassuring," Gwen replied. Leaving your six, soon-to-be-seven-year-old child in the custody of strangers is fraught with anxiety. At least it was for her. Jackson was only concerned about the prestige the school produced. *Had he considered safety?* she wondered. Each time she tried to approach the entire school subject with her husband, he shut her down. His modus operandi was to simply walk out of the room. Just like the time when she wanted to discuss parenthood: case closed.

Her next concern was how Madison would adjust to this new life. Her home was posh. Comfortable. Easy. There would be many challenges now. Then she wondered how well *she* would do with the new living situation. It was going to be a big adjustment for all of them. Except Jackson. He was barely there. She also wondered what it was going to be like when Lincoln left home. She squashed a shudder and smiled at the woman who stood behind a desk.

"Gladys, this is Mrs. Taylor and her daughter, Madison."

"Hello, Madison." Gladys acknowledged the little girl first. "I'm Gladys."

"Nice to meet you, Gladys." Madison held out her hand the way her mother taught her.

Gladys then turned to Gwen. "Nice to meet you, Mrs. Taylor." Gladys was the stereotypical housemother: mid-fifties, maybe sixties. It was hard to tell with her short, gray, curly locks, her reading glasses on a chain, rosy cheeks, and sensible shoes.

Gwen felt comfortable immediately. "Likewise." They shook hands.

"I hear you are going to be joining us next month." Gladys beamed. "They'll be thirty-five of you staying here during the week. And there are lots of fun things to do besides schoolwork." Gladys winked at Madison, who broke out in a big smile.

"I am going to give them a tour. See you in a few minutes." Mr. Bridwell motioned for the Taylors to walk through the small, well-lit lobby. Two modern sofas joined a corner table that contained several art books. A staircase and elevator were to the right. Mr. Bridwell pushed the UP button. "The living quarters are on the second floor. Most of the children are encouraged to take the stairs. We try to promote conscious physical activity. But we'll make an exception today. Just for fun." Bridwell was the consummate ambassador.

"We have stairs in our house," Madison said. "But we do not have an elevator. Well, there is one in the building, but not in our apartment."

The elevator opened to a large community room. There were sofas and plush chairs arranged in several configurations to encourage conversation and socializing. A small television was nestled in the middle of a series of shelves, flanked by bookcases. Two large pocket doors opened to another space with a Ping-Pong table on one side and a pool table on the other. Madison could barely see over the top of it. "Several of our older students play regularly. They're quite good." He motioned for them to follow him down the hall.

"Each student has their own room." He unlocked one of the doors. "I believe this is going to be yours, Madison."

Madison slowly entered the space that was going to be her home away from home. It was bright, with a window that overlooked the quad. A twin bed was on one side of the room, a desk with a lamp, and a dresser on the other. A beanbag chair sat in the corner. "You can decorate it any way you'd like. You can even put posters on the wall."

Madison got excited. "Oh, Mommy. We can hang the collage we made!"

"That is an excellent idea, sweetheart." Gwen was pleased that her little distraction meant more to Madison than she expected.

Gwen surveyed the room. "May we bring our own linens? Toss pillows?"

"Absolutely. Whatever makes Madison feel comfortable."

"There is an adjoining bathroom to the room next door. That's where your Buddy will be living. You'll each have your own sink but will have to share the other facilities. You can also lock the doors when you want privacy. Just try to remember to unlock your Buddy's side before you leave." He gave a little chuckle. He didn't mention that the Buddy would have a key to both doors in case of an emergency. He wanted Madison to feel safe but not suffocated or invaded.

"Looks like we have a little shopping to do on the way home," Gwen said to Madison. "Think about what color bedspread and towels you want."

Madison thought carefully. "Could we wait until we get to the store?"

Relief filtered through Gwen's psyche. Her daughter was going to be fine. Madison was astute and easygoing. She didn't make a fuss. Ever. Except for the clowns. And who could blame her?

As they proceeded down the hall, back to the elevator, Mr. Bridwell pointed out the phone at each end of the hallway. "Children can call their parents anytime, and incoming phone calls will be fielded by whoever is on duty."

When they returned to the lobby area, Gladys asked Madison how she liked the place so far. Madison gave her an affirmative answer followed by, "And we're going to pick out a new bedspread."

"How exciting!" Gladys grinned. "We'll see you in a couple of weeks." She walked over to Gwen and took her hand. She gave her a reassuring squeeze. "Madison is going to be well taken care of here."

Gwen believed it.

Mr. Bridwell walked them back to the main building, where their car was waiting. He bent down to look Madison face-to-face. "Do you have any questions for me today?"

"Nuh-uh. I mean, no sir." Madison remembered her manners.

"Well, if you think of anything, tell your mom and she can phone me." He turned to Gwen. "Naturally, that goes for you as well." He held out his hand. "It was a pleasure spending time with both of you today." He shook Gwen's first, and then Madison's.

"Thank you, Mr. Bridwell," Madison said, as she climbed into the back seat of the limo.

Gwen also thanked him. "I am sure you know how much angst this causes, having a parent put their child in someone else's hands, but I feel very reassured she will be just fine here."

"I have no doubt," Bridwell agreed. "She's very inquisitive, which we strongly encourage. She is also quite articulate for her age."

"And she has a bit of talent, too, but I'm sure every parent says that about their child," she said, chuckling.

"You'd be surprised. Some parents can't wait to drop their kids off and speed out of the driveway."

Gwen caught her breath. That's exactly what Jackson was doing with his children. She consoled herself with the knowledge hers would be home for the weekends. At least she had Lincoln full time for the next two years, unless Jackson had a different plan he wasn't sharing.

Mr. Bridwell gave Gwen the address of the shop where Madison could get her uniform. The administration believed that if everyone wore the same clothes, it would blur the class lines. Some children came from very wealthy families, while a few were there on special grants or scholarships. Having a uniform did exactly what it meant: everyone dressed uniformly. Gwen was surprised that Madison didn't put up a fuss. Madison loved clothes and putting together her outfits. But having a uniform was fine during the week. She could get creative at home.

It was also a plus that there wouldn't be any contests for who had the nicest things. Madison would become uncomfortable when the friends her father chose for her became competitive. It was always a challenge about who had the prettiest dress at a party. It was never an issue with Olivia. If Olivia admired one of Madison's dresses, Madison would ask her mother if it would be alright if Olivia could have it after she wore it. Gwen was often taken aback by Madison's generosity at such an early age. If Madison was okay with it, then Gwen could not object. Most party dresses were only worn once if they were going to be in the company of the same people. Jackson insisted. Gwen thought it was ridiculous, almost vulgar, but Jackson wanted to make sure everyone knew they were dripping in money. For him, it was all about conspicuous consumption.

The weekend before Madison was to leave for school, her mother planned a lunch date and a puppet play with Sandra and Olivia. The girls squealed to their hearts' delight as puppets flew on "invisible" wires across the stage and above their heads. Gwen loved it when Madison could be just a kid, playing with her best friend. After the play, they stopped at the iconic Serendipity, known for its whimsical décor and decadent, luscious desserts. It was a perfect day.

Madison and Olivia hugged each other and said their farewells, sad that they would miss each other, but vowing to see each other soon. That was Gwen's promise to Madison. Even if she had to sneak behind Jackson's back. Not that he would notice.

Madison packed her favorite books and some casual clothes for when she was not in class. Of course, she could not leave Mr. Jinx behind. He was her favorite stuffed animal. She remembered asking her mother when Mr. Jinx was born. "He is the same age as you are, honey. Uncle Kirby gave him to you. Remember?"

"Yes." Madison furrowed her brow and pursed her lips. "How come we don't see Uncle Kirby very much?"

Gwen wanted to say, "Because your father is a snob," but settled for, "He lives a long way from here." It was a little less than two hours, depending on traffic, but to a kid, that is a long way away.

When Madison finished putting her things together, her mother carried the suitcase down the stairs and placed it in the entry. Madison bounded down behind her. "Where's Daddy?"

"He's working." Gwen gave the robotic answer, whether he was working or not.

Madison shrugged. She was used to him not being around except when they had lavish parties. She had a piano recital a few weeks before, and he was a no-show. Odd thing for someone who insisted his daughter have piano lessons. Madison thought he wasn't proud of her, but she knew her mother was.

After Madison finished a perfect performance of "Für Elise," Gwen, Sandra, and Olivia leapt from their chairs and cheered. Even at her young age, Madison appreciated the connection of friendship. She observed the bond her mother and Sandra shared, and she felt the same kind of kinship for Olivia. The people who cared about you were always there for you, no matter in body, mind, or spirit. Even her little brother Lincoln, who was too young to attend, gave her hugs and kisses before she left the house. Yep. Actions often speak louder than words, just as much as a lack of it can show.

Madison gave Phoebe a hug. "Don't let Lincoln turn into a brat," she said, and giggled at the housekeeper.

Phoebe leaned over and wrapped her arms around the little girl. "We will see you on the weekend, honey. Have fun!"

Gwen and Madison climbed into the town car that was waiting for them. The two sat close together. Gwen held Madison's hand. "You know, sweetie, you can come home any time you want. I mean it. Whenever you want. And if you really don't like it, we can figure out something else."

"It's okay, Mommy. I liked the school. Mr. Bridwell seems nice, and I like Gladys."

"What about your room? It's not like the one you have here."

Madison gave a little shrug. "It's okay. I have a new bedspread and some cool pillows."

"Yes, you do. I particularly like the one you made from leftover felt."

Madison nodded. After one of the Taylor's extravagant parties, there were pieces of felt left over from the decorations. Madison asked if she could have them. She cut the felt into smaller pieces, made a felt mosaic of the letter *M*, and sewed it to an old toss pillow. "That's so I know it's mine." She giggled.

Gwen was relieved that Madison showed no signs of anxiety or fear. It reminded her of the brave move she had made when she moved to New York. She knew her little girl would be fine.

As they pulled into the long drive of Hackley, several other vehicles were arriving with students and parents. Mr. Bridwell and Gladys stood on the walkway and greeted everyone. There was a buzz of excitement in the air. Gwen's concerns were further alleviated.

Mr. Bridwell immediately welcomed Gwen and Madison and introduced them to another girl the same age as Madison. "This is Niko. Her family is from Japan. They work at the United Nations."

"Niko, this is Madison and her mother Mrs. Taylor."

Niko bowed. "*Hajimemashite.* Nice to meet you."

Madison did a little curtsey. "Nice to meet you too, Niko."

"Both of you will be staying here during the week," Mr. Bridwell announced. "You'll be across the hall from each other."

Madison was pleased she had already met someone her age. "Have you seen your room yet?" Madison asked with excitement.

"No. Today is my first day here." Niko's diction was precise. Deliberate.

"There's a game room, and craft room, and all kinds of things." Madison took Niko's hand. "Come with me." Madison was in charge. She walked over to Gladys. "Is it alright if I show Niko our rooms?"

Gladys was taken aback. In a good way. "Of course you can. You remember where to go, right?"

Madison nodded. "Niko's room is across the hall from mine." The two girls gaily walked into the building as Gwen watched on.

"I guess she's going to be alright." Gwen chuckled.

Gladys nodded in agreement. "It's nice that Madison is so outgoing. Niko is new to the States, and having a pal her age is terrific."

"Are her parents here?" Gwen looked around.

"No. They had to fly to London or Scotland, somewhere in the U.K. Poor child arrived with her nanny."

"Oh?" Gwen sensed an undertone.

"The nanny didn't even bother to take Niko's suitcase to her room." She jerked her head toward a lonely piece of luggage sitting on the sidewalk.

Gwen knew all too well about certain types of nannies. There were those who really loved children and wanted to care for them; then there were those who used it as a gateway to America; and then there were others who used it to gain access to the wealthy, and often their husbands.

Mr. Bridwell picked up Madison's and Niko's suitcases. "Let's see how they're settling in, shall we?" He led the way while Gladys stood guard for the new arrivals.

Gwen had the linens for Madison's room delivered several days before. Madison and Niko hurriedly rummaged through the shopping bags. Madison yanked on the package with her new white comforter with the gold stars.

Niko smiled in approval. "Very nice. Shiny."

Madison wrapped it around her like a shawl. "It feels so snuggly."

"Speaking of snuggly," Gwen said, standing in the doorway. "Mr. Jinx?" She handed the stuffed cat to her daughter.

"This is Mr. Jinx." Madison held him up. "They say the word *jinx* is a jinx, but not him! He's my lucky cat. My uncle gave him to me."

"We have lucky cats, too." Niko unzipped her bag and carefully unwrapped a white cat with one paw in the air. "His name is Maneki Neko."

"Niko, Neko! Niko, Neko!" Madison responded in a singsong.

"My name means 'kindness.' His means 'luck,'" Niko explained.

Gwen leaned against the doorjamb with her arms folded. "I think that is a wonderful combination. Kindness and luck."

"We have two lucky cats!" Madison exclaimed.

"And two lucky girls!" Gwen added.

Gladys appeared in the doorway. "Niko, would you like me to help you unpack the rest of your things? We can take them to your room."

Niko had been completely engrossed in her interaction with Madison that she forgot she hadn't been to her room yet. "Yes, please. Apologies."

"No need to apologize," Gwen jumped in. "You girls are having fun. I'll help Madison, and Gladys can help you. When you're both finished, we can take a walk, or . . . ?" She looked up at Gladys, begging for a suggestion.

"Go down to the pond. There are a whole bunch of baby ducks splashing around."

Madison looked at her mother with wide eyes. "Can we?"

"I don't see why not. What do you think, Niko?"

"I must wait for my parents to call." Her face turned sad.

"I'll tell you what," Gladys broke in, "you go with Madison and Mrs. Taylor. When your parents call, I'll get you. How does that sound?"

Now Niko's eyes went wide. "That would be very nice, Miss Gladys. But my father may be disappointed."

"I'll snatch you up real quick. I can run pretty fast for an old lady." Gladys chuckled. "Come on. Let's get you unpacked and ready to have some fun."

Gwen smiled at Gladys. She was a good egg.

It took the better part of an hour for Madison to unpack her clothes and decide how to drape her comforter, and where to place the pillows.

Gwen thought it was interesting how Madison had an eye

for detail, and placement, from her room to her clothes. Madison was particular, but at the same time, not fussy.

When Niko returned to Madison's room, the three of them went to the lobby area, where Gladys was waiting with two small bags of cracked corn. "The ducks love this." She handed each girl a packet. Gwen, Madison, and Niko strolled through the gardens and then on to the pond, where they spent a half hour enjoying the hatchlings. Gwen spotted Gladys scurrying toward them. "Looks like your parents may be on the phone." She nudged the girls in Gladys's direction, and Niko ran quickly toward her. Gladys waved and then took Niko's hand as they bounded back to the residence.

Gwen and Madison stayed until there was no corn left. "Mommy? Do you love Daddy?"

Gwen stopped abruptly. That was a question she had not anticipated. She didn't know how to answer honestly. She remembered something her mentor taught her: "When in doubt, answer a question with a question." So, she did. "Honey, why do you ask?"

Madison looked a little sheepish and shrugged. "I dunno." And that was the end of the brief conversation, although Madison wondered for the next ten years.

By the time she was in fifth grade, she asked for access to a sewing machine where she would tailor other student's uniforms. It had started with Niko, who was petite and thin. Her uniform hung on her like an oversized bedspread. Madison pinned, tucked, and sewed it to fit her as if it were custom made. Not only did Niko look more polished, but it also elevated her self-esteem. When the other girls heard about Madison's magical talents, they pleaded with her to do the same for them. Over the years, Madison became active in the school theatre. Not as an actor, but as the head of costumes and wardrobe. It inspired her creativity and made her one of the most popular students at the school. By the time she was a junior, she made up her mind to go to one of the best fashion design schools in the country. Not only was she accepted to FIT, but she also won a scholarship for a design she created as part of her entrance exam. There was nothing her father could say or do to keep her from pursuing her goals. Not that he cared.

Chapter Four

Lincoln

Lincoln Taylor was born two years after his sister. By that time, his father was considered a very wealthy man, and Lincoln enjoyed a cushy childhood. His mother and sister doted on him with affection, but not to the extent that Lincoln was self-centered. He was bright and developed an interest in building things with his LEGO sets. His father hoped his son would become a keen athlete and then a financier, but Lincoln would rather assemble things than kick or throw a ball around. Jackson enrolled Lincoln in tennis lessons, but like his sister, he had little interest. He did it to please his father, but his heart wasn't in it.

When Jackson recognized his son wouldn't excel in sports, he took less interest in Lincoln's projects or schooling and happily shipped him off to the Hackley School as soon as possible.

Hackley didn't have a first grade, per se. They started the children with the curriculum of what is taught in second grade in most schools. It was an accelerated program intended to challenge and advance students so they would have a competitive advantage when they completed their education. Naturally, Jackson wanted his son to excel at something and hired tutors to prepare him while he was in kindergarten, and the summer that followed.

Lincoln was a smart fella and a quick study. He surely did not want his sister to be smarter, so he was diligent about the assignments his tutors gave him. By the time he enrolled at Hackley, he was ready academically, although he was a bit shy socially. It was due to the limited access he had to other children. When he wasn't in school, his father insisted he study, which didn't give Lincoln the opportunity to develop friendships. Now, being away from home, the only person he felt comfortable with was his sister.

Madison was thrilled to have her very bright brother down the hall from her, and she made sure she included him in activities with the other kids. It didn't take long for Madison, Niko, and Lincoln to form an alliance. They called themselves the Three Mushcateers, named after the oatmeal they had for breakfast every day.

With Niko's parents traveling as much as they did, Madison invited her to stay at her house on several occasions. She introduced Niko to Olivia, and the house was filled with children's laughter on the weekends. Gwen looked forward to those precious days when their squeals of joy echoed through the massive co-op.

Lincoln enjoyed playing with his sister and her friends. Even though he was the youngest, they would often let him be in charge and decide what games they would play. Once, when Jackson questioned why Gwen allowed Lincoln to spend so much time with "the girls," Gwen took her cue from him. She walked away, but not without a glancing blow of, "It builds character, Jackson. Something you may want to consider developing." He would respond with something trite, but she would be sure she was out of earshot. After ten years, she was beginning to recognize his faults, which were growing in concert with his fortune.

Lincoln was as observant as his sister. As he got older, he could recognize the tension between his parents. Eventually he would discover the phrase *passive-aggressive*. Lincoln also discovered he really didn't like his father much. When he was younger, he didn't have the awareness, but once he went to school and observed how other people treated one another, he realized his father wasn't very nice. And he did not like the way his father treated his mother. His father was dismissive, although it would be a few more years until Lincoln learned what that word meant, as well.

Mr. Bridwell took a special interest in the Taylor children. For having come from a wealthy family, Bridwell was impressed by the way the children treated each other and their peers. They were kind. Friendly. Responsible. Bridwell met Jackson Taylor on very few occasions and attributed the children's standards to Gwen. She was not a mother hen by any stretch of the imagination. She was loving but not smothering. She didn't treat her children as if they were walking on water. Lincoln and Madison knew what was expected of them and were conscious about pleasing their mother and making her proud. By the time they were teenagers, they knew trying to make their father proud was a dead-end street.

When Lincoln turned twelve, Bridwell asked him if he had any interest in learning how to play golf. Finally, there was an outdoor activity that sparked Lincoln's interest. Basketball and football had no appeal. Both seemed too rowdy. Not that Lincoln was a sissy. He preferred a more subdued activity, like the time Uncle Kirby took him fishing when he was younger. Yes, golf could be something he could explore.

When it came to his studies, his favorites were math and science. The hints from his father about going into finance were not subtle, but Lincoln was more inclined to academia. He enjoyed the structure and camaraderie among the faculty of Hackley and wanted to pursue a degree in higher education. Unfortunately, his father put the kibosh on it and told Lincoln he would not pay for his college education if he was just going to become a teacher. "You'd be better off working on the railroad."

It wasn't until years later when Lincoln discovered his father had greatly exaggerated their lineage. True, his grandfather served in World War II. But he was not a decorated hero who died of war injuries. No. His grandfather had been a union worker for the New York Central rail line and died because of injuries sustained in a car accident while he was driving drunk. Lincoln also discovered they were not remotely related to President Zachary Taylor.

By his senior year, Lincoln made a loosely veiled gesture and enrolled in Pace University with a major in finance. He could change it at some point, but if not, he could continue to grad school once he finished there and major in whatever he wanted. But until that time, he had to toe the line.

Lincoln and his sister were model students and graduated with honors. Both applied for scholarships, not because they needed financing, but because their father thought it would look good on their résumés. Scholarships for high achievement.

It was September 1996 when Lincoln began his first year of college, and Madison was entering her junior year at FIT, the Fashion Institute of Technology. That's when everything changed.

Chapter Five

Changes

Madison Taylor was considered one of the most talented students at FIT. She had a knack for mixing and matching patterns that would not normally go together and experimenting with color. Everyone agreed she had a bright future ahead of her. Until she got the call from her mother.

"Madison, honey. I want you to listen very carefully. Do not ask any questions. Just promise you will do what I ask." Gwen's voice was strained but steady.

"Mom? What's going on?" Madison rarely heard her mother sound rattled, but she could hear cold, tense fear.

"Your father has been arrested . . ."

"What?" Madison shrieked. "What do you mean, arrested?"

"Madison, please, just listen to me," Gwen said evenly. "The U.S. Marshal service was at the house with a search warrant. They confiscated all my jewelry and whatever cash we had."

"Can they do that?" Madison was stunned.

"Apparently so. They are seizing assets, so he cannot dispose of evidence or ill-gotten gains."

"What ill-gotten gains?" Madison was having a challenging time processing this bizarre information.

"Please, just let me finish, and we can talk later." Gwen let out a big sigh. "It has something to do with fraud, mishandling of funds."

"But he didn't go to trial yet, right?" Madison insisted on asking questions.

"Madison, please. No, not yet, but they think he is a flight risk."

"What about his lawyer?" Madison kept pushing.

"Sidney said that I should get out of town before the press starts stalking me for information. His arrest is going public as we speak."

"Where are you?" Madison asked.

"I'm at the airport."

"Where are you going?" Madison's eyes welled up.

"Wherever the next flight is going out of JFK."

"What about Lincoln?" Madison's thoughts were in disarray. "What about the apartment? Where can we go?"

"You can go to the house and collect some clothes. There is a U.S. Marshal in the lobby. Show him your identification, and he will escort you to the apartment. I must warn you; he will be watching every move you make." Gwen paused. "You and Lincoln should go together. For moral support."

Madison was nodding at the phone and taking notes. "Maybe I can crash at Olivia's for a few nights."

"I don't think that is a good idea. You do not want her privacy to be compromised."

"Good thinking," Madison responded.

Gwen continued, "Use the credit card attached to my account and get a hotel room. Lincoln, too. As soon as I can figure things out, I will let you know. But for the next few days, I will be out of reach." Gwen was breathless. "You might want to contact your grandmother and stay with her and Pop-Pop this weekend. I should have more information by then."

Madison thought this must be a bad dream. "Mom? I love you."

"I love you too. You and Lincoln are all that matter to me, and I want you to be safe from gawkers and the press and who knows what. From what Sidney told me, there are a lot of incredibly angry clients, and I don't want them harassing you."

"Okay," Madison regrouped. "I will call Nana and tell her to expect me and Lincoln this weekend. Please be careful."

"You too, my sweet, darling daughter." Gwen ended the call.

Madison stared at her phone for a good, long time. *Why was this happening to her family?* Then it dawned on her that she was less surprised than she should have been over her father's arrest. When she was a child, her father was aloof. Distant. It wasn't until she was in high school and took a basic psychology class at Hackley, that she was able to put a name to his behavior: *detached*.

She was grateful for the love and affection her mother demonstrated toward her and her brother, and the clandestine outings she planned for her children to spend time with their real friends. Now, at twenty, she was able to see past the posh and protected life she had grown accustomed to. She and Lincoln thought their lives were normal until they were old enough to distinguish one's version of normal from another. In any case, having your father sitting in jail for fraud was not normal.

Madison checked the Cartier tank watch her mother had given her when she graduated from high school. She wondered if getting a five-thousand dollar watch at age eighteen was normal, too. She then realized she had a lot of real-life learning to do, because her life at that moment was a real-life nightmare.

She had a class in an hour and decided to check in with her brother and grandparents before she did anything else. Lincoln answered on the second ring.

"Maddie! I just got off the phone with Mom. What is going on? Dad's in jail? What happened?" His questions were rapid-fire.

"Did she explain anything?"

"Not really. Just that she was at the airport, Dad got arrested, and you and I must go to the apartment and get some clothes." Lincoln was always on an even keel, but this threw him for a loop.

"We can't stay at the house."

"Why not?"

"I will explain later. What time are you finished with your classes today?"

"Three."

"Okay. Good. Meet me at the house at three thirty. Bring your ID."

"Why?"

"Because we have to show it to the marshal who will escort us up to the apartment."

"Okay. Wow. This is blowing my mind," Lincoln replied.

"Mine too. I will see you at three thirty. And Lincoln? Do not speak to anyone. Mom thinks as soon as this news breaks, the press will be all over us with questions."

"Okay. Gotcha. See you later. Love ya."

"Love you more." Ever since they were children, they always signed off with an expression of affection.

Madison had been sitting in the student lounge when the disturbing call came from her mother. She looked around to see if anyone might have heard her conversations. There were several contemporaries a few yards away, deep in their own dialogues. None of them had taken any notice. She quickly gathered up her portfolio and made a beeline to her next class, constantly checking over her shoulder for any paparazzi. She kept repeating "No comment" to herself. That was the only answer she planned to give anyone: friends, acquaintances, or foes. She'd throw in "family emergency" if necessary. But there was one person she really wanted to talk to. It was her best friend, Olivia. But should she? She debated the question as she hurried to class. Her cell phone rang. It was Olivia. *Was it possible Olivia knew what was going on?* Would her mother have told Olivia's mother? Madison didn't know if she should answer it, so she decided to let it go to voicemail.

She arrived at her seat breathless. "You alright?" her teacher asked.

"Huh? Oh, yes. I thought I was going to be late." Madison leaned into the back of the chair. Surely no media would be storming the classroom. After all, it wasn't she who had been arrested. Madison wondered how quickly news traveled. She was sure she would find out by the end of the day, or when she and Lincoln showed up at the apartment.

Her professor looked at Madison again. "Are you sure you're alright?"

"Huh? I'm sorry. I'm a little distracted. Family stuff." There. That was good enough. Her professor would surely find out during the evening news, and then there would be no escaping the questions. Another troubling thought occurred to her. *What if she had to move out of town?* No. It wouldn't be that bad. After her father's story, the media would be on to the next one. She took a deep breath and convinced herself that the frenzy would eventually blow over, and life would go back to—what? Normal? Now there was something that would remain to be seen.

What about her mother? She would be taking the brunt of the questions. What if she got arrested, too? Madison knew her mother would be questioned eventually. Would the authorities view Gwen's leaving as a sign of guilt? Madison tried to maintain a level of optimism. Sidney would have given her mother advice. But what was the advice? Beat feet? Madison made a mental note to phone Sidney between classes. As classmates began to fill the room, Madison knew she wouldn't be able to focus on anything. The "family issue" thing would work on her professor. She decided to take a chance and got up from her chair. "Excuse me, Mrs. Clarkson. Do you think I could be excused from class today?"

"You said there were family issues?"

"Yes, but I'd rather not discuss them right now." She nodded toward the growing number of students.

"I understand. Of course you can be excused. You know what this week's assignment is, correct?"

"Yes. A collage." For some reason, saying those words gave her hope. It reminded her of the time when she and her mother bonded over torn pages from magazines, poster boards, and Elmer's. Madison made another mental note: *Find the colarge.* She chuckled to herself, recalling how she mispronounced the word. Funny how the memory of one small incident sticks with you. It was also a moment when she made up her mind to articulate and pronounce words properly. Madison was not a precocious child. She imagined some people may have thought she was. To be more accurate would be to say she was observant and tenacious. *Nothing wrong with that.*

Madison thanked her teacher and hustled to the student center again. She looked for a cubicle where she could phone her grandmother in private. The cubicles had once been phone booths. But with the growing popularity and use of mobile phones, the school remodeled them. Now they were wider with a seat and a shelf, and only two had payphones. The faculty thought they should keep at least two in operation in case of an emergency, or if a student was not fortunate to have a cell phone. Naturally, Madison was one of the fortunate ones. Everyone in her family had one. This year it was the Motorola Flip, until the next new model came out. That was one thing she could depend on from her father: the newest, and in all probability, the most expensive one available.

She pulled out a small notebook where she kept addresses and phone numbers. While she fumbled through the pages, she passed Niko's number and recalled the first day they met at Hackley and how they had bonded over their toy cats. Madison's was a plush toy named Mr. Jinx, and Niko's was a white porcelain cat named Maneki Neko. He was supposed to be for good luck. Again, another vivid memory from her childhood. She thought about the word *luck*. Now *that* was something to contemplate: *What exactly is luck, or to be lucky? Not being on that train when it derailed? Or being shoved in the opposite direction of an oncoming bus? Or having immense worldly comforts only to have your father get tossed in jail?* She could use a Maneki Neko right about now.

She wondered how her friend was doing in Japan. After Niko's parents' terms were over at the U.N., the family moved back to their homeland. She and Niko tried to stay connected, but thousands of miles can be challenging in maintaining a friendship. Madison opened her planner and jotted down a note to send Niko a card. With everything spiraling out of control, Madison was grateful she had something to keep track of where she was supposed to be and when. She also wrote a note to call Sidney, the family lawyer, and to be sure to pack Mr. Jinx. She had kept him in decent shape all these years. But first things first. Call Nana.

Her maternal grandmother answered after two rings.

"Nana? It's Madison." She knew she was stating the obvious.

"Madison, dear. I just got off the phone with your mother.

I'm not sure what is going on, but we think you and Lincoln should come here this weekend so we can figure out a plan for both of you."

"A plan?" Madison blinked several times. Of course. A plan. "Did mom give you any details?"

"Only that everyone had to get out of the house, and your father is in jail." Her grandmother's voice was stiff. Initially she'd thought Jackson was a good catch, but he turned out to be a shark. "We should have more information by the end of the week. I hope. You and Lincoln should plan to get here Friday night. I will cook your favorite."

"Short ribs and popovers?" Madison smiled. A home-cooked meal at her Nana's would be a salve on this sting of upheaval.

"Your mother loved to go to Patricia Murphy's when she got her paycheck." Mrs. Wainwright was referring to the restaurant owned and operated by Patrica Murphy on East 49th Street. It was known to be a gathering place for "ladies who lunch." Gwen and Sandra would splurge once a month to "see how the other half lived." Little did she know at the time that she would become one of the other halves. Now, Gwen was on the run from all of it.

"I remember her stories about her first couple of years in the city," Madison recalled. "I hope she is okay. She sounded really rattled on the phone."

"Your mother is resilient. She is one tough cookie."

Madison chuckled. Her mother was even-tempered, but if you knew Gwen well enough, you could see the blaze in her eyes when pushed against a wall. "You got that right, Nana." Madison noticed another student pacing in front of the booth. "I must get going. I'm meeting up with Lincoln in a little bit. We are going to the house to rescue some clothes."

"Where are you going to stay for the rest of the week?"

"I am not sure. A hotel somewhere between our schools. SoHo, the Village, or Gramercy Park."

"Okay, sweetheart. Call me later and let me know how you made out getting your things from home, and where you will be staying." She let out a sigh. "It is going to be okay. We will get through this."

"Nana? Do you know where Mom was going?"

"Someplace where she could think, I suppose. You know the press will be stalking her until they find another story to follow."

Madison chuckled. "We are all on the same page. No pun intended."

Mrs. Wainwright smiled at the phone. "You are quite the wit. Be careful. We will chat later."

"Thanks, Nana. Love you." Madison ended the call and exited the small booth.

Madison checked her watch again. Almost noon. Maybe she would grab some lunch. The time she had to wait to meet up with her brother was excruciating. As she walked through the common area, she wondered if anyone had heard the news yet. One thing was certain, it would be all over the networks at five o'clock. Better to reserve rooms at a hotel now so she and Lincoln would have a destination once they left Sutton Place.

She left the building and decided to walk in the direction of the SoHo Grand Hotel. It had recently opened and was convenient for both to attend classes. It would take about twenty minutes by foot. She planned to book two rooms for four nights, and for the following week. That should give them enough time to figure out more permanent housing. This way, they could leave most of their things, what little they could carry, with the bellman at the hotel, instead of dragging everything back and forth to Connecticut. And what, exactly, was everything? She wondered how much the marshal would let them take. She sighed. She would eventually find out.

Instead of stopping at a restaurant, she decided to go against one of her rules: do not eat anything from a street vendor. But today was different. If she interpreted her mother correctly, they could be eating hot dogs, or "dirty water dogs" (as some people called them), for a long time. She might as well get used to it. When she arrived at 23rd Street, there were a half dozen food carts. Falafels. Sausages. Hot dogs. Chicken kebabs. A plethora of aromas from all the mystery sandwiches you could ever want filled the air.

On the other side of the corner were two men with knock-off designer purses laying on top of a blanket. They looked legit from a distance, but Madison could easily tell a real Prada from a fake one. She ordered a hot dog with sauerkraut and mustard. As the vendor was handing her the hot dog, loud voices roared from the corner where the imitation handbags were. The two men gathered their wares quickly and jumped into the back of an unmarked, beat-up van, which had been idling a few feet away. The getaway vehicle peeled out of the space as the men fumbled to pull the doors shut. A police car was half a block away but did not seem to be in any hurry to catch them. She guessed the police had better things to do than confiscate some fake accessories. She smirked. *They were busy arresting white-collar criminals.*

Madison continued to walk down Seventh Avenue as she licked the mustard from between her fingers. She could not walk into the hotel smelling like she took a bath in the vendor's cart. She stopped at Loehmann's department store and used the ladies' room to freshen up. On her way out, she made sure she sprayed herself with one of the perfume samples.

As she approached the hotel, she took in a few deep breaths and centered herself. They had no idea who she was or from whom she was running. Not yet, anyway.

She walked into the lobby with her head held high. The concierge greeted her. "Good afternoon, Miss. May I help you?"

Madison gave him her winning smile. There was no sign of dismay on her face. "Good afternoon. I would like to see if you have two rooms available for the remainder of the week."

"Certainly. This way, please." He walked her over to the front desk. "Miss?" He waited for Madison to respond. She was not sure what name she should use. But she really had no choice. The credit card said Gwen Taylor.

"Miss Madison Taylor. A room for me and my brother Lincoln." She wondered how long it would take the hotel staff to put the pieces together. *Never,* she hoped. "We would like to stay until Friday and then return Sunday evening. Is that possible?"

The clerk behind the front desk typed a few things into her computer. "We have availability for the next four nights. When do you think you will be returning? Afternoon? Evening?"

"Whichever is most convenient," Madison said. She was at the hotel's mercy at the moment. The trains ran regularly, so transportation would not be an issue.

"Check-in is at three o'clock, but we can put you in for a later arrival if that is more convenient for you."

"Let's say six?" Madison calculated the train ride in her head. Plus, she would need time with her grandparents to sort things out as much as possible. Hopefully, her mother would make contact by then, as well.

"Absolutely." The associate typed a few things into the system.

"We would also like to check our luggage with the bell captain, if possible. We are visiting our grandparents for only two nights and don't need to bring everything with us."

"Not a problem. When you check out on Friday, just ask the bellman to take your things to the captain. You can pick up the ticket on your way out."

Madison was relieved. She was able to buy ten days of shelter. At least she had some of the bases covered. For now. She knew she could depend on Lincoln to be level-headed and proactive. Even though he was not as much of an extrovert as his sister, he had strength and stamina. More importantly, he had integrity. And so did she. They would muddle through this together, regardless of where their mother was now. It did not matter if all they had left were the shirts on their backs. Madison knew her mother would never abandon them. At least not emotionally. Considering what was going on, that was a plus, especially since she did not know the finer points of the situation.

The woman behind the desk finally looked up. "Would you like the bellman to bring your bags to the room?"

"I do not have them with me. I will be picking them up this afternoon."

The clerk did not flinch. Many people would check in without luggage and have it delivered later. Or never. It depended whether it was a legitimate guest, or a clandestine meeting of a highly paid executive and an "escort," as they wish to be called.

The associate handed Madison the key. "Do you want to take the key for your brother's room, as well? I have both of you checked in right now."

"Yes, that will be fine. Thank you." Madison checked her watch again. Another two and a half hours to go.

"Would you like someone to see you to your room?" the woman asked.

Madison smiled. "No, thank you. I believe I can find it."

"Enjoy your stay," the clerk called out as Madison walked toward the elevators.

Their rooms were on the twelfth floor. If the press were in the lobby, and Madison and Lincoln had to sneak out of the hotel, they could take the elevator to a lower floor and then use the stairs. *But how would the media know where they were staying?* It took less than an instant for Madison to realize they might be swarming the front of the apartment building at this very moment. Even though she was only nine years old at the time, she remembered a big hubbub about one of her father's acquaintances. The man's name was Boesky, and he'd been arrested for insider trading. She didn't know what it meant at the time but read about it when she was in high school. She also remembered how her father was on edge for a while. But then again, he was always either on edge, reticent, or invisible.

When she got to her room, she found a plush robe hanging in the closet. So far, it was the highlight of her day. Or was it the hot dog? It dawned on her that the men selling bootlegged handbags were no worse than her father. That is, if what he was accused of was true. In her heart, she believed it was. She was beginning to feel uncomfortable with the thoughts she was having about her father. He was an enigma. It was due to the things he was doing in the shadows, which included cheating on her mother. Unfortunately, his affairs were not the big secret he tried to hide. *Men can be so stupid. Or was it arrogance? Most likely the latter.*

Madison turned on the shower and opened the small bottles of BVLGARI shampoo, conditioner, and body wash. The warm water streamed over her body, cleansing the street dirt and the emotional dirt from her being. If only she had purchased a new outfit when she stopped at the department store. After her shower, she blew out her shoulder-length hair and pulled it back in a ponytail. She hung her clothes on the back of the bathroom door and ran the shower again, hoping the steam would freshen her clothes. At least she would smell good when she met up with the U.S. Marshal. Not that it mattered what he thought. It was simply something she always tried to manage. Put on a good appearance, even if it is just for your own sake and self-esteem.

Madison realized her clothes were beginning to get damp

from all the steam and began to run the blow-dryer up and down her pants. *This has been some kind of day. And it ain't over yet,* she mused.

Again, she checked her watch. She'd managed to tick off another hour. She had ninety minutes to go before she met up with Lincoln. It would take about that long if she wanted to walk the three miles to the soon-to-be former apartment. She'd probably be a sweaty mess by the time she got there. Maybe she'd walk through SoHo and then grab a cab. But then again, maybe not. She had to be careful of how she spent her money until she knew exactly how much there was left. She checked her wallet, found a few MTA tokens, and decided she would take the bus uptown and then walk across town. That should get her there in plenty of time with a few minutes to spare.

She checked herself in the mirror. She was beginning to look increasingly like her mother. Some said Gwen resembled Jessica Lange. Madison could live with that. She remembered one night they were playing "Who do you look like?" and her brother was flagged as Jeff Daniels, who had recently starred in the film *Pleasantville*, but Lincoln preferred Nick Carter of the Backstreet Boys. Madison responded with a sarcastic, "You'll get over it, when you realize how dumb that is."

It also occurred to her they had not included their father in the game. It was because they rarely got a good look at him. She snickered. But if she had to choose someone, it would be Jeff Bridges. It was not a secret that her father was handsome. That, along with his charm, is what got them into this fine mess.

As she walked to the bus stop, she kept looking over her shoulder, waiting to be accosted by some hungry journalist looking for a juicy story. She realized she was being paranoid, but she saw how the press could take over people's lives. No wonder so many celebrities paid people to keep them out of the paper. Yet, there were those who paid loads of money to make sure they were always in print. *What a world.*

There weren't many people on the bus, and she managed to get a seat. She perused the crowd and wondered how many of them were happy. Worried? Anxious? Angry? Content? Madison looked at one woman who sat with a bag on her lap. The woman was expressionless. *Was she sad?* Madison wondered. Whenever she and Lincoln were bored, they would make up stories about other people around them. People they did not know. If they were at a restaurant, Lincoln would lean in and whisper something outrageous, such as, "They're private detectives pretending to be husband and wife while they tail a cheating husband." Or, "Bank robbers stopping for a bite to eat to throw off the police." Madison would howl. Lincoln was the quiet one, yet always had something witty to say when no one else was paying attention. She wondered what kind of mood he was going to be in today.

When the bus arrived at 57th Street, Madison exited through the side door and walked east. She slowed as she approached the neighborhood, looking in each direction for gossip predators. But was it gossip? She remembered laughing with Olivia, "If it's true, then it isn't gossip." Madison knew her world was changing at a rapid pace. She hoped she could keep up.

Madison was relieved to see her brother waiting at the front entrance. He was chatting with Reggie, the door attendant. Neither of them looked dismayed or bothered. Lincoln was smiling and nodding. That's her brother—relaxed, cool. Of the two of them, he represented calm. Not that Madison would become hysterical; she was simply more animated. She kept her head down, and her eyes darted side to side. "There she is," Lincoln announced, and put his arm around her shoulders. "Good talking to you, Reggie. See you in a bit." Madison was always impressed by how mature her brother appeared, and his impeccable manners. It was Hackley. And their mother. Gwen taught them about having good manners at an early age.

"Hey, Reggie," Madison managed with a strained smile.

"Good afternoon, Miss Madison." Reggie always referred to her as *Miss* before her first name. It started when she was around twelve. One afternoon he referred to her as Miss Taylor. Madison insisted he call her Madison, so they compromised with "Miss Madison." Reggie was a good old transplanted southern gentleman. She had no idea how old he was. Her grandfather's age?

Reggie opened the door for the siblings, who moved swiftly to the front desk where a U.S. Marshal waited. One of the prune-faced co-op board members gave them the stink eye as she passed them on her way out. "Hello, Mrs. Greenwood." Lincoln paid no attention to the old battle ax's sour puss. She huffed a response. Lincoln elbowed Madison, who bit her lip to keep from laughing.

Lincoln and Madison showed the marshal their IDs, and the three approached the elevator bank. When they exited on their floor, Madison let out a big whoosh of air. "That is something I am not going to miss. Old crabby cakes."

"The building is filled with them. Or had you not noticed?" Lincoln joked. The marshal smiled at him. Lincoln went on to say, "I suppose this isn't the best time to be joking, but under the circumstances, it's better than crying."

The marshal simply nodded at the two young adults. They did not seem the least bit smug or spoiled, something he would have anticipated, given the surroundings. Another guard was sitting in the hallway. The two greeted each other, and the guard unlocked the apartment door. "I'm sorry, but I am going to have to escort both of you to your rooms and monitor what you pack. Who wants to go first?"

"She'll take the longest, so let's start with her," Lincoln said, jerking his thumb at his sister.

"Ha ha. Very funny," Madison deadpanned. She looked at the agent and nodded ahead. "My room's this way." The three climbed the stairs to the second floor. Lincoln leaned against the doorjamb, while Madison tossed a few pairs of jeans, blazers, T-shirts, and underwear into a Gucci suitcase. Then she stopped abruptly. "Is it alright for me to use this bag?" Not that she had any alternatives. The marshal gave her an affirmative shrug. He could tell these kids were victims of their father's wrongdoings. It was not their fault that the world as they knew it was coming to an abrupt halt. Chances were good their father would be spending a long stint behind bars. The government usually does not go after high-profile people unless they have a good case; otherwise, it would be a waste of valuable resources.

Madison went into her private bathroom and piled her makeup and beauty products into a travel bag. Then she continued to pack her leather boots, loafers, and a pair of sneakers. She knew she could not bring her entire wardrobe with her. "Will I be able to come back for some of my things at a later date?"

"It's possible, but you may have to get a court order," the agent replied.

Madison's stomach turned. *A court order?* Things were getting more complicated. She checked and double-checked for things she could not live without, including Mr. Jinx and the collage. She tucked both precious pieces under her arm and left the suitcase at the top of the stairs. "That should be it for me. Lead the way, dear brother."

The three walked down the hallway to Lincoln's room. While Madison's room reflected her artistic flair, her brother's was more minimalist. Lincoln took little time packing a few shirts, slacks, jeans, jackets, underwear, and socks. He tossed his Dopp kit on top of his clothes and zipped up the Tumi luggage. He also did a quick once-around to be sure he was not leaving anything important behind. Unlike his father, Lincoln was not interested in gold cufflinks, heavy link bracelets, or pinky rings. The only piece of jewelry he owned was a Cartier watch like his sister's. It was a gift from his mother when he graduated from Hackley.

"That should do it for me." Lincoln heaved the bag off the bed and started back toward the stairs. "I suppose you want me to carry that for you?" he half-joked with his sister.

"I'll get it," the marshal offered. Again, he was beginning to feel sorry for them.

When they reached the bottom of the stairs, Madison decided it was time to navigate one of her fears and turned toward the agent. "Do you think there will be any press?"

"Not yet, but certainly after the evening news. If you feel you are being harassed or stalked, let me know, and I will try to arrange for security." He handed her his card, and then gave one to Lincoln.

The gravity of the situation was starting to sink in. It was one thing to hear about it over the phone. It was another when you were rushed into packing your necessities for what could be the last time. The apartment was eerily quiet. They had no time to prepare for this separation. Emotionally, intellectually, or physically. Their lives had been driven off a cliff. The only thing they could do was pray for a soft landing. Not that there was any expectation of going back to the way things were. There was no doubt that wasn't going to happen. They would have to be able to brush off the dust, heal their wounds, and move on with life with as few scars as possible.

Madison was much more concerned about her mother. She was the one who spent the last twenty-two years living in a fantasy world. Of course, Madison existed in a world of plenitude, but attending Hackley during the week removed her from the twenty-four-seven, in-your-face opulence. Her personal surroundings at Hackley were minimal. Her schedule, demanding. Madison knew she had many more years to recover from this humiliation and degradation. Her mother? Sure, Gwen could be steely. But she was also human.

As they were about to enter the elevator, the agent drew his cuff to his face and spoke into his shirtsleeve. "All clear?" It was then when both Lincoln and Madison noticed the earpiece. They were too engrossed in what they had to do in a short amount of time to pay attention to the marshal's head. They looked at each other with raised eyebrows.

The agent looked at them just before the doors opened into the lobby. "Follow me. Speak to no one."

Madison started to get nervous. *Here it comes*. But when the doors opened, there was only one scraggly-looking guy with a camera and a portable recording device. "Excuse me! Excuse me! Are you the Taylor kids?" In one way, she was relieved to find there was a lone reporter waiting. But in another way, she knew this was just the beginning.

The marshal got between the overzealous reporter and the siblings. He did not have to say a word. The reporter immediately backed away when the agent stared him down. He opened the service door. "Wait here," he instructed, indicating they should stand against the wall. Madison and Lincoln said nothing and did what they were told. The marshal counted for about twenty seconds. He looked through the small window of the door. "He's gone around to the side. We are going out the front."

The agent got another "all-clear" from the other marshal who was standing with the door attendant. They hustled to the cab Reggie hailed for them. The trunk was open and ready for their luggage. Reggie quickly opened the rear passenger door, and the two hurried in. As Reggie began to close the door of the taxi, Madison let the tears roll. She squeaked out, "Thanks for everything, Reggie. I am going to miss you."

"I shall miss you too, Miss Madison." He leaned into the

window. "Good luck to you. And your mother." He tapped the roof of the taxi, as it pulled out of the circular drive.

Madison tried to keep herself from sobbing, but holding back gave her the hiccups. Lincoln put his arm around her. "It's going to be okay, sis."

Madison rested her head on his shoulder. "I hope you're right."

The driver looked into the rearview mirror. "Where to, kids?"

Lincoln turned and peered through the rear window of the cab. He, too, was beginning to understand how exposed they would be for the next few days. Probably more.

"SoHo Grand," Madison said, sniffling.

"Isn't that a bit pricey, considering the circumstances?" Lincoln quizzed her.

"Mom said to use her card. Unless they throw us out on the street, we are registered."

Lincoln checked every few blocks to see if anyone was following them. Traffic was beginning to build as people began their commute from work. Even if someone were following them, they, too, would be stuck in the daily transportation torture.

Fifteen minutes later, they arrived in front of the hotel and were greeted by a bellman. Madison gave him their room numbers, and they followed him to the elevator, as he wheeled their remaining possessions to the twelfth floor. Lincoln thanked and tipped him. Again, Madison was impressed with the maturity of her little brother. He was eighteen going on thirty.

"What do you want to do about dinner?" Lincoln asked.

"Room service?" Madison answered quickly. "We can watch our family be humiliated on the five o'clock news."

"Do you think they'll hound us at school?" Lincoln asked.

"I am going to the dean's office first thing. By then they

will know what is going on, and I will inform them that I still plan on attending classes."

"I'll do the same thing." Lincoln nodded. "I am going to unpack. See you in thirty." Lincoln took his bag to the room across the hall.

Madison placed her suitcase on the rack, unpacked, and hung her clothes in the closet. She changed into one of the two tracksuits she brought, moved to the desk, and phoned Sidney. "Hi, Sidney. It's Madison." She slumped down on the bed, hoping she might hear some good news.

"Hello, Madison. How are you and Lincoln holding up?"

"Okay, so far. We went to the apartment and got some clothes. We are at the SoHo Grand right now."

"Good. You know the routine. Do not speak to anyone. 'No comment' is your only comment. Do not engage in any conversation regarding this matter."

"With anyone?" Madison wanted to be certain what the limitations were.

"Not if you can help it. Your family is one thing, but the less said, the better. You do not want any of your friends called as witnesses."

"Witnesses to what?" Madison was genuinely confused.

"Your lifestyle, for one," Sidney explained. "They are going to be showing how extravagantly you lived."

"But . . ." Madison was still unclear. "It was my father, not me, my brother, nor my mother."

"You and your brother are going to be okay."

"But Mom?" Madison's heart sank.

"It is going to take a lot of convincing that your mother knew nothing about your father's business."

"But she didn't." Madison's voice got louder. "He was barely around."

"Yes, but she was living under the circumstances of your father's income."

"Is she going to be arrested, too?" Madison thought she might faint.

"Not likely. But she will be asked to give a deposition."

"When?" Madison started to doodle on the pad next to the phone.

"We don't know that yet."

"Do you know where she is?" Madison asked.

"I can't say."

"Can't or won't?" Madison had an excellent grasp of semantics.

"The less you know, the better. For now." Sidney cleared his throat. "I want to hire private security for you and Lincoln."

"Why?" Madison did not think her life was threatened until Sidney explained.

"Your father hurt a lot of people. People are angry. If they can't take it out on him, they may come after you and Lincoln."

Madison dropped the phone and vomited into the trash can. The thought of revenge had not occurred to her. She had been engaged in anticipating the breaking news and her next move. But this? This was beyond disturbing.

She could hear Sidney's voice coming through the phone that landed on the floor. "Madison? Are you alright?"

She wretched again and mumbled, "Yeah. Give me a minute." She went into the bathroom, rinsed her mouth, and wiped her face. "I'm coming, Sidney. Hang on," she called toward the place where her phone was lying on the rug. She held the damp washcloth to her face.

"Madison?"

"Yes, Sidney. I am here." She fumbled with the phone and placed it next to her ear. "What do we do now?"

"I recommend you stay with your grandparents for a while. I don't think anyone will track you to Connecticut."

"But what about school?" Madison asked.
"You may have to put your studies on hold. Temporarily."
"But Sidney, Lincoln just started his freshman year. I have huge projects coming up. I am supposed to assist at the Met Gala."
"I'm sorry, Madison. But your safety is of the utmost importance. Best you and your brother stay under the radar."
Madison's head was reeling. "For how long?"
"A couple of weeks at the least." Sidney paused. "I know this is an extremely difficult situation to navigate, especially coming out of left field. But it is imperative you take the necessary precautions. Both of you."
"Sidney? Can I call you right back? I want to get Lincoln so we can talk this through together."
"Certainly."
"Give me five minutes."
Madison peeked through the fish-eye lens of the door. The hall was empty. She flipped the swing bolt to keep the door ajar and knocked on her brother's door. He opened it immediately. "What's up?"
"You have to come to my room. We need to talk to Sidney."
"Sure." He grabbed his room key. "You okay? You smell like puke."
"Very observant." Madison pushed her door open and locked it after they entered.
"Are you alright?" Lincoln saw how pale his fair-skinned sister looked.
"Just a reaction to Sidney." She shoved the trash can into the bathroom and shut the door. "I'll deal with that later."
"I'll call housekeeping." Lincoln dialed the number using the house phone. "Good afternoon. My sister took ill and had a mishap in the trash can. If you don't mind, I am going to leave it in the hallway covered with a towel." He paused. "Yes, fresh towels would be appreciated. Thank you."

Madison hit the speaker button on her cell. "Sidney. I have Lincoln here."

"Lincoln. How are you holding up?" The voice of Sidney Rothberg floated toward him.

"I'm alright. Baffled, but alright."

"I told your sister that you should both be aware that there may be some people who seek revenge."

Lincoln shot Madison an inquisitive look. She nodded for him to listen.

"Revenge?" Lincoln asked with an even tone.

"As I explained to Madison, your father made a lot of enemies, and there may be some people who want to get even with him."

"By doing something to us?" Lincoln asked.

"It is possible. While there haven't been any overt threats, we need to take precautions. I suggested to Madison that you suspend your studies for the time being."

The cool, calm Lincoln balked. "Sidney, I just started. Where am I supposed to go? I can't transfer now."

Sidney sighed. "I understand. But please give it some thought. Baruch? No one will think about looking for you at a city college, even though it has an outstanding business program. I know some of the senior faculty members. I am certain they can offer assistance."

Lincoln looked at his sister. "What about Madison?"

"She has a higher profile than you do."

"Meaning?" Lincoln asked.

"Meaning, if the press is going to tail anyone, it will be her. She has garnered some publicity in the fashion pages."

Lincoln could not argue. Madison had been featured in *Women's Wear Daily* during their spring round-up of promising students. She was getting attention in the use of mixed media in patterns and textiles.

"I suggested you spend some time at your grandparents'."

"Yes, we're planning on heading up there Friday afternoon."

"That's four days from now. News will be breaking in less than an hour."

"Are you suggesting we leave tomorrow?" Madison chimed in. "I was going to speak to the dean. Can't they stop people from entering the school property?"

"They can try, given it's a small campus." Sidney paused for a moment. "How about this, we hire private security for the remainder of the week. That should give both of you enough time to sort out your classes. Once you get to your grandparents' house, we should have a clearer picture."

Madison shook her head. For the first time in her life, she was stupefied. "I cannot believe this is happening." She paused. "Sidney? You are the family estate lawyer. Who is going to be our father's criminal attorney?"

"There have been a few names bandied about. Unfortunately, his assets are frozen. He has also been remanded due to being a flight risk."

Madison sat up straight. "What about tuition? Lincoln and I have scholarships. They cannot be transferred."

"Your mother had the good sense to put money aside in a trust for your education. She also had the good sense to have her own bank account. I do not know her exact financial situation, but she will be okay for a while." He waited for the siblings to absorb this new information.

Madison was the first to speak. "So, let us go down the list. You are going to hire private security for us for the remainder of the week."

"Correct."

"And then?" Madison asked.

"And then you'll discuss your housing situation with your grandparents."

"I can move in with Tyler. He's still looking for a roommate, and he lives near Tribeca."

"That would be convenient if you transfer to Baruch," Sidney offered.

"It's not exactly upstate from Pace," Lincoln said sardonically.

"You finish your first year at Pace and then transfer to Baruch. Even with the scholarship at Pace, there are some heavy expenses. At least with Baruch, you will use less trust money, which will enable you to do graduate work if you wish."

The words *graduate work* rang in Lincoln's ears. That was something he planned to do. He hadn't discussed it with anyone yet.

"What about me?" Madison asked.

"Madison, I am a little more concerned about you than Lincoln. He has a lower profile, and it will be easy for him to blend into the neighborhood near Baruch."

"What happens to the scholarship money at Pace?" Lincoln asked.

"The balance will revert to the school. Think of it as giving another student an opportunity."

Lincoln could not argue with that.

"Hello? Remember me?" Madison was dreading the answer.

"Rhode Island School of Design?" Sidney winced while making his suggestion. It was a private school and much pricier.

Madison could not argue with the ranking of RISD. It is considered one of the finest in the country. But that meant uprooting herself. Reestablishing herself. She had put so much time and effort into her undergraduate work so far. But she could bring her projects with her. She would be the new kid on the block, but she was also prepared. At least she did not have to worry about Gerard, her ex-boyfriend. It would be good to be far away from him, and not have to plan her social schedule around when he might be hanging out at their usual haunts.

Madison was ticking off the pluses and negatives. Olivia was attending school in Boston. She would have a friend an hour's train ride away. Madison was making a valiant attempt to put a positive spin on this very ugly, overwhelming situation. What mattered was her artistic creativity. She could bring that with her regardless of where she landed.

Lincoln looked pensive. "Let me get this straight. I go to Pace for one year and then to Baruch. Madison goes to RISD now? I live with Tyler and Madison lives with who?"

"I can stay with Nana and Pops until I get settled." Madison was already getting her head in gear.

"Sidney, if you think you can make this transition as painless as possible, there's really no other option, correct?" Lincoln stepped into his adult shoes.

"Correct."

"You mentioned security," Lincoln prompted.

"We will set you up with a private company and monitor the fallout. If we can keep your names out of the papers, there's less chance you'll be on other people's radar. What kind of building does Tyler live in?"

"Doorman."

"Are you sure he's serious about having a roommate?" Madison interjected.

"I'll call him now." Lincoln pulled out his cell phone and dialed his friend's number. "Ty. LincLinc. You serious about a roommate?" Lincoln listened and nodded. "Long story. I will catch you up tomorrow." Another pause. "Sounds good. Thanks, man." The air in the room lifted.

Lincoln turned to his sister and the speakerphone. "We're good. I have to pay for the utilities. His folks are paying for the loft. It's in Tribeca. Just south of Canal, close to Chinatown, so there will be plenty of places for us to eat!"

The idea of food made Madison's stomach turn again.

Sidney gave a slight chuckle and continued. "Two security guards will meet you in the lobby tomorrow morning. They will escort you to school."

"That's going to look kind of goofy, no?" Madison asked.

"These guys are paid to shadow you. Their job is to have their eyes and ears peeled. You can just pretend they're not there," Sidney reassured them. "Madison, you should plan on RISD. With your credits and GPA, you should have no trouble transferring. Fortunately, you are only three weeks into the semester, and I know you are a quick study."

Madison thought she might hurl again but was able to keep whatever was left in her stomach inside her stomach.

"I know this is hard. But I have known the two of you since you were little kids. You are going to be okay. It is another one of life's adjustments. I will call you tomorrow afternoon to see how things are moving along. In the meantime, if you need anything from me, just call. Cynthia will find me."

"Thanks, Sidney," Madison replied. Lincoln followed.

"And Mom? Can you tell us where she is?"

"The less you know, the better. She is okay. She will be in touch later this evening. Now, get something to eat, and try to get a good night's sleep. You have a lot of work ahead of you."

"Goodnight, Sidney," Madison spoke into the phone.

The two sat in silence for a few moments. Lincoln put his arm around his sister. "Well, kiddo, it's not like this is the first time we've been exiled from our domicile."

"True, but at least we had one on the weekends." Madison sniffed, but she was not going to cry. No. She had to save her strength for the days, weeks, and months ahead.

Lincoln opened the leather-bound directory and flipped to the Room Service page. "Now that you emptied your stomach of that street dog, how is your appetite?"

"How did you know I ate a hot dog?" Madison furrowed her brow.

"Evidence: trash can. Your breath." Lincoln elbowed her.

"Maybe soup and a club sandwich."

"You bet. Who is paying for this?" He was half joking.

"I guess Mom." She shrugged. She pulled the portfolio from her brother's grip. "I wonder how their burgers are." Madison's appetite rebounded. "I think this calls for extra crispy fries."

"Talk about a one-eighty!" Lincoln gasped.

"What can I say? I am hungry now that my stomach is empty. But just to be on the safe side, I will order a ginger ale."

She placed their order and flopped on the bed. She steeled herself as she clicked the TV remote. "Fasten your seat belt."

The announcer came on:

> "We have breaking news. Two of Wall Street's most influential financiers were arrested today and charged with fraud. Jackson Taylor and Raymond Gershon, of Taylor-Gershon, have been charged with twelve felony counts, including wire fraud, money laundering, securities fraud, and false filings with the SEC. Both men are being held without bail. More on this story after these messages."

Lincoln and Madison watched their handcuffed father as he was escorted into the criminal court, his Gianni Versace suit jacket pulled over his head, hiding his face. Gershon was similarly attired.

"This is surreal," Lincoln commented. "But this is probably the most I've seen of him lately," he said, and snickered.

Madison threw a pillow at him and laughed. "This is what it must be like in the *Twilight Zone*."

"You know something, Maddie? We were *living* in the *Twilight Zone*. Now, we have been thrust into reality."

"Quite a trajectory, I'd say." Madison got up and pulled Mr. Jinx from her bag. Lincoln grinned.

"Interesting."

"What?" Madison sat down on the bed.

"Stuff that is important to us. Of all the things you could have taken from the house, you picked Mr. Jinx."

She pulled out the collage and unrolled it. "And this. My first piece of art." She climbed back onto the bed. "What did you grab?"

Lincoln handed her a small box. Inside was a golf tee.

"What's this?"

"A golf tee. Surely, you have seen them before," he joked.

"No. Never. Duh. But why this one in particular?"

"It is the one I used when I finally broke one hundred. I always carried it for good luck."

"Obviously, you were not carrying it today."

"But I am now."

Their conversation got interrupted by a knock on the door. A muffled voice called, "Room service."

Lincoln checked through the pinhole. He opened the door and let the waiter roll the cart into the room. As he was setting up the table, the news returned with "more on the story."

"Can you believe those two?" the waiter commented. "Stealing money from old ladies. Families. Retirement accounts? Shameful." He *tsk*ed. "They should throw them in the slammer for a very long time." Lincoln maintained a straight face, added a tip, and signed the check. The waiter thanked them and left the room.

"Throw them in the slammer!" Lincoln parroted, and they both burst out laughing. Not that any of it was funny.

Later that evening, Gwen made a quick call to Madison. She told Madison that she had opened a savings account many years ago in both her and Lincoln's names when she set up the trusts for college.

Madison furrowed her brow. "I wonder why Sidney didn't mention that to us."

"Because he does not know about it. No one does except your grandmother. There should be around twenty thousand dollars in there to split between the two of you." Gwen paused. "After the Ivan Boesky thing, with your father's growing paranoia, I was getting a little nervous about your father's business dealings, so I started to stash a little money away whenever I could."

"What about you?" Madison asked. "Do you have any money?"

"I have enough to get by for now."

"How long is *for now*?" She could hear noise in the background.

"Sweetheart, I do not want you to worry about me. You and your brother do what you need to do. Nana said you can stay with her until you can decide where you want to live."

"I suppose transferring to RISD is a foregone conclusion?" Madison sighed.

"It is for the best. I know you will shine there."

"I guess you spoke to Sidney."

"Yes, and he said he discussed all of this with you and Lincoln. I am so sorry the two of you are going through this."

"It's not your fault," Madison said wearily.

"In some ways, it is. I should have gotten out a long time ago."

"Mom? Can I ask you something?" Madison queried.

"Of course. What is it?"

"What did you see in Dad? Why did you marry him? Were you in love?"

Gwen went silent for a moment. She had not been expecting that sort of question. "When I met him, he was an up-and-coming financial maverick. Most men his age were still in some kind of hippie phase. Long hair. Smoking lots of marijuana and doing other kinds of drugs. Your father was clean-cut. Wore nice suits. Charming. And good-looking." She thought for a moment. "There was a time I wanted a career, but your father dictated our lifestyle. And quite frankly, it was a lifestyle that was easy to get used to. Honestly, my biggest disappointment is with myself. I should have walked out years ago."

Madison stared blankly at the phone. "I don't think I realized how unhappy you were."

"But you and your brother made me incredibly happy. And proud. That is something your father cannot take away from me."

"Where are you going to go?" Madison asked softly.

"Out of the country for a bit. It is going to depend on how soon they will want a deposition from me."

"Did you know he was doing this?" Madison asked.

"Not the particulars, but I had my suspicions. Many. It was hard to keep track of his indiscretions, so I made like an ostrich and buried my head in the sand."

Madison's eyes teared. "Mom, I am so sorry."

"Sweetheart, do not apologize to me. I am the one who is sorry for all of this. Just keep your head high."

"According to Sidney, I need to keep my head down." Madison eked out a chuckle.

Gwen snickered, as well. "Yes. Be careful. Sidney told me he was hiring private security."

"Can you—we—afford it?"

"We will manage. But first, you and your brother need to get settled. Sidney told me Lincoln was going to move in with Tyler, finish out his year at Pace, and then transfer to Baruch."

"Yes. We have a plan." Madison was doodling on the pad again.

"Okay, honey. I must get going. They are boarding my flight now."

Madison thought her mother was at an airport, and now she confirmed it. Madison made out the announcement. *Morocco?* Interesting choice. Then she remembered that Morocco did not have an extradition treaty with the U.S. She knew this tidbit from the news she watched earlier. They explained the reason her father was remanded as a flight risk, and they named a few of the countries that would not extradite him to the U.S. The plot was as thick as any episode of *Law & Order* or *FBI: International*.

"I love you, sweetheart. Give my love to Lincoln. Stay safe. Stay optimistic." She ended the call.

Madison stared down at the floor. There was much to grasp. Her mother's honesty about her feelings toward her father; her mother going on the lam; Madison and her brother finding new housing. And she had to transfer. If it had not been so utterly overwhelming, she could cry. But there wasn't anything left. She grabbed Mr. Jinx and gave him a huge hug.

PART II

Chapter Six

Moving On

As she suspected, a half dozen reporters were hanging around the entrance to FIT. Two school security guards stood at the top of the steps. Madison glanced up at one of them, who gave her a subtle nod, indicating she should walk to the side entrance. She looked in the direction of her security guard, who motioned for her to follow him. They managed to circumvent the throng of gawkers, cameras, and microphones. Madison's security detail hustled her into the building without being accosted by any of the rubberneckers. He escorted her to the dean's office, where she was rushed in, and the doors were closed behind her.

She was unusually calm. It was the comfort in having someone watching her back. Front. And side.

The associate dean and a counselor flanked the dean. "Good morning, Madison. Please take a seat." He motioned to the chairs in front of his desk.

"Thank you." Madison had total composure. "I understand our family attorney, Sidney Rothberg, was in touch with you late yesterday afternoon."

"Yes. Incredibly sad news."

"Sad? I think *disturbing* would be more apt," Madison replied. "It is not necessary to rehash your conversation with Sidney. Mr. Rothberg. At his urging, I must transfer to RISD."

"Madison, I want you to know that we, the administration, and the faculty are working to get your records sent to them as quickly as possible. I spoke to the dean at RISD last night and explained the situation. And I gave him a glowing recommendation."

Madison interrupted, "Thank you very much. I appreciate it." She paused. "If anyone had been watching the news last night, they would have a clear idea of the situation. Not all of it, but an overview."

"Correct. We printed out your file and faxed it last night and made a copy for you. They asked if you could report to the administrator on Monday."

"I plan to go to Connecticut on Friday. There should be no problem getting there. My grandparents live about thirty minutes away from the school."

"You have a very promising career ahead of you, Madison. I know you will do quite well. We shall miss you, of course."

Madison thought she might tear up but bit the inside of her lip to maintain her equanimity. "I shall miss everyone, as well."

"Mrs. Fischer boxed up your things. We can ship them to your grandmother's if you wish."

"That would be extremely helpful. Thank you." Madison wrote down the address.

"I am sure you'll want to say your goodbyes to some of your professors?"

"I would like to, yes." Madison got up from her chair. She held out her hand. "Thank you again for making this a little less painless." She tucked her file under her arm and shook everyone's hand while her security detail waited in the hallway.

As they proceeded to the classrooms, several students cast disapproving looks in her direction. Madison's thought balloons were popping in her head, while she controlled saying them aloud. Most of her classmates were kinder, gave her hugs, and wished her well. When they approached the exit, more paparazzi were waiting. She looked at the agent. "What should we do?"

"Up to you. Want to barge through them?"

"Do you think it's safe?"

"Ringo and I have you covered."

"Ringo?" Madison did not recall another agent.

He patted the inside of his jacket.

"Oh . . ." Madison didn't know if she had ever been that close to a gun before. It was likely, but she had never been aware of one. "You don't think you'll have to use that, do you?" Her hands began to sweat.

"No. You will be alright. I know Mr. Rothberg was concerned about retaliation, but you will be out of here before anyone has an opportunity to come near you."

"I trust you are right," Madison said with some trepidation.

He took her elbow with his left hand. "Let them get their photos. They will beat feet to their offices to see who can get their pic out there first."

About a dozen reporters started calling her name and firing questions. "Miss Taylor? Did you know about all the money your father was stealing?" She remained mute.

"Madison? How does it feel to have your old man arrested for fraud?" Still no answer.

"Where is your mother?" Again, she did not reply.

The security agent gave them a look that said, *Get out of the way*. He was an imposing sort, and they parted, giving Madison clearance to get into a cab.

Once they were safely in the taxi, Madison let out a long exhale. "Wow. That was intense."

"Now you know why Mr. Rothberg was concerned."

"I suppose getting out of Dodge is the only thing for me to do." She sat back. "I hope Lincoln is going to be alright."

"We have someone on him. Fortunately for him, his face is not as widely known as yours."

"Oh, lucky me." She heaved another big sigh. "Well, I guess I'll have to find something to do for the next three days."

"You should plan to go to Connecticut early tomorrow. There will be more press coverage tonight, and you do not want them to be on your heels."

"You're right. I will call my grandmother and let her know when to expect me. I will also have to let Lincoln know. Your men will be keeping an eye on him, correct?"

"Correct."

Madison felt reassured.

The agent told the cab driver to make several detours to throw off anyone who might be following them. But then again, it was New York City traffic. No one was going anywhere in a hurry.

They pulled in front of the hotel. The security guard got out first and sized up the entrance. One bellman, and a couple on vacation. He could tell by the fanny packs they were both wearing, baggy shorts, and T-shirts. The man wore black knee-high socks with sandals, and she was in clunky white sneakers. *They wouldn't be white for long*, he thought.

The agent opened Madison's door and escorted her inside. Some of the staff greeted her. Obviously, they had not made the connection. Or they had but did not care. That was the more likely of the two. It was, after all, New York. Nothing much fazed them.

The agent entered the room first. It was better to be cautious than surprised, at least under those circumstances.

"You can come in," he said, and gestured to her. "I'll be in the lobby until six, when the next agent will clock in. If you need anything, hit this button." He handed her something that looked like a pen with a button on the top. "Just push this." He made a motion with his thumb. Then he showed her a similar-looking object in the inside pocket of his jacket. "You push that, and this will buzz."

Madison gingerly took the object from him. "This is double-o-seven stuff."

"Keep it handy, but don't try to write with it." He chuckled. "I will be downstairs, and I will call you when Bennie comes on duty. You should know what he looks like. But I am better looking." He grinned, then turned toward the elevator. Madison closed and bolted the door.

It wasn't even noon. What was she going to do with all her time? She threw herself onto the bed and stared at the ceiling. And stared. And stared. And stared.

Her phone rang, and she sprang to her feet so quickly, she almost lost her balance. It was Olivia. She forgot to return her call the night before. Now that the cat was out of the bag, she had no reason not to speak to her best friend.

"Livvy! I am so sorry I did not get back to you yesterday."

"Are you alright? I mean, are *you* alright? Geesh. Now that was some kind of news. My mother called and told me to turn on the television. Holy cow."

"Holy cow is right. I'm okay. A little discombobulated but doing the best I can." Madison settled in one of the club chairs. "I really don't know much about any of it, except my father was arrested for fraud, remanded because he's a flight risk, my mother is off to parts unknown, I am heading to my grandparents, and Lincoln is moving in with Tyler."

"Wait. Start again. Slowly, please," Olivia requested.

"Mom called me yesterday morning and told me my father was arrested. That much you already know. They froze all our assets, which means we no longer have access to the apartment unless we get a court order. Lincoln and I threw some clothes together. I can almost say we are getting away with just the shirts on our backs. Literally. And, of course, Mr. Jinx." She pulled her plush kitty closer. "The good news/bad news: I am transferring to RISD beginning Monday," she continued.

"Is that the good news or the bad news?" Olivia asked.

"Kinda both," Madison clucked. "Yes, good news is I will be closer to you. The rest? You be the judge." She chuckled again. "No pun intended."

Olivia was speechless. Then she took a breath. "Do you think your mom told my mom? All she said to me was, 'Turn on channel seven.'"

"I have no idea. She did not have much to say except she was getting on a plane." Madison kept the destination a secret. As Sidney had put it, *the less you know, the less they can get information from you.* Or something to that effect. "Lincoln and I were planning to go to Nana's on Friday, but the security agent they assigned to me suggested I get out of town tomorrow. The sooner the better."

"Security agent?" Olivia was mystified.

"Yes, Sidney hired someone to escort me and Lincoln until I leave town and the story dies down a bit."

"But why?"

"Sidney mentioned retaliation. People trying to get even with my father. I should make a public service announcement: 'Hello to all of you who have been screwed over by my father. Please know that he could not care less what happens to the family, so do not bother getting yourself into trouble by trying to get even.'"

"Wow, oh wow." Olivia was trying to process the news. She hadn't grown up with the same creature comforts and luxury, but Madison never acted spoiled. She knew this was life-changing for her friends.

"You know something, Livvy? As much as the money provided us with all the material things one could wish for, there was always this black hole of emotions. My mother had double duty in dishing out family love."

"Is she going to be alright?" Olivia was deeply concerned about her favorite people.

"I think so. Ya know, I had a heart-to-heart with her last night. Not ideal circumstances, as you can imagine, but she told me—confessed, really—how miserable she was, and that she should have left my father years ago."

Olivia repeated her previous, "Wow, oh wow." She paused. "Can I be honest?"

"I wouldn't expect any less," Madison urged.

"Your dad? I was not a big fan of his."

Madison burst out laughing. "Truth be told, I do not think you have exclusivity on that. And he was not much of a fan of anyone else, either. He sucked up to people with money, but he was sorely lacking in compassion and empathy."

"I believe the word is sociopath, with a huge scoop of narcissism." Olivia was in her junior year at the University of Massachusetts. She wanted to become a psychologist and work with underprivileged kids who came from broken homes, or with women in crisis. She felt blessed by the love her family shared and wanted to help young people who were not as lucky as she was. "Sorry. But that is how I always viewed him. I just recently learned the lingo and the labels," she said, snickering.

"I suppose I was using the same technique as my mother. I call it ostrich syndrome. I, too, buried my head."

Olivia explained, "Routines become routines because it gives one a sense of security knowing what to expect. People look for consistency, good or bad. For me, if things were bad, I'd like to think I would rather take a chance at change for the better, but people are afraid of change." Olivia sighed. "Fear. It is an extraordinarily strong motivator. I have two more years to figure it out." Olivia gave a wry chuckle. "Also, remember you didn't know better." Olivia was trying to be sympathetic.

"Not true. Can I be honest?" Madison asked.

"I wouldn't expect any less." Olivia repeated Madison's words back to her.

"I preferred having dinner with you and your family. There was always laughing, joking. Lots of tasty food. In my house, we rarely ate dinner as a family. I cannot remember the last time we had dinner together. Holidays, but they were catered. During the week, we stayed at Hackley. Weekends were social activities for my parents." Madison's family interactions were playing like a sad film in her head. "It's not as if I am going to miss him. But Mom? If she wasn't available over the weekends, when Lincoln and I were home, she would take a car up to Hackley during the week. She was very engaged in our education and activities," Madison mused.

"Well now you can have dinners with me and my family when we go back to New York," Olivia said.

"Uh, I don't know if I am ever going to be able to go back to New York. At least not any time soon. This is just the beginning of the drama-rama. There'll be depositions, and then the trial, which could be a long way from now. I already had a group of reporters waiting for me at school this morning."

"What happened?" Olivia was intrigued with this new chapter in her best friend's life.

"The security agent Sidney hired snuck me in and then pushed our way out of school, and he then brought me back to the hotel." Madison sighed. "Oh, and yesterday afternoon, when we went back to the apartment, we dealt with a U.S. Marshal. I have to say he was nice."

"Well, it isn't exactly your fault."

"True. I think he almost felt sorry for us."

"Heck, *I* feel sorry for you," Olivia answered.

"It's odd. I don't feel sorry for myself. I am shocked. Stunned. But sorry?"

"You are shocked, alright. Give it some time to set in."

"What am I going to miss? Expensive clothes? I'll make my own." Madison grunted. It was at that moment when she set her course. It would be the beginning of a stellar career.

Olivia chuckled. "You were always the one to change things up. Prada would be apoplectic if they saw what you did to one of their outfits."

"Right! Remember when I turned the white pantsuit into a white capri pantsuit?"

"White was always a good color for you. Or is it the absence of color, my friend?"

"I think clear is the absence of color." Madison was finally starting to relax. It was good to have a long talk with her dear friend.

"Listen, I am going to call Nana and let her know I will be coming up tomorrow. Might as well get out while the getting is good. Hey, why don't you jump on a train and visit?"

"You are going to need a little time to sort things out. How about the following weekend? Or maybe if you are up to it, you can come to Boston. There is lots to do here."

"I'm already liking this new arrangement." Madison was smiling. "Gotta get going."

"Keep me posted. Whatever you need, you know I will be there for you."

"I love you to the moon and back!" Madison said cheerfully. Then she dialed her grandmother's number and gave her an update and an estimated time of arrival.

"Honey, I am so glad you are coming tomorrow. You need to be around family."

Madison caught herself when her thoughts went to *Family? Where is my mother?* Instead, she said, "Lincoln is going to stay here until Friday. Well, not here at the hotel. He is moving in with his friend Tyler. He is bringing his things over there tonight."

"What about school?" Nana asked.

"The plan is for him to complete his freshman year at Pace, and then transfer to Baruch." She took a breath. "I must report to RISD Monday morning. If it is alright with you, I'll stay with you and Pops until I can find a place."

"Don't be ridiculous. You can stay as long as you want."

"Thanks, Nana."

"And you can borrow my car to get to school. Since your grandfather retired, we really don't need a second car, although I wish he'd get out from under my feet once in a while."

Madison laughed. "Mom said you're volunteering at the library."

"Yes. That is one of my excuses to get out of the house." She laughed. "I keep telling him he needs a hobby. Then he says that *I am* his hobby. Zip-a-dee-do-da."

"So that's where my mother got that expression?"

"We don't have a copyright on it, dearie," Nana chuckled. It was good to hear her granddaughter was in a light mood. All things considered.

Later that evening, Lincoln checked in with his sister. "All settled in. You okay?"

"Yes. Did you check out of your room?"

"I called the front desk. They said you told them to put everything on the card."

"Correct, and I am checking out in the morning. I am taking the ten o'clock train."

"Is your watchdog still in the lobby?" Lincoln asked.

"As far as I know. He is supposed to accompany me to Penn Station. I ordered room service again. It will be nice not to feel like a hostage."

"Yeah, it's kind of creepy." Lincoln knew his sister bore

the brunt of the chaos. He was glad he had maintained a low profile in the swirling society of New York money. "Let me know when you get to Nana's."

"Will do. And Linc? Please be careful out there. Just because they have not zeroed in on your scent yet does not mean they won't."

"I am thinking about changing my appearance. Maybe get a mullet."

"That is so 1980s!" Madison teased.

"A bowl cut. A little fringe in the front. Maybe bleach it blond."

"You? Going grunge?" Madison cackled.

"Well, no one would recognize me."

"True. How about a baseball cap and call it a day?" she joked.

"I'll think of something," Lincoln reassured her.

"Okay, bro. I will check in with you when I get to Nana's. And whatever you do, do not talk to strangers." She chuckled.

"Roger that. You be careful, too."

"No worries. I have secret service agents," she said wryly.

"Love you."

"Ditto."

Madison checked her watch. It was time for the evening news. She clicked on the remote to see if there were any further pieces of humiliation. Sure enough, the charges against her father were beginning to become known. She watched with detached curiosity. She knew he was not a nice person. Cordial, yes. Nice? She had no trouble processing the situation he had created for himself and her family. Now she had to move on from the shame.

The more she thought about it, the less she felt the indignity. It was not her fault. She could not bear any of the blame. This was something she was going to have to remind herself of now, and for the years ahead.

They say if you are not part of the solution, then you are part of the problem. Could she solve it? Absolutely not. But she could not do the math to conclude she was part of the problem, either. It was *his* problem. Yes, there would be financial repercussions as far as her lifestyle, but she could maneuver them. Hackley had been more than an academic education. At least she could be thankful for the one thing her father insisted upon. It taught her independence and individuality, and that was something she could take with her. And Mr. Jinx.

Chapter Seven

Making a New Life

Madison and Lincoln's maternal grandparents had never been particularly fond of their son-in-law and avoided any conversation about him if possible. As far as they were concerned, if they never had to hear his name again, it would be a blessing.

Gwen had returned to give her deposition and easily agreed to a lie detector test. She was compliant and wanted the feds off her back. Once they were satisfied, she vanished again. This time it was Canada. Morocco was a bit too exotic for her cosmopolitan taste, and she wanted to have easier access to her children. She had pangs of guilt for abandoning them, but she also knew they were equipped to manage things. Regardless of all the creature comforts that were availed to them, her kids had grit. Despite her husband's material indulgences, she did not raise entitled brats. There was a great possibility his absenteeism had worked in their favor.

Madison was about to graduate from RISD, and Lincoln was finishing his sophomore year at Baruch. It had been two years since the arrest, and the trial was about to begin. As the evidence of their father's misdoings unfolded, with it came a media circus. Nana and Pops suggested it would be in the siblings' best interest to change their last name. They decided to adopt their mother's maiden name, and at twenty-two, Madison Taylor became Madison Wainwright, and Lincoln Taylor was now Lincoln Wainwright.

Their father was sentenced to one hundred years in a federal penitentiary for wire fraud, grand larceny, and tax evasion. Neither his wife nor his children ever saw him again. Except for the chaos he created for the family, it was as if the man had never existed.

While Madison was attending RISD, she spent many weekends with Olivia in Boston. One night when they were at a St. Patrick's Day celebration, she met Eric Fuller, who was studying to be a marine biologist.

After their year-long, long-distance, train-travel relationship, Madison embarked on finding a job and moving to Boston. With her credentials from FIT and RISD, she secured an entry-level position at a high-end design house. She never mentioned or referred to her family. Not even with Eric. She would talk about her brother but kept the family name on the down-low. She was far enough away from New York and several years from all the publicity, and she took the opportunity to begin to reinvent herself. She was now Madison Wainwright, assistant designer.

She had a keen eye for style and began to make her own clothes from leftover fabric and notions. Her boss recognized her potential and began to give her more complicated assignments.

Metallics were all the rage. Anything shiny, from pants to shoes. But Madison did not care for a discombobulated look and began to design separates, with a mix-and-match theme. Using similar color palettes and design elements, the customer could choose a skirt, top, jacket, and pants that could be intermingled. It was just like when she made her first collage as a child. You could create several different looks with the same four pieces.

The company loved the idea and allowed her to create her own line of clothing under the banner of Valencia Fashions. Her simple approach to building a wardrobe became all the rage, and the line collected blow-out reviews designating Valencia Fashions ahead of the game in ready-to-wear.

However, Madison's name was rarely mentioned in the publicity, nor did she share in the profits. When push came to shove, she got shoved out the door.

Madison refused to be squashed. Maybe designing clothes was not in the cards, but reviewing them became her platform. It kept her in the fashion world and afforded her the opportunity for a little revenge.

She started a website called Where Are You Going in That?, aimed at fashion faux pas. She took her cues from Joan Rivers, who was gaining additional fame critiquing the stars on the red carpet prior to award shows. Some of it was tongue-in-cheek, and some of it was downright scathing. Similarly, Madison used humor, but she would always offer constructive criticism. *Take it or leave it. But if you leave it, you should leave those clothes at home, too.*

Her professional network grew, and she was offered a job at *La Femme*, a highly regarded, major fashion magazine, but it meant moving back to New York.

Her relationship with Eric went sideways when he discovered she was related to the scoundrel Jackson Taylor. It wasn't about who her father was, but that she'd kept that important fact from him. He could not forgive her for what he considered lying, and they parted ways. Thankfully, they had not moved in together or made any lifelong commitment. Now, the new job and move were exactly what she needed. The best part was that Olivia was moving to New York, too. She had gotten a job in a women's shelter and would be doing what she always dreamed of.

When Madison was living in Boston, her brother visited frequently and developed a deeper relationship with Olivia. It was a long-hidden truth that Lincoln carried a torch for his sister's best friend, and he was thrilled that two of the three most important women in his life were moving back to New York City. Lincoln was beginning his master's program at Baruch. A new chapter was unfolding for all three of them.

From 2002 through 2008, Lincoln continued his studies working toward a Ph.D. in wealth management. He did not want others to become victims of people like his father and his cronies. He and Olivia got married in 2004 and had their first child in 2006. The women's shelter where Olivia worked had a day-care center, and she was able to bring Giada with her.

By 2008, Lincoln earned his degree and secured a job at Fordham University. Real estate was still within reach at the time, and they purchased a brownstone in Inwood, on the northern tip of the borough of Manhattan, near the George Washington Bridge.

Madison's life was just as fruitful. With her new name and new attitude, she threw herself into her work and created a new persona. She worked her way up from fashion reviewer to assistant editor, then on to executive editor. By the time she was forty-four, she was editor-in-chief.

Madison was known for her unmistakable all-white wardrobe, the opposite of most career women in New York. Her short, platinum blond hair was chin-length, and she kept one side tucked behind her ear. Madison Wainwright became a force to be reckoned with.

Chapter Eight

Moving Ahead

When Madison began to make over six figures, she decided she could afford to exchange her small Hell's Kitchen studio for something more spacious. She had no desire to move back to something like Sutton Place. Too pricey, too snotty, too bougie. But when she heard Tyler was moving out of his loft in Tribeca, she thought it would be perfect.

Fifteen hundred square feet of space, where she and her cats would have their own bathrooms; she could stretch her arms without hitting a wall. Situated in a desirable part of the city, it was a quick subway ride to her office, or she could take a nice, slow thirty-five-minute walk to work, weather permitting.

Her loft was also an easy forty-minute subway ride to her brother's. At this point in her life, she appreciated how to spend her hard-earned money. Limos or town cars were no longer an option unless it was a gala. Except for the occasional taxi, buses were more her style now.

The next few years were quiet. Routine. Gwen visited during the holidays, and Madison and Olivia took turns hosting their dinners. Life was steady. Peaceful.

Madison had a few boyfriends over the years, but none of them were able to hold her interest. She had an excellent job, an active social life, and a cool apartment. She also managed to dodge any references to her past.

Now in her late-forties, Madison had meticulously reinvented herself. She had to admit, keeping up a front was often exhausting. Her only confidantes were her brother and Olivia, and of course, her mother.

Around the same time, Olivia was in burnout mode from the strife and horrors of the abuse she observed at the shelter. Giada was in college, and Olivia needed a change. Madison's assistant was promoted, leaving an opening in Madison's office, and she offered Olivia the job. "I know I can be riding my broom a lot, but you know me better than anyone. Please say yes."

Madison's reputation was that of a tough but fair boss. She expected people to do their job, but she was not without compassion, and she would keep things highly confidential if anyone were in a bad situation. It was an easy decision for Olivia. She and her best friend/sister-in-law would be a team.

Madison was overjoyed to have Olivia working with her. She knew she was a hard worker, but more than that, she knew she could trust her with her life. Madison was fiercely loyal, and she expected people to treat her the same way. If you wanted to see hellfire and brimstone, just cross Madison with betrayal. If there was one thing she would not, could not tolerate, it was disloyalty.

That was how her last breakup occurred. She had been dating a younger man named Seth. He was eight years her junior and exceptionally good-looking. He was polished and articulate and he knew how to make her laugh. They had been seeing each other for almost three months when he met her in her office after work one evening. They planned to go out for drinks. Seth was sitting across from her when she excused herself to freshen up.

As Madison walked down the hall, she realized she had left her keycard on her desk. She turned around, and as she approached her office, she caught Seth looking through her computer and writing something into a small notepad. She stopped short. "What are you doing?" she demanded.

He was red-faced. "Uh, trying to get on the internet."

Madison quickly crossed the office and got a glimpse at what he was looking at. She flung her arm toward the door and shrieked. "Get out!"

Olivia heard the commotion and dashed into Madison's suite as Seth jostled past her in the doorway. The notebook launched from his hand, and Olivia quickly snatched it up.

"What's this?" She saw the name of a company embossed on the cover. A competing magazine. She held the pad high above her head as Madison tackled Seth to the floor. Not about to let go of the evidence, Olivia bolted to her desk and called security.

In one fell swoop, Olivia tossed the notebook into her desk drawer, locked it, and shoved the key into her bra. Within minutes, a security guard appeared. Olivia pointed to Seth. "Have this man arrested."

"Arrested? For what?" Seth roared.

"Corporate espionage." Madison leaned against the doorframe.

"Corporate what?" Seth was getting redder by the minute.

"And trespassing," Madison added.

"Trespassing? You invited me here!" Seth continued to protest.

"You trespassed into my computer." Madison was passionless. "It took you three months to find the opportunity, and I played right into your plan."

He said nothing.

"Take him downstairs and wait for the police," Madison instructed the security guard. "Tell them we have the evidence locked up. They can send someone to retrieve it." Madison turned away from the men and walked back into her office. Olivia followed and went over to the sideboard, where Madison kept a few glass carafes of whisky, vodka, bourbon, and port. It was there for the celebrities and the advertisers. That evening, it was for Olivia and Madison.

Olivia poured two fingers' worth of bourbon into two double old-fashioned tumblers.

Madison was sitting in one of the club chairs. "I knew he was too good to be true." Madison took the glass from Olivia. "Thanks. He was too good-looking."

"What, to be a spy?"

"Exactly, he had to be a spy. James Bond is not an ugly dude."

Olivia let out a nervous laugh.

"That was some stunt you pulled." Madison clinked Olivia's glass. "When did you learn to move so fast?"

"There were a few occasions when outraged husbands found their wives, and we had to go into overdrive."

"Well, you certainly mastered that skill."

"You weren't so bad yourself."

"Maybe professional football is in my future." Madison clicked her tongue. "How could I have been so foolish?"

"It's not easy to ignore a pretty face."

"And he was charming." Madison took a sip. "And he made me laugh." She took another sip.

"You were very calm and collected."

"On the outside. Inside? I wanted to smash that pretty face into a rubble of flesh." Madison finished her drink. "Come on. Let us have a fabulous dinner."

"I'll tell Lincoln he has to fend for himself," Olivia said.

"He'll be fine. I know you made a batch of something scrumptious over the weekend."

"For occasions like this one. I can leave him to his own devices and not feel a pang of guilt."

"Guilt? Do not be ridiculous. You are the best thing that ever happened to my brother." She got up from her chair. "And me. Come on. I hear some roasted oysters calling my name."

Once they settled into a booth at Carne Mare, they ordered octopus carpaccio, tuna tartare, and roasted oysters, along with a crisp, cold bottle of sauvignon blanc.

"So, what do you think he was really after?" Olivia asked, as she dug into the raw tuna topped with lemon zabaglione and shaved bottarga.

"He was not lying about trying to get on the internet. He was looking up Jackson Taylor, family relatives."

"Whoa! What do you suppose made him do that?"

"We were at a cocktail party when I ran into one of my old professors from FIT. He came over and exclaimed, 'Madison Taylor, is that you?' I cringed and then said, 'Wainwright.' I tried to give him a sign that he should not continue the line of conversation, but you know how some people can be. Rehash the past. I immediately excused myself and grabbed someone else to talk to. Seth asked what that was about, and I said that the man was confused."

Madison sat back against the leather seat. "With the latest publicity about having some of the money recovered and divided among the victims, Seth most likely did the math."

Olivia wrinkled her nose. "So, wait. Do you think he originally started dating you to get company secrets and stumbled upon what he thought was an even bigger scoop? I wonder if he planned to sell the info to his boss or the press. Make a name for himself." Olivia shook her head, still not quite believing what just happened.

Madison took a sip of wine. "It is almost difficult to comprehend that it has been almost thirty years since my father was arrested. I thought it was in my rearview mirror until the latest. And it reminded me of how much contempt I have for what he did to those families. You'd think I could just close that chapter and move on. I've had years to recover."

"And you did it brilliantly. You created a very cool, sleek image with your all-white wardrobe of bow blouses, jumpsuits, slim skirts, cardigans, blazers, military jackets, trousers, tunics, and moto jackets." Olivia smiled. "You're the Tom Wolfe of fashion." She was referencing the author of *The Bonfire of the Vanities* and *The Right Stuff*, who was always seen in a white suit and often a white fedora.

"You forgot about the white patent stilettos, which kill me, by the way."

"I don't suppose you'd trade them in for something more comfortable?"

"I have white boots." Madison leaned in. "Besides, that is simply my work costume. You know I have a few other items in my closet that I wear as a disguise."

"Ah, but which is the disguise? The lady in white, or the gal in the gray tracksuit, sneakers, and baseball cap?"

"You ask a very interesting question." She held up her wineglass and clinked it against Olivia's. "Right now, I am Madison, forty-eight, five feet seven inches, having dinner with my best friend."

"Cin cin!" Olivia matched the clink.

Chapter Nine

The Inheritance

Present Day

It was Wednesday morning, and Madison was reviewing a couple of articles for the upcoming edition when Olivia stuck her head in Madison's office. "Sidney is on the phone."

Sidney Rothberg had retired from his regular law practice but maintained a few special clients. Over the years, he had grown particularly fond of Madison and Lincoln and was proud of how they had managed to pick themselves up and move ahead with their lives. It would have been traumatizing for most people, especially if you came from the lush and privileged. He had to give Gwen credit for that. She too was steely in all the fallout. She gave her testimony and never had to see her husband's face again. Ever.

"Sidney! How nice to hear your voice. How are things? Everything alright? How is Edna?"

"Madison! So nice to hear your voice, as well. All is well in grandpa and grandma land. It is hard to keep up with three little ones, but I love it. I get to spoil the heck out of them, and then pack them up and send them home after an exhausting but wonderful day."

"I know what you mean. When Giada was little, she could run me ragged. But three? I could barely keep up with one! Tell me, to what do I owe this pleasant call?"

"I anticipate this is going to come as a surprise to you. Remember your Uncle Kirby?"

"Of course. I was just thinking about him a few days ago. Why?"

"We were informed that your uncle left you his marina in his will."

"His marina?" Madison was perplexed. She knew he did a lot of fishing work, but she could not recall anyone speaking about his marina. "I don't understand."

"You and your brother are now the proud owners of Kirby Taylor's Marina in Smuggler's Cove in Navesink, New Jersey. The town is nestled between the two rivers, the Navesink and the Shrewsbury, along the Jersey Shore."

Sidney reminded her that the eponymous show was not an accurate depiction of the area.

He continued in defense of the often-derided state of New Jersey. "Did you know the people on the show were not even from the area? The locals thought the depiction of the Shore and their outrageous activities have given the residents and the beautiful coastline an unbelievably bad rap."

"Sidney, you should be on the board of the chamber of commerce," she teased. "You do not have to sell me on the idea."

Sidney chuckled. "Many people have a preconceived notion of where I spent a lot of my summers as a kid."

"Oh, Sidney, you have known me long enough to know I am not judgmental. Only when it comes to fashion."

"That's our girl. Now, as I was saying, your uncle left his marina to you and your brother."

"Tell me more!" Madison urged.

"Yes. From what information I have, he won it in a bet. That part of it is vague, but the deed is real."

"How long had he owned it?" Madison was doodling.

"About ten years." She heard Sidney rifling through the pages.

"Wow. Now *this* is news," Madison quipped.

"I suggest you and Lincoln get down there as soon as possible. See what needs to be done. Put it on the market."

Madison had not gotten that far. She was still absorbing the information. "Sell it?" It was more of a statement than a question.

"I don't suppose you and Lincoln would want to be dockmasters?" Sidney joked.

"That would be a *no*, but I would like to check it out, discuss with Lincoln, and then decide. We do not have to do that right now, do we?"

"No. Not at all. I know how immersed you are with your job, and Lincoln with school, and dear Olivia, who must deal with you every day," Sidney teased.

"Very funny, Sidney," Madison shot back with a chuckle. "Things are routine. A change of scenery might be good for all of us." Madison became thoughtful. "Maybe we will keep it. Hire someone to run it. It would be nice to have a place for the summer. I am so over the Hamptons. Yes, it is beautiful out there, but that's part of the issue. It is out there. *Way* out there. I can almost fly to Miami in the time it takes me to get to Sag Harbor," she said, and snickered. "Plus, it's filled with people from New York!"

"Well, that will not be the case at this marina. It will be filled with people from New Jersey." He laughed.

"A marina. At the Shore. How exciting!" Madison was pumped. "Tell me more about it." She was animated.

"I really don't know much, which is why I suggest the two

of you get down there as soon as you can. I will have all the paperwork sent over to your office."

"Thanks, Sidney. You are a gem!" Madison jumped out of her chair. "We should get together for dinner next time Mom is in town."

"I would like that very much. I am sure Edna would, too. You take care. Have fun at the Shore. And remember, if you need anything, just call."

"Thanks again." Madison ended the call with a *whoop*!

Olivia stuck her head in the door again. "Something you wish to share?"

"Yes, I do." She gestured to one of her side chairs. "Please sit."

"Okay"—Olivia gave her a suspicious look—"what's going on?"

"We, as in you, Lincoln, and I, are now the proud owners of a marina."

"A what? Marina? How? Why?" Olivia was noticeably bewildered.

"Uncle Kirby. He passed away several months ago and left his marina to me and Lincoln. And since you are married to Lincoln, that makes you a dock mate. That is what they call water colleagues."

"Water colleagues? I know you just made that up." Olivia chuckled.

Madison grinned. "Sidney is sending over the papers and said we should go down and take a look."

"Down where?" Olivia still did not know the location of this new treasure.

"The Jersey Shore." She looked at her notes. "Smuggler's Cove on the Navesink." She turned to her computer and pulled up Google Maps. She entered *Smuggler's Cove* into the search bar, and then her office in the directions search bar. "It's about an hour and a half with no traffic."

"That's not too bad," Olivia considered. "So, back up, please. You and Lincoln got this from Uncle Kirby?"

"Yes. He 'acquired it.'" Madison used air quotes. "Either in a card game or a contest. But according to Sidney, all the paperwork is properly filed, and the deed has been transferred to us. Uncle Kirby did that before he passed away." Madison slowly shook her head. "I had no idea."

"Think about it. You and your brother were the only family he had."

"As far as we know!" Madison snickered. "There could be more surprises."

"For instance?"

"An ex-wife? A kid? An illegitimate kid he knew nothing about?"

"You've got to stop reading those British mystery novels," Olivia joked.

"You stop." Madison waved a hand. "Anything is possible." She grew thoughtful. "From what I remember, Uncle Kirby was the salt of the earth. Ha. I suppose I should say he was the salt of the river." She laughed out loud. Then she looked up at the ceiling. "Just kidding, Uncle Kirby. And thank you." She put her hands together in a prayer position. "We've gotta call Lincoln. Do you know if he is in class now?"

Olivia checked the time on her phone. "Not sure. I will send him a text and tell him to call me ASAP."

Nothing bad but call quick. She typed out the message and hit the SEND button. Within a minute, her phone rang.

"Liv? Everything alright?" Lincoln sounded a little out of breath.

"Yes. Just peachy. And I mean it." She started to giggle. "I am going to put you on speaker. I'm with Madison."

"Seriously. Are you okay? Drunk? What's up?"

"Well, Professor, if you'd shut it for a minute, I'd tell you," Madison chided.

"Yeah. Yeah. Continue, madame," he joked in return.

"I just got off the phone with Sidney."

"That can't be good news."

"*Au contraire.*" Madison was being cheeky. "He informed me that you and I were in Uncle Kirby's will."

"Really?" Lincoln was dubious. Not that there were ill feelings between them; it just never occurred to Lincoln that his uncle owned anything, nor did he think his uncle would leave anything to them.

"Yes, dear brother. He owned a marina in Smuggler's Cove on the Navesink. And he left it to us! Isn't that exciting?"

Neither Olivia nor Lincoln could remember the last time Madison was this animated.

"Exciting? My word is more in the area of *surprising*."

"Okay, I shall take both. But listen. Sidney wants us to go down there . . ."

"Down where?"

Madison filled him in on the sparse details and recommended they take a ride the following day. "What's your schedule?"

"My last class is at eleven. I can meet you there around two. Does that work for you?"

"Perfect. I will hire a car."

"Now, let's not get fancy, dearie." Lincoln had a glimmer of their previous life of extravagance.

"Oh, it's just one day. Do not be a party pooper. Besides, we now own a marina!"

"Alright. Livvy? Will you please accompany my sister? I do not want her to get lost or into any trouble before I get there. You know how some of these city women can be when they leave the Big Apple."

"I've got it covered." Olivia winked at Madison.

Madison whispered, "We'll leave early and have lunch somewhere down there."

"What did you say?" Lincoln was not sure if Madison was speaking to him or trying to avoid him hearing what she was saying.

"Just figuring out what time to leave." Madison gave Olivia a sheepish grin and looked at her schedule. "I have a meeting at ten. Should last about an hour. Tops."

"Okay. Text me the address, and I will meet you there in the afternoon. I will let you know my ETA."

"Excellent! This is so exciting!" Madison could not hold back her enthusiasm.

"You need to tone it down a bit. You do not want the staff to know that you can be a fun person."

"Ha, ha. I *am* a fun person." Madison pouted.

"Not when you're in your white uniform." Olivia winked again. "Which reminds me. You never answered my question about disguises."

"What about it?" Madison cocked her head.

Olivia rolled her eyes. "You're incorrigible."

"Another one of my disguises," Madison tossed back. "Okay, so let's make a plan."

Olivia arranged for a car service and then checked the internet for restaurants in the area. There was a lovely spot called One Willow on a nearby marina. Olivia stared at the photos. She forwarded the link to Madison's email. "Hope this is what Uncle Kirby's place looks like."

Madison opened the link and checked the photos of the restaurant. "Wow. I'm with you, sister."

Chapter Ten

A Rude Awakening

The following day, Madison blasted through the meeting and hopped into the car with Olivia. She clutched the portfolio with all the legal papers.

It took a little over an hour to arrive at One Willow. The place was spectacular. Floor-to-ceiling windows with a view no matter where you sat. There was an outdoor dining deck and a dining dock, and a captain's bar. The manager, Jason, introduced himself and showed them to a table.

"Is this your first visit with us?" he asked politely.

"Yes, but we hope it will be the first of many." Madison was still high on the idea. "My uncle owned a marina in Smuggler's Cove. Unfortunately, he passed away, but he left the place to me and my brother." Jason furrowed his brow, trying to recall a marina in Smuggler's Cove. "On the Navesink."

"Yes, that's where Smuggler's Cove is. On the Navesink." He laughed. "Enjoy your lunch."

"Shall we have a prosecco? To celebrate?" Madison suggested.

"I suppose it would be appropriate," Olivia agreed. Normally neither drank during the day, but one glass of bubbly to toast their new legacy could not hurt.

After they finished their lunch and paid the bill, Jason thanked them for coming in. "Good luck with everything. Hope to see you again soon."

"I am sure you will," Madison cooed.

The women got back into the car and headed in the direction of Smuggler's Cove. When the driver approached the waterway, Madison kept looking back and forth, but saw nothing but dilapidated docks, a few gas pumps, and a dozen or so clam boats. Insisting this could not be right, Madison got out of the car and proceeded to the dock to ask where the Taylor Marina was. Someone pointed to a sign that confirmed that the dilapidated bunch of wood *was* the Taylor Marina. She would have stomped all the way back to the car, but one of her stilettos got caught between the dock planks and propelled her forward. It was a mortifying and graceless splat, with her white suit now marred with bait and slime, and maybe a few clams. Lincoln arrived in time to help her up as she raged against the disgusting inheritance, insisting they would put it on the market the very next day.

Her clothes were a mess; her shoes were broken. She urged her brother to help her to the vehicle. She just wanted to go home. Then it occurred to her she could not sit in a car for two hours reeking of fish.

One of the clammer's wives took pity on the city girl. "C'mere, hon." The weatherworn face of a woman smiled at her. She handed Madison a pair of freshly rinsed Crocs. "Follow me."

Madison glumly picked up her broken Jimmy Choos and tossed them into a bucket of fish scraps that was sitting on the dock.

"Hey, hon, we use that for chum." The woman stuck her

gloved hand into the bucket and pulled them out. "Oh, such a shame. These are nice. I mean, they *were* nice." She *ts*ked. "Couldn't get my fat foot into one of these." She pulled out a plastic bag from her back pocket and handed it to Madison. "Here ya go."

Madison grumbled, "Thank you," and placed the soon-to-be-trash shoes into the bag. She followed the woman past an old pickup with a truck cap bolted over the bed. The woman opened the back and took out a clean pair of cargo pants and a flannel shirt. Madison was not sure which was worse—the slime or the clothes. She gave them a cursory sniff. At least they were clean.

Madison stood there, speechless. Where was she supposed to change? She leaned toward the woman's parched face as if to ask.

The woman understood the gesture and jerked her head toward a dilapidated shed. "Come on. I'll show you around," the woman said with a big smile, as if Madison had any interest in spending one more excruciating minute on the dock. "Name's Hannah."

"Madison. Kirby was my uncle."

"Sorry about your loss. He was a good man. Loved the water." She waved her arm in a sweeping motion. "Loved this place."

Madison had been so traumatized, she had not taken any notice of the beauty that was before her eyes. "It *is* pretty," she sighed, but there was no way Madison would ever set foot anywhere near the property again.

The two women entered a small wooden building that had to be decades old. The wood was splintered. Weathered. And smelled like fish. There were faded tide charts hanging by clothespins on a fishing line against one wall. Several crab traps were piled in a corner, and a few clam rakes stood in a bucket. A tiny octagon window faced east. There was a toilet and a sink in a space the size of a linen closet. The toilet tank was in dire need of purging. Madison held her breath as she quickly changed her clothes.

Hannah lit up a cigarette. "Ya mind?"

Madison thought the cigarette smoke might camouflage the stench, but it did not. Now it just smelled of fish, smoke, and dirty toilet.

"This here was your uncle's office." Hannah snickered and waved her cigarette around. Madison wondered if it was a fire hazard. *Maybe it wouldn't be so bad if the place went up in smoke,* she mused. Hannah waved her hand in front of her face. She, too, was getting a lungful of stink. "I been after Charlie to call Johnny on the Spot to swap out that tank, but he didn't want to touch anything until you all came by."

"That is an excellent idea." Not that Madison planned to use it, but it might make selling it easier if it did not smell like a septic tank with notes of dead fish. "If you do not mind, I would appreciate it if Charlie could handle that. We will pay him for his time."

"Don't be silly. We're happy to help." Hannah nodded toward the open door and the half-dozen small, shallow boats. "Your uncle used to rent out them skiffs tied to the dock. Clammers, if they missed the morning run from the depuration plant, or tourists who want to go crabbing."

"Depuration?" she asked, as she was snapping the cargo pants. They were several sizes too big and several inches too short. But you do not complain when your own clothes stink to high heaven.

"It's where they clean the clams. We got the biggest one on the coast. You wanna get fresh clams, you just drive around under the bridge. The place will sell you a bushel for practically nothing."

As interesting as Hannah was trying to make it sound, Madison wished she had never asked.

Hannah handed Madison a wet wipe, the only civilized thing in the cramped space. "Thank you. Again." Madison was beginning to feel a pang of guilt at her inner voice screaming *get me out of here!* The woman had been so kind.

"Me and my husband Charlie run a little food truck." She nodded toward another vehicle that looked as old as everything else. "We make po'boy sandwiches for the clammers and anglers. Somethin' my grandaddy taught me. He used to do a lot of shrimp boating. But shrimp ain't always easy to come by so we make it with clam strips. Them, we got plenty. You should try one."

The thought of eating a clam strip at that moment churned the bile in her stomach. "Thanks, but we just had a big lunch."

"Ya think your brother would like one? I can whip one up real quick." She grinned. "I make a mean tartar sauce, too."

"That would be lovely." Madison wondered how Lincoln would react to a clam sandwich.

Once Madison was as cleaned up as she could be, the two went over to where Lincoln and Charlie were standing. "Can I offer you a clam strip sandwich?" Hannah looked at Lincoln.

It took him by surprise. He wasn't sure how to respond. He didn't want to be rude, but he also was leery about eating something off a food truck. He hesitated but also had to admit it smelled delicious. "Sure. Why not? Thank you."

Madison shot him a dubious look as if to say, *I am not cleaning up your vomit, bro.* Lincoln knew his sister well enough to read her mind. He chuckled.

Hannah walked over to the food truck and hopped inside. The oil was still hot and simmering when she dropped a handful of breaded strips into the vat. Madison could not deny there was something about the aroma of fried food. You wanted to eat it, but you knew it was going to do any number of things, such as clog your arteries, make your face break out, give you gas, or make you fart. She was glad Lincoln was driving his own car.

Lincoln offered to stay behind and wait for the real estate agent to arrive. He knew Madison could not get out of there fast enough.

Madison thanked Hannah for her help and piled into the town car. "See you soon!" the woman said, and waved.

"Not if I have anything to do with it," Madison muttered under her breath, and gave the woman a weary wave in return.

Madison was silent all the way home. She was deflated. When they got to the Holland Tunnel, she finally said two words: "This stinks."

Olivia could not help but laugh. "The situation, your clothes, or your hair?"

"All of it. I cannot believe this. What a dump."

"Well at least Uncle Kirby didn't pay for it, and neither did you."

Madison groaned. "Taxes. We are going to have to pay inheritance tax. Ugh!" She kicked the bag of ruined clothes with her borrowed hot-pink Crocs.

Olivia patted Madison's hand. "It's going to be alright. You can sell it, pay the taxes, and come away with a little money."

"Yeah. Five dollars, I'm sure." Madison felt as if she had been flung off a Ferris wheel. "How could something that sounded so good be so terrible?"

"It is called *life*, and you know well how life throws curveballs."

"I do indeed." Madison looked down at the flannel shirt and rubbed the fabric between her fingers. "Pretty soft, actually."

"It was very nice of that woman to loan you some clothes."

"I know. And I feel like such a jerk. I was so ungracious and rude."

"You were mortified. And in a bit of shock."

"I will buy her some new shirts and a couple of pairs of cargo pants and send it with a humbling note."

"Now there's the Madison we know and love."

Twenty minutes after they were out of the tunnel, the car brought them to Madison's loft, where she greeted her cats, Mario and Luigi. They were much more interested in the soiled clothing in the plastic bags than they were in saying hello to their mommy. She grabbed the bag with her broken shoes, walked out her door, down the hall, pulled open a stainless hatch, dropped them in, and listened as they tumbled down the metal chute. She metaphorically was throwing the marina out, too. She would tell Sidney to find a realtor to put it on the market, and that would be that.

About an hour later, Lincoln arrived. Just as he was walking into the apartment, Madison's phone rang. As she picked it up, she pointed to Lincoln's shoes, reminding him to take them off. Madison developed the habit of leaving her shoes at the front door when she moved back to New York—too much yuck on the streets—and she expected guests to do the same. She knew it was annoying, but she didn't have many visitors anyway.

She answered her phone. "Hello. This is Madison."

A deep voice spoke. "Madison Wainwright?"

"Yes. Who is this, please?"

"This is Detective Burton. Smuggler's Cove police department."

"Yes, Detective. How can I help you?" She looked at Olivia and Lincoln and shrugged.

"I understand you are the new owners of Kirby Taylor's Marina."

She put her hand over the receiver and whispered, "Word travels fast." Then she continued. "Yes, my brother Lincoln and I inherited it from our Uncle Kirby. What can I do for you?"

"I was told you and your brother were down here a few hours ago."

"That is correct." She was beginning to feel as if she were being interrogated. "May I ask what this is about?" She was being very polite. When it was time to sell the property, she wanted all the support necessary, including from the local police. She knew how persnickety small-town folks can be when it comes to their community. And rightly so. But all she wanted was to dump the dump and walk away.

"There has been an unfortunate incident."

"Incident?" She sat up straight. Lincoln leaned in. "I am going to put you on speakerphone, if that's alright. My brother is with me."

"Yes, of course," he replied.

Madison hit the button, and everyone was able to hear everyone else's voice. "Please continue."

"Sometime around six, a body was spotted floating under the dock. We do not have any other details, but we will need both of you to come down to the station tomorrow for a statement."

"Sorry? Did you say a body?" Madison wasn't sure what she was hearing. "A dead body?"

"Yes, I'm afraid so."

"Detective, I can assure you this is the first we have heard of this incident. Why do you need a statement from us?" She was baffled. They had nothing to do with whatever this situation was. Simply because a body was found nearby, surely there was no reason for them to be brought into it.

"Because you are the owners of the dock he was found tangled under."

"But we had nothing to do with this. We were there for less than an hour. We left around four." Just when Madison thought her day could not get any worse, another head-spinner. At least she was on dry ground this time. "I'm sorry, Detective, but we don't know anyone in the area."

"I understand; however, as I mentioned, you own the property." He cleared his throat. "We need a statement."

"Of course. Sorry. I did not mean to sound heartless. I am simply in shock." For the second, make that the third, time that day. First was the discovering the ramshackle dock, then a face-plant on the deck, and now this. Could it get worse? She was afraid to ask.

"When do you want to see us?" She was rolling her eyes, furrowing her brow, and twisting her mouth.

"The sooner the better. How is tomorrow? One o'clock?"

"I have to check my schedule."

"Ms. Wainwright, I don't mean to be harsh, but your schedule will have to wait. A man is dead, and we don't know how or why."

"Of course. Of course. How insensitive of me." Madison was truly embarrassed. "It has been a long, long day."

"I understand."

"Does anyone know who the poor man is?" Madison was regaining her sense of sympathy.

"Not yet. He had no identification on him, and by the looks of it, he had been in the water several days."

Madison's face went sour. "How awful."

Olivia sat with her mouth agape. She reached for Madison's hand. Then Lincoln's.

"Yes. This is not an unusual occurrence around here, but unfortunate, nonetheless."

"Of course. Can you text me the address, please? We will be there by one. Thank you for calling. Again, apologies if I was a bit terse."

"No apologies necessary. See you tomorrow." The detective ended the call.

Madison slouched on the sofa. "Talk about a fine kettle of fish."

Chapter Eleven

The Investigation Begins

The next morning, Madison decided to dress more appropriately for her jaunt to clam-town, and of course, the police department. White capri pants, white tank, white cardigan, and white skimmers with a rubber bottom. If she were going to fall on her face, at least her shoes would not be to blame.

She checked the labels of the borrowed clothing—extra large—and then quickly walked to the Rag & Bone down the street from her loft. She suspected Hannah didn't have anything from the high-end store, but it was the closest place to her apartment, and it was a small gesture to repay the woman's kindness. She decided to buy two shirts and two pairs of pants for her. An hour later, Lincoln and Olivia picked her up, and they headed to Jersey. Traffic was light, and they arrived before their appointment.

"Do you think we should visit the crime scene?" Lincoln asked.

"Our entire life has been a crime scene, or hadn't you noticed?" Madison said sarcastically, and rested her head against the window.

"Easy, girl. We will give them our statement and then get out of here."

"With all the commotion, you never mentioned anything about the real estate agent. What did she say?"

"There are some legal hurdles before we can sell it."

"Oh, please don't tell me this."

"It has something to do with the water rights."

"What do you mean?"

"Riparian rights. Tidewaters, etcetera," Lincoln replied.

"What does that have to do with us? The marina?"

"Since the transfer to Uncle Kirby was a result of a gambling debt, we need a clear title."

"But I thought all of that was taken care of." Madison was losing hope of ridding herself of this debacle.

"Yes and no. We must get the area surveyed."

Madison began to moan.

"Listen, we don't have to do anything for the moment. We give them our statement, and then we can work on the survey and everything else some other time."

"Are there taxes due on the property?" Madison asked.

"Doesn't seem to be."

Lincoln slowly drove past the marina. There was yellow crime-scene tape marking off two of the three piers that jutted out into the water. Onlookers were trying to get a glimpse of the area where the body was recovered. Madison slumped down in her seat. "They're not looking for you," Lincoln teased her.

"Not yet," Madison scoffed. "At this pace, I will be arrested for assaulting the deck with my shoes. Or my face."

"Oh, stop it." Lincoln laughed.

Madison huffed and slinked up a bit to grab a peek. There were several police officers, a police boat, men in slickers, and some in underwater gear. "I hope they removed the body." She turned her head.

"I am sure they did." Lincoln looked over at Olivia and rolled his eyes.

Lincoln continued to the police station where Detective Burton, a stenographer, and another officer were waiting.

Detective Burton was over six feet tall and robust, clean-shaven with a bald head. He seemed to be in his early 40s. He wore a crisp white shirt and tie, looking very official. "Thank you for coming in. I realize this is not exactly what you had planned when it came to your uncle's marina."

"That is for certain." Lincoln jumped in before his sister had a chance.

"Right this way, please." He showed them down a sparkling clean hallway, with bright light shining through the glass. "New office. We got wiped out during Superstorm Sandy, and it took ten years to get us moved out of the 'temporary' trailers."

"That storm did quite a number on the shore. And Lower Manhattan," Lincoln added.

"There were some anomalies. Most of the town was six feet deep in water, yet there were a few streets that had nothing. Take your uncle's place, for example. We joked and said, 'He was at the right place, at the right tide.' The shack took a soaking, but nothing fell over."

"Was that before or after he won the bet?" Madison was curious.

"It was actually *the* bet," Burton began to tell the story. "Your uncle predicted that the water line was not going to damage the shack. Billy Bob disagreed and said—I'm paraphrasing here—'If that shack is still standing, then it's yours, along with the marina.'"

"Almost sounds like a local legend," Lincoln said, with a bit of curiosity.

"We have plenty of those, but we also had a few witnesses. Billy was a man of his word and turned the deed over to Kirby. Besides, he was planning to move to Florida to be with his daughter and grandchildren. The tax and insurance were draining him. He was quite happy with the outcome."

At least somebody was, Madison thought to herself. *And here we are.* She continued to follow the detective down the hall.

Burton opened a door to a small conference room. Madison noticed how chilly it was in there.

The detective noticed Madison's reaction to the temperature. "It keeps people awake and alert." He chuckled. "Please take a seat. Can we get you coffee? Tea? Water?"

"Water, thank you," Madison replied. Burton reached over to a tray of bottled water that sat on the sideboard and handed one to her.

The commanding detective opened a file. "We still have not been able to identify the deceased. The bloating made it tough for the coroner to pull fingerprints."

Madison hoped the ghastly details would remain at a minimum.

"We also do not know if it was foul play, suicide, or an accident. The body was in unbelievably bad shape."

Madison gritted her teeth. "What happens now?" She was hoping for a quick resolution.

"We are trying to identify the body, and the coroner will have to determine cause of death. It could take days. Weeks. Months, if it was foul play."

Madison was taking long, deep breaths. *Months?* "I see." She wanted to get the show on the road. "What can we do to help?"

"Just a few questions. For now. Do you have a list of your uncle's contacts? Friends? Associates? Other family members?"

Madison looked at Lincoln. "Honestly, we do not. I hesitate to say we were estranged from Uncle Kirby, but the communications became less frequent over the years."

"I understand. Families can be like that." He clicked his pen and jotted down a few notes. "Can you recall the last time you spoke to your uncle?"

Madison looked at Lincoln again. "Several years, I think."

"And how did you come to find you inherited the marina?"

"Our family lawyer."

"And did he mention how he came into that information?"

Lincoln spoke up. "No. It hadn't occurred to me to ask." He turned to his sister. "Maddie?"

"I didn't think to ask, either. Does it matter?"

"Hard to say, but there had to be someone who knew how to get in touch with you after your uncle passed away."

"I'll call Sidney," Madison offered. "May I?"

"Yes, of course," Detective Burton answered. "If you don't mind, you can use this." He slid the black flying-saucer-looking phone in her direction. "Please put it on speaker."

Madison shivered. *Were they suspects?* She pulled out her mobile and looked up Sidney's private number, then dialed via the conference room phone.

"Sidney Rothberg," he answered with a questioning tone.

"It's Madison." She paused.

"Madison. I did not recognize the number." Sidney's voice floated into the room.

"Lincoln and I are at the police station in Smuggler's Cove. We are sitting with Detective Burton."

"Are you alright? What happened?" Sidney's voice was tense.

"After we got back yesterday, Detective Burton phoned and informed us that a body had been found tangled in some fishing lines under Uncle Kirby's dock."

"How dreadful." Sidney's voice lowered. "What happened?"

"No one knows. They do not know who the person is, either."

"What can I do?" Sidney asked.

"Detective Burton was curious as to how you got the information about our inheritance. We do not know any of Uncle Kirby's associates."

"Interesting you should ask. I didn't think anything of it, but the package was delivered by hand. It contained a letter of introduction from your uncle, which was handwritten, along with a copy of his will. I had everything checked out, and you and Lincoln are the owners of the marina. I sent you copies of everything."

Lincoln chimed in. "There seems to be some question about tidewater rights, but we can discuss that later."

"According to the paperwork, you own the dock and the building. I will check into the water rights as soon as we get off the phone. I apologize. It had not occurred to me."

"Me either," Lincoln said. "It was the real estate agent that brought it up."

"I will get on it right away, but it may take some time. Bureaucracy moves slowly."

Detective Burton snorted. He knew all too well.

"Do you still have the original envelope the paperwork was in?" Sidney asked.

Madison reached into her portfolio. "Yes."

"Return address?"

She turned the large manila envelope over. "No. Just your name and address on the front. You said it was delivered by hand?"

"Yes."

"Was the delivery person wearing a uniform?" Burton asked.

"That, I cannot say. It was dropped off at reception."

"Do you have security footage?" Burton asked.

"Yes. I will check with our IT guys and see if they can pull up anything. And I can check with the front desk in the lobby. They should have something. People cannot get in the building without showing ID." Sidney sent a quick text to both.

"That would be a big help," Burton replied.

Madison wondered why, but Burton quickly answered her thoughts and turned toward her. "Until we can figure out what happened here, we need anything that is connected to your uncle."

Madison remained calm, while her inner voice was screaming. She'd spent half her existence dodging drama and building a new life. She did not ask for any of this: from her father's financial crime spree, to a decrepit marina, to a dead body. *Why? Why? Why?* Had she not paid her dues? Had she not fought back well enough so she would no longer have to fight? They say there is a reason for everything. Now, Madison thought she must have been a horrible person in a previous life.

Burton could see the concern on her face. "Ms. Wainwright, I realize this has been very disruptive and unexpected. We will get to the bottom of it. All I ask is that you be patient, and of course, cooperate." Burton's impression of the siblings was that they were well-educated, polite, and sincere. He had them checked out after he phoned them the night before. He called his go-to private investigator, Ross Licitra, who gave him the skinny on them. She was a successful editor; he, a well-respected professor. Burton also knew their lineage and how they'd fended for themselves after their father's arrest and conviction. At least they did not seem spoiled and entitled, another thing he was often surrounded by. He didn't know which was worse—old money or new money.

"Detective, you can be certain we will do whatever we can to assist you," Lincoln assured him.

"We appreciate it."

They could hear voices in the background, coming from Sidney's side of the call. "We have a photo of a young man. Signed in as Josh Hanover."

Burton looked at Madison and Lincoln. "Ring a bell?"

Madison shook her head. "I have no idea."

"Doesn't ring a bell for me," said Lincoln.

Burton typed something into his tablet. A few seconds passed. "Josh Hanover. Eighteen. Lives nearby." He typed something into his cell phone.

"Do you think Uncle Kirby gave him the envelope and asked him to bring it to New York?"

"It's possible," Burton answered. "I'm sending an officer over to his house now."

Things were becoming more mystifying as the minutes passed. "This is all so very strange," Madison ruminated. "Sidney? Uncle Kirby died of a heart attack, correct?"

"Yes. Why?"

"The timing of everything. I wonder when he gave this fellow the package."

"Good point," Sidney agreed. "The will was dated June of last year."

"But he could have given the package to Hanover at any time and said to deliver it when he passed away," Lincoln added.

"Let's see if young Mr. Hanover can enlighten us." Burton looked down at his phone. It was one of the officers. Hanover was out on a tuna boat. He let out a huff of air. "However, we are going to have to wait for him to return from the tuna trip."

Madison was now sitting on the edge of her seat. "What time will he be back?"

The detective gave her a wry smile. He knew she was not going to like the answer. "Fifteen to twenty days."

"Fifteen? Twenty? Days? Can't you send the Coast Guard to fetch him?" Madison's eyes were bugging out.

Burton laughed. "No. He is not under arrest. At least not yet."

"Well, if he is a suspect, shouldn't you go and get him?" Madison was trying to keep her voice at a normal octave.

Burton laughed again. "Ms. Wainwright, please. You are going to have to be patient. We do not know if a crime has been committed. Not yet, anyway." Burton wrote down a few more notes. "When you went to the dock yesterday, did you notice anything out of order?"

Madison burst out laughing. "Sorry. I had never set foot on the property before yesterday, and if you saw the inside, you would not be able to tell if it had been ransacked or not." Madison regrouped. "There were maps, and papers." She omitted the stinky part. "Not that I asked, but if something were amiss, I would think Hannah would have mentioned it. But I will be happy to ask her."

"That's alright. We'll be going over to the area in about an hour for some follow-up questions. I can ask her myself. But thank you." Burton scribbled another note.

Madison was bouncing her knee up and down under the table. Olivia placed her hand on Madison's thigh, hoping to reduce the possibility of levitation. Madison sat straight. She took a deep breath. "I guess we are going to have to see how things unfold."

Lincoln suppressed a grin. He knew his sister was about to hit the ceiling, figuratively and literally.

"I'm afraid so, Ms. Wainwright. It's going to take some time. But we will keep you up to date on our progress."

"Thank you," Lincoln said, nodding.

"Yes. Thank you," Madison added.

Olivia knew her work was cut out for her. Madison would be moving full bore trying to settle this. Olivia would have to keep her friend on an even keel. For everyone's own good. When Madison got something stuck in her craw, you had to either follow or get out of the way. Madison was not one to wait for people to get things done.

"I have something I want to give to Hannah," she said to Burton. "Would it be alright if we go over to the dock?"

"As long as you don't go past the crime-scene tape," he said flatly.

Madison imagined being wrapped up in a roll of it.

"Thanks again for coming in." They stood, shook hands, and reassured one another they would keep everyone up to date.

When they got back in the car, Lincoln turned to Madison and smiled. "I'm going to have another one of those clam sandwiches."

Madison shivered.

They returned to the small parking area across from the dock. People were still gathered, chatting, smoking. Olivia elbowed Lincoln and nodded at the NO SMOKING sign next to the gas pump. It was a mystery to see so many people with cigarettes, especially young people. Then again, no one among the throng seemed to be using sunscreen, either. It was a different world.

The three got out and walked toward Hannah and a small group of people. "Hey! Didn't think we'd see you back here so soon!" Hannah gave them a wave.

"Me, either," Madison answered, gritting her teeth. Then she reminded herself that Hannah was a nice person and did not deserve a chill from her. Madison pulled on a smile. "I'm sorry I didn't have a chance to launder your clothes, so I got you these." She handed the confused woman the bag. "As a thank-you."

"For me?" Hannah gingerly took the bag and peeked inside. "For real?"

Madison's face went soft. "Yes. For you. You were truly kind, and I was kind of a—well, you know." Madison hesitated to use foul language. At least with people she didn't know.

"Aw, shucks. You didn't have to do this." Hannah peered deeper into the bag and pulled out an incredibly soft, red and black, buffalo-plaid flannel shirt. "Ooh. But I'm glad you did. I was just telling Charlie I needed to go to the Tractor Store and get some new things. You saved me the time." She plucked out the second shirt, which was a green plaid.

"I thought it matched your food truck." Madison grinned. Always the fashionista.

"Well, it sure does." Hannah held it up to her chest. "Charlie. Look." Charlie ambled over to where the women were standing.

"Ms. Madison brought these for me. Wasn't that nice of her? A thank-you present."

When the crew from New York first arrived, Charlie didn't think much of the tall, white-clad woman in high heels.

"Who goes to a fishing dock in high heels?" he'd said gruffly after they left.

Hannah tried to defend the hapless city woman. "She didn't know what this place was. I could tell."

"Whatever," he said, and shrugged.

But in the new day's light, he saw that he may have jumped the gun with his opinion. Hannah had a point. Plus, now they had a dead body and all.

"Yep. Nice of her." He nodded.

"And look! New cargo pants!" Her excitement for something so simple was touching. "Madison, you are one classy lady." She stuffed the clothes back into the shopping bag. "Come on. Clam sandwiches. On the house!"

Madison's eyeballs rolled back in her head. This was going to be a lot tougher than she imagined.

Several people were hanging around the front of the food truck. " 'bout time, Hannah," one of her dining guests teased. "My stomach is making all kinds of noises."

"So will the rest of your intestines later," another angler joked.

"Are you saying there is something wrong with my clam rolls?" Hannah slapped her towel at him.

"It's not your clam rolls. It's his belly roll." People chuckled. Apparently busting chops was a normal occurrence around those parts.

Hannah hoisted herself into the truck. "Come on, Charlie. Hop to it."

There was a small picnic table nearby, where Olivia, Lincoln, and Madison took a seat. For some odd reason, Madison felt a sense of relief. Madison was a go-getter and get 'er done kind of woman, but in spite of what people perceived, she also knew when it was time to let things go. Everyone was doing what they had to do. The challenge now was being patient, a skill she was still trying to perfect at her age.

Madison finally had the opportunity to drink in the atmosphere. The scenery was magnificent. A large, winding river was surrounded by lush vegetation, high hills toward the south, and the water gently lapping against the shoreline. It reminded her of the Renoir painting, *The Skiff*. The difference was that the two women in the painting were fashionably dressed, and tranquil. Neither of them was fishing or clamming. She glanced at the group gathered by the food truck. Another painting came to mind. It was *Luncheon of the Boating Party*. Again, in the painting, the women were fashionably dressed for an afternoon soiree, but the two men were clad in sleeveless shirts and straw hats and looked more like her immediate circle of characters.

Yes, the people she had encountered over the past twenty-four hours were an interesting lot. There was the button-down Detective, who Madison would bet did not smoke. Then there were the crusty dock people, who smoked, dried their skin to leather, and ate fried food every day. True, they were quirky, but there was a fellowship among them. They looked out for one another.

Madison noticed an exceptionally large bird with a fish in its beak, gliding over the water, when someone from behind said, "It's an osprey." Madison blinked. She hadn't heard the person approach and turned toward the voice.

"Good afternoon. I am Captain Viggo Eriksson, U.S. Coast Guard. You're the Taylor family?"

"It's Wainwright." Madison stiffened.

"Apologies. But you are, were, related to Kirby Taylor?"

Madison held her hand above her eyes to shield them from the sun. The officer stepped up to create a shadow. "Yes. He was our uncle."

"Sorry for your loss."

"Thank you," Madison replied.

Lincoln stood and shook the captain's hand.

"I'm working with the town's local police and the State Police Marine Services in the investigation."

Madison was hopeful that having the Coast Guard involved would hurry along the process. "Looks like we are keeping you busy." She smiled. The officer was quite handsome, with classic Norse looks. A full head of wavy light brown hair with streaks of blond from the sun, steel-blue eyes, light skin but slightly tanned, straight nose, high angular cheekbones, with a closely cropped well-trimmed beard. From where she was sitting, she thought he might be five feet ten, maybe eleven inches tall, with a trim, athletic build. Her eyes darted to his left hand. No wedding band. *Now why did she do that?* she wondered. His raw manliness reminded her of what it would be like to be with one. It had been such a long time.

"Normally we don't get involved in local situations. We mostly concentrate on smuggling, search, and rescue. That sort of thing."

"What brings you to Smuggler's Cove?" Madison laughed nervously. She realized he had already told her. "Sorry. All this fresh air. And the"—she paused—"situation."

He snickered. "Understandable. Just doing some investigative work. We need to make sure that he was not involved in anything that fell within our authority. But we still don't know who he was and what he was doing here."

For the first time, Madison wasn't in such a hurry to get answers, but she decided to ask a question anyway, even if it was to keep the conversation flowing. "Tell, me Captain Eriksson, do you really get a lot of smugglers here?"

"You would be surprised. Drugs. Contraband."

"I guess I was thinking more about pirates," she said, suppressing a giggle.

"We have them, too. But they don't wear bandanas and patches over their eye anymore." He smiled. "This area is steeped in pirate and privateer history."

"What's the difference?" Madison knew the answer but asked anyway. She simply wanted to hear the man's deep, sultry voice again.

"Pirates are considered bandits and live outside the bounds of the law. Privateers are commissioned by the government or sovereign power to legally do their pilfering." He shifted his weight to keep the sun out of Madison's eyes.

"Interesting." She gave him a wry smile. "Sounds like insurance companies." She giggled. *Was she flirting?* Her best friend Olivia seemed to think so by the little nudge she gave Madison under the table.

Captain Eriksson laughed. "You have a point, Ms. Wainwright."

"Please. Call me Madison."

"Certainly, Madison." He nodded.

"Detective Burton told me there was a young man who carried my uncle's papers to New York. He is out on a tuna boat, and we have to wait until he gets back. I do not suppose there's any chance you could go out and fetch him?" she asked innocently.

Eriksson chuckled. "Sorry. No chance. Unless they get capsized, which doesn't seem likely. They have good weather predicted."

It was worth a shot, Madison thought to herself. "Of course. I suppose I am a little anxious about all of this."

"Understandable," he replied.

Lincoln noticed a scraggly dude hobbling in their direction. He was wearing a Grateful Dead T-shirt that had to be as old as the hills behind them. His shorts were ripped above the knees, and his tanned feet clomped in a pair of flip-flops. "Howdy! The name is Crusty," he said, and snickered. "For crustaceans."

Madison had a different interpretation, then silently admonished herself for having a mean thought. He held three wrapped clam sandwiches in his hands. "Hannah says I should give these to you. You're Kirby's kin?"

"Yes. I am Lincoln. This is my sister, Madison, and my wife, Olivia." He availed himself of the rolls with the crispy seafood.

"Good to meetcha." Crusty wiped his hands on his shorts. "We was sorry about Kirby. He and I used to fish every morning until my lumbago started acting up. So, I'd wait for the boats to come back and help clean the fish and the traps."

"I am sure he is going to be missed." Lincoln was getting a better picture of his uncle and his friends. The opposite from his father. Lincoln wondered if his father ever had any real friends.

"Well, I'll let you fine folks enjoy your lunch. Hannah makes a mean roll. And her tartar sauce"—he kissed his fingertips—"good stuff." He turned and began to walk toward the food truck.

"Crusty?" Lincoln stopped him. "If you don't mind, perhaps one day you can tell me more about my uncle. We hadn't seen him in an exceptionally long time."

"Sure thing, young man. You can find me here most any day, except during a nor'easter." He shuffled his way back to his gang.

Captain Eriksson cleared his throat. "I should be going. Enjoy your lunch." He reached into his pocket and pulled out two business cards. He handed one to Lincoln and Madison. "I'll be in touch. In the meantime, if you think of anything, or have any questions, please feel free to reach out."

Madison quickly rifled through her bag, but before she could dig deeper, Olivia was handing one of Madison's cards to the captain. He looked at the card and then at Madison. "Editor in Chief." He tapped the card against his fingers.

"And, if you have any questions . . ." She let her words hang in the air.

He smiled and placed her card in his breast pocket. "Enjoy the rest of this beautiful day."

Olivia waited for the striking officer to be out of earshot. *"Muy caliente!"* She raised her eyebrows at her sister-in-law and fanned her face.

Madison smiled. She could not have agreed more.

They took their time enjoying the local cuisine and atmosphere. Lincoln nudged his sister. "Good clams, eh?"

"I must admit it. This is delicious." She wiped some tartar sauce from the side of her lips. "Not even greasy." She made favorable noises as she took another bite.

"I think this place is starting to grow on you," Lincoln noted.

"Let's not get ahead of ourselves." Madison laughed.

They finished their lunch and went over to the truck to thank Hannah and Charlie and bid their farewells.

"Thanks again for the clothes. That was mighty sweet of you." Hannah was grinning from ear to ear. "You need anything, you just give me and Charlie a jingle." She pulled out a card that said:

CLAMS ON WHEELS
& A PINCH OF CRABS
by Hannah and Charlie
We Bring 'em, Fry 'em, Serve 'em
908-555-2784

Madison chuckled. "Clams on Wheels. That is something people will remember."

"I hope so. With the dock all locked up by the police, I hope we can get some parties or festivals to make up the difference."

It had not occurred to Madison how this situation was going to impact other people. She had been caught up in her own drama, which had little, if any, impact on her daily life. Again, she felt a little embarrassed about being selfish.

They said their goodbyes, but Madison secretly hoped she would be back. Not for fish, but for that catch—Viggo Eriksson.

Chapter Twelve

Ship Ahoy

Captain Viggo Eriksson was born in Norway, along with his four siblings, from generations of anglers and sailors. Even though a seafaring life was common for the family, Viggo's mother fretted every time his father went out on the cold waters of the North Sea, hoping her husband would return unscathed.

By the late 1980s, many of their relatives had migrated to New England. A large distribution company in the fishing industry had recently opened a new facility in Gloucester, Massachusetts. There were already a handful of Erikssons who had relocated and encouraged his father to bring the family there. It paid well, overhead was reasonable, and it was a much safer environment. Everyone spoke fluent English, so there would not be a communication issue. There was truly little, if any, reason not to go, and when Viggo was eight years old, they immigrated to the United States, and when eligible, his parents completed the process to become naturalized citizens.

When Viggo turned fifteen, *he* began the process of becoming a naturalized citizen, He wanted to integrate himself into the new culture, and when he was old enough, he got a part-time job working with the delivery crew of the fishing company.

Viggo enjoyed the camaraderie but not the smell. He loved being on the water but did not like baiting a hook. At some point, he had to figure out how he could make an aquatic living and still maintain a less fishy aura. Coming from an immigrant family, Viggo was also interested in the process and the ways and means people employed to come to America. Much of it was illegal due to the backlog in processing. It was a problem, but Viggo wanted to learn more.

In his senior year of high school, Viggo applied to Salem University, where he studied criminology. His goal was to join the OCS in the Coast Guard and become a response officer. It entailed shore-based Coast Guard operations, law enforcement, emergency management, search and rescue, coastal security, and environmental response.

His diligent work and studies paid off and eventually earned him the rank of captain by the time he turned thirty. Over the years, he had been assigned to various stations across the country, particularly those that experienced more than their share of natural disasters. After crisscrossing from the West Coast to the East Coast and the Gulf of Mexico, he eventually landed in Virginia Beach, where he lived with his girlfriend Brittany for several years.

During the pandemic, there were more shifts and changes in base personnel, and once again, Viggo found himself reassigned. This time it was Sandy Hook, Gateway National Park, New Jersey, the southern part of the triangle that constitutes the gateway to New York Harbor.

New York City's looming skyline of concrete and steel skyscrapers seemed like a stone's throw from the station, yet Sandy Hook was eerily quiet at night. The sounds and bustle of the city that never sleeps is hushed by the narrow ten-mile spit that provides a deep channel for ships to enter New York Harbor, one of the busiest seaports in the country.

Viggo was always in awe of the juxtaposition of high-density living and the dirt roads where deer wandered regularly. There was a sense of peace and serenity on the long, narrow peninsula that was previously an active military installation.

The York Colony built the lighthouse in 1764 to assist ships entering the harbor. Today it still boasts of being the oldest working lighthouse in the country. Now it is home to the U.S. Coast Guard and MAST, the Marine Academy of Science and Technology, a four-year public high school. But before you get to the lighthouse at the tip of the hook, the seven-mile drive from the entrance to the fort provides many beaches and recreation for visitors. The winters are sparse except for the die-hard fishermen. The summer months are the most challenging, brimming with sunbathers, kite surfers, more fishermen, cyclists, joggers, and sightseers. Lots of people were running boats without having a clue how to operate them. They didn't know starboard from *Star Trek*. Then there were the yahoos on their personal watercrafts—WaveRunners or jet skis. Those were serious trouble on a Saturday night. Normally the Coast Guard is not called unless it's an emergency, but with the influx of tourists, the local police and state police had their hands full, from the Raritan Bay all the way down the intercoastal waterway. Miles and miles of stupidity, and too often, drunk stupidity. The holidays were the worst.

Then there are the day trippers, who have no idea that there is a difference between low tide and high tide. They would drag their beach gear out to the sandbar that jutted out from the west side of the park and into the bay. They were unaware that within a few hours they, and their coolers, would be floating away. There is at least one rescue during a normal week. It was not so much a risk of drowning; more likely, it meant some nitwit stranded waist-deep for six hours. Luckily for most, the fine people who live on the hillside would notify local authorities when it was obvious the hapless holidaymakers were not getting off the sandbar without the assistance of a boat.

The park is adamant about keeping the land pristine and limits the amount of people and traffic, and it closes at sunset. If you do not get there before nine a.m., chances are you will not get in.

In 2022, when Viggo was transferred from Virginia to New Jersey, he thought Brittany would follow. They had been together for several years, but the subject of marriage never came up. Viggo decided if Brittany was not in a hurry, then neither was he. But her lack of interest in marriage apparently reflected a lack of interest in him. When she broke things off, he resigned himself to bachelorhood.

He was in his early forties when he moved, with fifty not too far down the road, and "daddy time" was quickly slipping away. He occasionally wondered if he had made the right choices, but then could not imagine himself running after a kid when he was in his fifties. He settled into his singular path and was perfectly fine living alone with his Portuguese water dog, Diogo, named after the Portuguese explorer Diogo Gomes.

When he first came to New Jersey, Viggo rented a small fixer-upper cottage in one of the local shore towns. He had already put in almost twenty years with the Coast Guard and decided if and when he retired, he would continue to live in the area. The following year, he purchased it from a family who wanted to move south.

The cottage was just on the other side of the bridge to the hook, which made it easy if he chose to ride his bike to work. He had everything he needed: a good job, a cozy work-in-progress house, a handful of good friends, lots of decent and reasonable eateries, swimming, and hiking; and, if he felt like it, there were many places with live music. Best of all, he had his roomie and pal, Diogo.

Every morning Viggo would fix his coffee and fill an insulated container. He also hooked a dog chew into his belt, and he and

Diogo would go for a jog on Popamora Point, which ran along the shoreline. It was part of the great Henry Hudson Trail. For Viggo, it was his favorite part of the day. Halfway down the path, they would stop for a quick rest. Viggo would finish his coffee while Diogo fetched his stick. Unless he was called to an early duty roster, it was his and Diogo's ritual every day.

Occasionally Viggo would bring Diogo to work and let him run in an enclosed area near the old officer's row of houses at Fort Hancock. It once served as living quarters for commissioned officers, but too many years of neglect left the buildings in a state of disrepair. It was shameful and pitiful to see incredible waterfront property tumbling into the bay. Finally, after twenty-plus years of rife between private citizens as to who should refurbish the declining community, someone began the process of restoration. It would still be several years before the area saw a renaissance, but each season breathed new life into the park.

As he was getting ready for his morning run, he emptied his shirt pocket from the day before.

Madison Wainwright
Editor in Chief
LE FEMME MAGAZINE
110 William Street
NY, NY 10038

He looked down at Diogo, who was waiting patiently. "She was a very interesting woman." Diogo *woof*ed in return. "I wonder what her story is. Her current one." Diogo tilted his head. "I know her father had some sketchy history, but she seemed to have landed on her feet." Diogo *woof*ed again and started beating his tail on the floor.

"Alright. Alright. I shall ponder this later." He grabbed the dog's lead, and they made their way to the door. Just before he stepped out, his cell phone rang, which was usually a bad sign that early in the morning. It was Burton.

"Hey, Rob. What's up?"

"Good morning, Viggo. Wanted to let you know we got an ID on the body."

"Anyone I know?"

"Maybe. We found his car down river. Wallet was in the glove box. Dennis Farrell. Ring a bell?"

"Yeah. He used to run with those treasure hunters."

"Obviously, not anymore. We're still not sure what happened. Coroner is still working on it. Just thought you'd like to know in case any of his cohorts start showing up."

"Thanks. I appreciate it," Eriksson replied. Over the years, there were rumors and legends that Captain Kidd, among others, left a bounty estimated at a million dollars somewhere along the riverbanks. Farrell and a handful of fortune seekers were on the lookout for a legendary map that would lead them to the hoard. In their quest, they would occasionally pull out tide markers, crab traps, and disturb protected watersheds. Often, Viggo and his colleagues would get called in to help the state police run down the pilferers. Eriksson didn't think there would be a call for homicide, but then again, it was a million dollars rumored to be at stake. What that had to do with Kirby Taylor remained to be seen, and how or why Farrell's body ended up under Kirby's dock was the latest question.

"Are you going to notify the Wainwrights, or should I?"

"Up to you. We're all involved until this gets sorted out," Burton said.

Eriksson seized the opportunity to reach out to Ms. Wainwright. "It's still early, but I'll call her after my run."

"Thanks. Keep me posted." Burton ended the call.

Viggo walked back into his bedroom, where he saw Madison Wainwright's business card on his dresser where he had left it. The day just got a bit more interesting.

Chapter Thirteen

Making Lemonade

Lincoln was not thrilled with the idea of telling his sister that getting clear title for the water rights was going to be a laborious process if they planned to sell it. If it remained in the family, they would be able to continue business as usual. The definition of *usual* escaped him, but they were going to have to make the most out of a challenging situation. Before he had the chance to rehearse his speech, his phone rang. It was Madison. He took a deep breath. "Hey, Sis. What is going on so early in the morning?" It was past nine, but Madison rarely phoned before eleven.

"I got a message from Captain Eriksson." Her voice was unusually buoyant. "They identified the body."

"What did he say?"

"I didn't speak to him. He left me a voicemail saying I should call him back and he would give me more details."

"And did you? Call him back?" Lincoln asked.

"Not yet."

"Why not?"

"I wanted to talk to you first."

"Because?"

"Because we have to have a plan."

"Meaning?" Lincoln knew this was where he was going to have to drop the news.

"Meaning, now that they've identified the body, maybe we can start to move forward."

"Did Eriksson say if they found the cause of death?"

"No."

"Maybe you should call him back and get all the information you can before we start on the next leg of this seafaring adventure."

Madison sighed. "I suppose you are right. I'll give him another hour before I call. Once I speak with him, I'll call you back."

"Good idea." Lincoln felt relieved. He knew the conversation was inevitable, but at least he bought himself another hour or two to craft his words, call the Tides Resource Council, and have a timeline that would not send Madison into a tizzy.

Lincoln's optimism waned when he realized the council was made up of twelve governor-appointed volunteers who worked under the purview of the Department of Environmental Protection. At best, it would be a nightmare dealing with another level of bureaucracy. Madison was not going to be happy.

Lincoln began doing some research on what it might take to replace or repair some of the deck and the shack. If it were going to take months to get the situation resolved, maybe they could eke out another summer and make a little money. He would have a chat with Charlie and Crusty to see if they would be interested in running the place. How hard could it be?

He trolled the internet and discovered there were dozens

of deck materials from poly dock boards to preconstructed lengths made of wood. He opened his folder of paperwork that Madison copied for him. He looked at the rough drawings and began to do the math. If they replaced all three docks, it would cost about seven thousand dollars in materials. A prefab shed would run around four thousand. He would have to figure in labor, but he calculated the entire job would run somewhere in the mid-twenties. Six new dinghies would bring the total close to thirty. Then add six outboard motors. That would be another six grand. They were looking at a forty-thousand-dollar investment. He knew Madison would go kicking and screaming and would rather set the place on fire. But what if he could make it work? The idea of rebuilding something was appealing. Plus, the family could spend the summers at the shore. Another expense. Throw in ten thousand to rent something. Okay, fifty grand for the whole enchilada.

He might be able to convince Olivia. Madison was going to be the hurdle. But just maybe he could get Olivia to help him coax his sister into taking a shot.

Lincoln had some savings and knew he could get funding through a home equity loan. He checked and double-checked the numbers. If he was right in his calculations, and there wasn't anything hidden underwater, this was doable. A burst of excitement coursed through his veins. He quickly put everything into an Excel spreadsheet, with names of suppliers and prices. He figured Charlie could help him with the locals and make recommendations, and he would gladly pay Charlie to supervise. *Add another five grand.* It would still be a sound investment, especially if they eventually were able to sell it.

Meanwhile, he would have to figure out a way to balance the books. They say it takes at least three years for a new company to start to see a profit. It could be risky, considering none of them knew one iota about running a marina, but Lincoln felt he would have the support of Uncle Kirby's circle of friends. It would be good for everyone. There is nothing like breathing new life into something people appreciate. Next would be convincing his sister and his wife.

Madison drummed her fingers on her desk, waiting for what she thought would be the right time to return Captain Eriksson's call. She had to admit she was a little nervous. But why? He was not going to arrest her. When she heard his message, she got butterflies. Maybe that was why. But why now? She was forty-eight years old. Wasn't she past having a crush on someone? *A crush?* She shrugged it off. She was too old for schoolgirl nonsense. But still. She called Olivia into her office.

"Captain Eriksson phoned."

"Ooh." Olivia wiggled her eyebrows.

"Okay, you stop that."

"My dear Madison, I have known you too long to not be able to recognize when you find a man alluring."

Madison laughed. "It has been so long I almost forgot what that was like."

"And? Did you speak to him?"

"Not yet. But the good news is they identified the body." She wrinkled her nose. "I suppose that really is not good news. A dead body and all, but at least that is one thing out of the way."

"So? What are you waiting for?"

"Moral support. Please sit with me while I call him back."

"Madison Wainwright! You are almost giddy."

"Exactly. I want to be cool, calm, and collected."

"As you always are."

"Ha! That is on the exterior, and you know it."

Olivia smiled. She was happy to see Madison excited again.

The disappointment about the marina knocked her a bit, but Madison was resilient.

Olivia pointed to Madison's phone. "Dial."

Madison sat up straight and hit the redial button. It rang twice. Each time, a line of goosebumps ran up her arm. She shook them off.

"Captain Eriksson," a smooth, deep voice answered.

"Hello, Captain Eriksson. Madison Wainwright returning your call."

"Good morning, Ms. Wainwright."

"Please, Madison, remember?"

"Yes, of course. Madison. What can I do for you?"

"I am returning your call. You identified the person?" She really did not want to refer to him as *the body*. It sounded so indifferent.

"Yes. Name is Dennis Farrell. Treasure hunter."

"Treasure hunter?" Madison asked.

"There is a group of them in search of a treasure map that is supposed to show where Captain Kidd buried his gold. Supposed to be about a million dollars' worth."

"How intriguing," Madison said slowly. "Do you know what happened to this treasure hunter?"

"Not yet, but at least we know who it is. Was." He paused. "They found his car about a mile downstream. They haven't found any watercraft, like a canoe, or kayak, which is what a lot of them use to navigate along the shore. No one has seen any of his fortune-seeking buddies either, so we don't know if he was on his own."

"Are they looking for the map or the treasure?"

"Both. There are a few books that describe certain areas, but they think if they can get their hands on this phantom map, they'll hit the jackpot. Did your uncle ever mention a map to you or your brother?"

"No. As I told Detective Burton, we had no communication with him for several years, but there were several maps pinned on some fishing line in the shack." She shuddered at the thought of the odoriferous ramshackle structure.

"I see. Yes, I noticed them when I was on the scene. I thought he may have kept a log or a journal. Most anglers keep a log."

"Captain, believe me. If I thought I had any information that would help this investigation, I would happily provide it. But unfortunately, I do not."

"It was worth asking. Sometimes people don't remember things right away. In any event, I thought you'd be interested in knowing that the investigation continues, but now we have one piece of the puzzle."

"Does this mean *you* are off the case?" Madison crossed her fingers, hoping for a negative response.

"Not yet. Not until the coroner sends over the report."

"Then I suppose we'll be seeing each other again?" Madison cringed at her forwardness.

"If you're in the neighborhood."

An awkward silence hung in the air. "I am sure my brother will drag me down there at some point," she said with a nervous giggle.

"You sound as if you don't appreciate our little enclave." He was half teasing.

"Oh, it is lovely. But I know nothing about docks, decks, jetties, wharfs, or piers."

"You seem to have the lingo down."

"Well, just don't ask me to describe what they are. All I know is that they are things in the water." She tilted the phone so Olivia could hear what he was saying.

"Next time you're around, I'll give you a primer."

"I'd enjoy that." She winked at Olivia, who gave Madison a thumbs-up.

"I have a meeting I have to get to but look forward to your

next visit," he said with a smile that she could not see but felt.

"Me, as well. Enjoy your day." Madison ended the call before she made a total fool of herself.

She threw her arms up in the air and spun herself around in her chair. "Woo-hoo!"

"I think someone likes you."

Then Madison put on a frowny face. "What if he has a girlfriend?"

"I don't think so," Olivia replied. "It sounded like a date to me."

"But he didn't exactly ask me out."

"True. But think about this: why didn't the detective call you? Technically he is the head of the investigation." Olivia raised her eyebrows.

"Maybe he was busy." Madison let out a big huff of air.

"Let's think positive," Olivia said. "And let's think of an excuse to go down there again."

"That's going to take some kind of planning." Madison started drumming her fingers again. "I have to let Lincoln know about poor Mr. Farrell." She hit the speed-dial button for her brother and put it on speaker.

"Linc, I just got off the phone with Captain Eriksson. The man's name was Dennis Farrell. From what he told me, he and a few other guys are treasure hunters."

"Doesn't look like he found any," Lincoln said glumly.

"But here is something interesting. Captain Eriksson said there is a rumor, legend, or something that there is a treasure map that marks where Captain Kidd buried a million dollars' worth of gold somewhere along the riverbanks."

"I imagine there are a lot of stories like that," Lincoln said, as he stared at the Excel spreadsheet, wondering when it would be a suitable time to bring up the subject.

"Anyway, he asked if Uncle Kirby ever mentioned a treasure map, and I explained that we hadn't spoken to him in years."

"Didn't you say there were several maps hanging in the shack?"

"Yes, but would it be that obvious? Something with a big X marking the spot?"

"Don't be daft. But there could be some clues there." Lincoln was becoming more intrigued with this newfound family business.

"I suppose, but I am not setting foot in that gross place again." Although, truthfully, she was trying to come up with a reason to go there without stepping inside the mung-box.

"Funny you should mention it," Lincoln said, finally pulling up some courage.

"What? The shack? What about it?"

"I have an idea I want to float past you and Olivia. No pun intended."

"How about letting the thing float down the river?" Madison said wryly.

"Such a comedienne," Lincoln groaned. "But seriously, can we meet for dinner?"

"Tonight?" She looked over at Olivia.

Olivia nodded.

"I don't have anything in the fridge, so we can do takeout or go out. Your choice," Madison replied.

Lincoln debated whether the conversation should be at home, in private, or in a public space. He decided on takeout. "How about that Lebanese place down the street from you?"

"Okay with me."

"I'll stop there on my way to your place. Text me what you want."

"Get the usual." She looked at Olivia. "Rice pilaf, sfeeha, manakish, kafta, and hummus." She loved their meat pies and meatballs.

"Sounds good to me. What time?"

Madison checked her planner. "I have a meeting at four. Should go about an hour. Say six?"

"Got it. I'll phone the restaurant and let them know I'll pick it up at six o'clock and be at your place by ten after."

"I'm getting hungry thinking about it," Madison said, and ended the call.

Madison was still ruminating over how she could get back to Smuggler's Cove without appearing desperate. Or was it anxious? Or artless? Insecure, perhaps? Her reverie was broken by the sound of her cell phone.

"Hello, this is Madison."

"Ms. Wainwright, this is Detective Burton. Did Captain Eriksson have an opportunity to speak with you today?"

"Yes. He said you were able to identify the man. Dennis Farrell?"

"Correct. I wanted to reassure you that we are diligently working on this matter."

"I have no doubt." Madison's words were chipper.

"As soon as we get the coroner's report, we will be in touch."

"Thank you, Detective."

"You're very welcome. Just one other thing. Every year. Smuggler's Cove has a seafood festival, and we would like to honor your uncle. The town has a fund that helps families when they lose a loved one as a result of an accident while working the waters. We hold a fifty-fifty raffle."

"That is a lovely idea. What can we do to help?"

"You can be in attendance when we give the check to the committee's fund." He hesitated when he realized he was pitching a small-town activity to a highbrow New Yorker. "It won't take up much of your time."

"That will not be an issue." She wondered if the Coast

Guard was invited. "Just text me the information, and we will be there."

"It's held over Memorial Day weekend. A kickoff for the summer, as if we don't have enough going on." He snorted. "I know everyone will appreciate the opportunity to celebrate your uncle's life here."

"Sounds wonderful." Madison was quite sincere. The response and support she had witnessed regarding her uncle was heartwarming. "We would be honored. Thank you."

"I'm sure you will enjoy the festivities. It's not the Macy's Thanksgiving Parade, but it's good fun."

"That is a relief! As much as I enjoy watching the parade on television, I will skip the crushing crowd."

"No crushing involved, except for crushed ice with lots of syrupy flavors. We call them 'snow cones.'"

"So do we, Detective." Madison chuckled. "We *do* live on the same planet."

Burton laughed. Maybe he was being a little too biased. "Yes. Yes, we do. I will send you the details this afternoon. Have a good day."

Madison was sure to have a good day. She now had plans for Memorial weekend. She snapped her fingers. She was going to help the committee with the planning. After all, Kirby was her uncle, and she had always been fond of him. This was her opportunity to make up for the time lost, if that is ever possible. At least the good intentions and positive energy would be there.

"What was that about?" Olivia asked. "You're smiling like the cat who ate the canary."

Madison snapped herself out of her reverie and told Olivia about the seafood festival and honoring Uncle Kirby.

"That's so nice. Ooh, we should probably get a hotel for the night," Olivia suggested. "For the weekend? You might want to hang around town a little." She gave her friend a mischievous look. "Don't think I don't know what that smile was really about."

Madison laughed. "You know me too well. But staying over the weekend is not a bad idea. What about renting a house?"

"Even better. I will get on it right now. I am sure many are already booked."

"Good point." Madison gazed out the window that overlooked more buildings and a blotch of blue sky. "You know something, Liv, I think I was a little too quick on the draw about my opinion."

"Which one? You have many," Olivia teased.

"Smuggler's Cove."

"Oh, really?" Olivia gave her a sideways look. "Could it be the handsome Coast Guard captain?"

"Yes, but that's not all of it. Everyone has been genuinely kind, and the scenery is absolutely beautiful."

"Do you mean the *scenery*-scenery? Or the Coast Guard scenery?"

"Can't I mean both?" Madison chuckled. "Listen, I am not a fan of the bait and tackle part of it, but the area and the people, it is quite charming."

"That's a good word for it." Olivia nodded. "And handsome mariners help, too."

"Will you please stop?" Madison was blushing.

"Nope," Olivia said emphatically.

"Okay, but promise you will not tease me in front of Lincoln. He would never let me hear the end of it."

"Lincoln and I share many things. *Our* secrets?"—she pointed to Madison and then to herself—"they belong to us, and us alone."

"Thank you."

"Hey, I love my husband, but we're best friends forever." Olivia winked. "Now, I have some house hunting to do."

"And I better call Linc and let him know about the festival and our plans."

Olivia went back to her desk, and Madison dialed her brother's number.

"Twice in one day?" Lincoln answered without saying hello.

"Hello to you, too," Madison snarked. "So, I got a call from Detective Burton this morning."

"Well, aren't you the darling of the local constables?"

Madison rolled her eyes. "Yes. Yes, I am. Get this. Smuggler's Cove has an annual seafood festival over Memorial weekend, and each year, they honor someone. This year they want to honor Uncle Kirby. There's some sort of fund for families who lost a loved one while working out on the water."

"That's pretty cool. Uncle Kirby. Who knew he was so popular?"

"Exactly. We surely didn't, and now it is time for us to make up for all the years we ignored him."

"It wasn't entirely our fault."

"Yeah, it was. We were grown up enough to stay connected with him."

"I hate to admit it, but when you're right, you're right," Lincoln said.

"Thank you. Anyway, they want us to go down and be part of the ceremony."

"Huh. What does that entail?"

"First thing is renting a house for the weekend."

Lincoln laughed out loud. "Of course. How foolish of me."

"Liv is working on it. I think it could be fun."

"Are you alright?" Lincoln asked suspiciously.

"What do you mean?"

"You swore you would never set foot over there ever again. And now you want to rent a house for the weekend?"

"Why not? Seafood festival. Sun. Beach. Uncle Kirby."

"I feel as if I'm missing something." Lincoln secretly was pleased that his sister had a slight change of heart about the area, but her enthusiasm was suspicious.

"Like what?" Madison tried to remain stoic.

"I dunno. But you rarely change your mind at the drop of a dime."

"What do you mean?" Madison asked.

"You're not one to change her mind so easily. What gives?"

"I was too eager to rush to judgment, that's all. The people are genuinely nice, and the area is lovely." She waited for her brother to continue. She did not want to implicate herself in any ulterior motives.

"Well, I am glad to hear it. I thought you were being a little too judgy."

"It's part of my job," Madison defended herself.

"It's not fashion week at the Jersey Shore."

"Is it ever?" Madison asked with a touch of cynicism.

"And there she is," Lincoln joked.

"Alright, already. Anyway, mark your calendar. Details to follow. See you at six-ten."

"Ten-four," Lincoln returned the shorthand. Convincing Madison of his plans may not be as difficult as he first thought.

By five o'clock, Madison was finished looking through cover shots and was ready to head home. "Shall we walk? It is such a nice evening."

"Sure." Olivia changed into her sneakers, and Madison yanked off her stilettos and swapped them for her new white skimmers. She liked the way they felt.

As they were leaving the building, Olivia gave her an update on finding a house to rent. "I found a few that look perfect for us. Four bedrooms, two and a half baths, and near the beach."

"I sense a *but* coming," Madison replied.

"But most want a month's lease, preferably the season."

"What kind of money are we talking about?" Madison asked.

"Five thousand for the month, twelve if we take it for three months."

"Yikes. Those are Hamptons numbers. Are any of them on the beach?" Madison was calculating in her head.

"Nothing is exactly on the beach. At least not near Smuggler's Cove. There is one that has a spectacular view of the ocean, a pool, and a jacuzzi. It's on one of those hills."

"And what kind of money are they looking for?"

"Fifteen thousand for the summer."

"Geez!"

"There's one house that's on the water, but there's no beach."

Madison sighed. "We will talk this over with Lincoln. I have a little cash I can spare, but I was hoping to use it for a trip to London."

"We can look further when we get to your place. I bookmarked the most interesting places."

Madison put her arm around Olivia. "You are the best."

It took them a little over twenty minutes to make it to Madison's apartment. As usual, Mario and Luigi were sitting on the long mission-style bench that ran along the wall next to the front door. "I don't know how they know I'm in the building," Madison said to Olivia, "but here they are." She leaned over and kissed them both on the head and scrunched their fur.

She tossed her tote near the cats, who were patiently waiting for more attention. "Come on, guys. Chow time." She kicked off her skimmers, left them by the front door, and slipped on a pair of Oofos. Olivia followed suit with her own pair of ballet slippers that she carried in her bag.

After the kitties were fed, Madison excused herself and changed into a flannel track suit.

"I see you are becoming a fan of this fabric." Olivia ran her hand down Madison's sleeve.

"I am. I think it is going to be a big trend for fall."

"It better be, considering it's the main story!" Olivia chuckled.

Madison cocked her head. "Interesting, isn't it?"

"What, flannel?"

"Yes, flannel. I had not given it much thought and really did not make the connection when Hannah loaned me her shirt. Ha. Hannah is fashion-forward. Who'da thunk it?" She flopped down on the sofa. "Wine or beer?" She looked up at Olivia.

"Why don't I fix us a Manhattan, and then we can decide when Lincoln gets here."

"Why did I ever let you marry my brother?" Madison laughed. "I should have kept you for myself."

"But we don't play on that team."

"Yes, but I could have hired you as my personal assistant."

"You already have." Olivia went into the kitchen and pulled out two large stainless-steel cubes from the freezer, then over to the sideboard and mixed two drinks.

Madison readjusted her position when Olivia handed her the cocktail glass. "Thank you. I did not mean to imply you were my servant."

Olivia curtsied. "I shall always be your servant."

"I prefer best friend." They clinked glasses.

The door attendant rang Madison's intercom to alert her that her brother was on the way, "With something that smells delicious!"

"Thanks, Marvin. I would be happy to share leftovers, but I doubt there will be any."

"I can understand. Have a good evening."

"Hey Marvin? Can you send the food up, and send my brother away?"

"Excuse me?" He was not sure if she was joking. Madison had a very dry sense of humor, and sometimes it was hard to know if she was kidding or not.

"Just kidding, Marvin. You have a good evening, too."

Five minutes later, Lincoln was struggling with his set of keys and eventually tapped his elbow on the door. "Delivery!"

"You can leave it outside. Thanks." Madison and Olivia giggled.

"You are on a roll," Lincoln called from the other side of the door. Olivia dashed over to let him in.

"Thank you." Lincoln gave his wife a peck on the cheek. "At least I can count on you to open the door."

"Only because you are bearing nutritious and delicious food." She giggled and returned the kiss.

Madison was already in the kitchen, gathering plates, forks, serving spoons, and napkins. "What is everyone drinking?"

"Beer, for me," Lincoln called, as he removed the well-sealed food from the shopping bags. "Hon?" He looked over at Olvia.

"What kind of beer do you have?" Olivia asked. She considered herself a beer snob. She would rather die of thirst than take a swig of Budweiser or Miller Lite.

"Stella Artois and Blue Moon," Madison replied.

"I will take a Blue Moon. Got a slice of orange?"

Madison rummaged through her refrigerator. "This is pathetic," she said to herself. "I have something that looks like it could be an orange, or a very old apple," she called out.

Olivia grinned at Lincoln. "Pardon me while I rescue your sister from domestic bliss."

For all her talent, Madison was not much of an artist when it came to the kitchen or cooking. Olivia took the wrinkled piece of fruit. "I think it's salvageable." She cut a wedge and put it in a beer glass, then poured her drink. Lincoln liked his out of the bottle. Once when they were in a pub, the waiter asked if he wanted it in a glass. Lincoln's response was, "But it's already in a glass." He used that joke over and over until it solicited moans from his friends.

Once everything was on the table, they each took a seat. "I'd like to say grace tonight," Madison offered.

"Are you sure you're alright?" Lincoln placed the back of his hand on his sister's forehead. Madison gently slapped it away.

"All this stuff with Uncle Kirby made me realize we should be thankful for what we have."

"Let's not forget how hard we've worked to get here," Lincoln added.

"Exactly. We were lucky enough to have the mental acuity, education, and integrity. So, please humor me. This may be the one and only time." Madison bowed her head and took Lincoln's and Olivia's hands in hers. "Thank you, Lord, for all the blessings in our life. We may not always show our gratitude, but I promise I will make more of an effort. Amen."

"Ditto and amen," came from Lincoln.

"I shall do the same," Olivia added. "Amen."

"See? That was not so hard." Madison held up her glass. "To Uncle Kirby."

They talked about the festival and if they should give a little speech. "Detective Burton didn't give me any details except the date. But I think I might volunteer."

Lincoln almost spit out his beer. "Are you sure you are alright? It was just a few days ago when you were totally disgusted. Now you want to play nice in the sandbox?"

"Ha. Sandbox. Get it?" Madison caught the pun before Lincoln did. She began to clear the table. "By the way, what did you want to talk about?"

Lincoln went back to the bench where he'd left his attaché case. "I've been doing some financial projections."

"Projections? What kind?" Madison asked, and then gave Olivia a side glance. Olivia was as much in the dark as Madison and shrugged.

"Did you know that Uncle Kirby took in around thirty-five thousand dollars last year?"

"From the marina?" Madison looked dubious.

"Yes, from the marina. There are a lot of people who like to go crabbing. He was averaging a thousand dollars per weekend in the summer months."

"Seriously?"

"Yes. And he rented out two slips to people who kept their boats there, at two hundred bucks a month, each. I checked around, and quite a few people will do that if they have riparian rights. For the boat owners, it's cheaper than a larger marina, and for the dock owners it was a little cash in their pockets."

"Is that legal?" Olivia asked.

"I didn't get that far, but my point is, that dilapidated marina had an income." Lincoln slid the paperwork toward his sister. "We don't know how long it's going to take for the water rights to be sanctioned, so why waste a summer's worth of income?"

"But the place is a mess," Madison noted.

"Which brings me to my next point. I ran some numbers. We can fix the place up for around sixty thousand dollars."

"Whoa, that's a bucket of money," Madison said.

"Yes, but if we sell Nana and Pop's house, we would have more than enough to cover the cost, plus rent a summer house."

Madison eyed her brother. "Continue."

"We know the people who are renting the house plan to move at the end of May. We can ask them if they wouldn't mind if we put it on the market. If it's too inconvenient, we can wait until they move out. In the meantime, we can get a home equity loan"—he looked at Olivia for approval—"then pay it back once the house sells."

Olivia was listening intently. "As long as we pay it back, I don't have any reservations, but what if the house doesn't sell right away?"

"Madison and I have been approached by several real estate agents over the past couple of years. There was no mortgage, so Maddie and I have been able to pay the taxes, keep the property maintained, and still share the profits three ways. We should make a tidy sum from the sale."

"What about Mom? She owns a third of it, too."

"I don't think she'd mind an influx of a hundred thousand dollars."

"You think we can get three hundred thousand for the house?"

"I looked online, and that seems to be the going rate for that size house and neighborhood."

"I'm all in," Madison said with the biggest grin. "Now let's look at those summer houses Livvy found today."

Lincoln hadn't realized how tense he had been until he felt his shoulders come down from his ears. "Wow. I don't remember the last time you were so agreeable."

"Now, who's being funny?" Madison took a pull from her glass.

"I will call the tenants tomorrow and ask if they would be willing to let people tromp through the house. I will give them an incentive. Half month's rent."

"That works for me." Madison was all atwitter at this new phase that was unfolding.

"Then I will call the agent that has been hounding me. She's probably called me every other month for the past year."

"Gail, right? Nice woman."

"It's an ideal neighborhood for a young family." Madison thought back to the days when she was a little girl and played on the swing her grandfather made from rope. She was happy it was still there and intact. Her reminiscence led to the days when she was in exile from New York. She sighed. "Lots of memories."

"Should I give Mom a call while we're on the subject?" Lincoln asked.

"Do you know what time zone she's in?" Madison chuckled.

"She is in Toronto. Same as ours."

"Daylight Savings Time always throws me," Madison said.

Lincoln pulled out his cell phone, dialed her number, and put it on speaker. Gwen answered after two rings. "Lincoln, honey. Everything okay?"

"Hey, Mom. Yes, everything is fine. Why do you think there is always a problem when I call?" Lincoln smirked.

"It's a mother's reaction," Gwen replied. "What are you up to?"

"I'm with Maddie and Olivia."

"Hey, Mom!" Madison called out.

"Hello, Gwen." Olivia was never comfortable calling her Gwen, and she also did not want to call her Mom. But when the girls were in their twenties, Gwen insisted on it.

"We went down to see Uncle Kirby's place. It's a bit of a mess, and so is the paperwork, but we will figure it out."

"Kirby was a good soul. He loved you and your sister," Gwen recalled. "Is there something in particular you wanted to discuss, because I know next to nothing about it."

"There's some legal mumbo jumbo we need to iron out about the water rights, which could take months. We thought rather than have the place just sit there for a season, we could fix it up, hire someone to run it, and make a little money." Lincoln moved the papers around. "According to his banking records, he took in almost thirty-five thousand dollars last year."

"Really?" Gwen sounded surprised.

"Yes, but the place could use a refurb." He looked to his sister and then Olivia for moral support. "We were thinking about maybe putting Nana and Pop's house on the market." He held his breath.

"I think that's a great idea." Gwen was reassuring. "You have been managing the place, and even though we get a small sum each month, I think it is a good time to sell it. I am sure we could all use a little extra cash."

Madison leaned closer to the phone. "There's a seafood festival on May thirty-first, and they are honoring Uncle Kirby. There is an emergency fund for families of fishermen. They do a raffle, and then they put his name on a plaque. It is rather quaint. I am sure Uncle Kirby would be proud to have his name on something besides an old marina. I have not mentioned this to Linc or Livvy, but if we go ahead and fix the place up, I think we should change the name from Taylor to Kirby's Marina."

"That's a wonderful idea," Gwen gushed.

Lincoln gave his sister a high-five. "Alright. We are good to go. I am going to call the tenants and the real estate agent tomorrow."

"Keep me posted. I love you!" Gwen signed off.

"Love you, too!" everyone said in unison.

As soon as they knew the call was over, Madison chimed in, "You forgot to mention the dead body."

"I am sure that is something she could do without knowing," Olivia put in her two cents. "She worries enough about the two of you."

Over the years, Gwen was in constant contact with Olivia's mother, Sandra. In the beginning, Gwen was incredibly careful about communicating with her children. It was her way of protecting them. Sandra played a key role in keeping Gwen up to date, and Sandra confided in Olivia, who was part of their underground communications. Olivia often felt she was keeping things from her best friend, but she also had an allegiance to her own mother. She comforted herself knowing that everyone was looking out for one another, and it was not important who knew or did not know.

"Now let's look at that house," Madison urged Olivia, who was pulling up the website.

It was a front-to-back split-level. When you entered the house, there was a large room to one side that could serve as a bonus room or a den. Across from it was a bedroom and bath. From there, you could go up a short flight of steps to the bedrooms, or down a short flight to the kitchen, dining area, and a great room. The entire lower level faced a large patio with a pool, which overlooked the bay to the left and the ocean to the right. There was a pool house to the side that could also be used for houseguests.

"I think I'm loving this place." Madison kept swiping through the photos. "Is this the one that's fifteen grand for the summer?"

"That's what it says."

"Sounds kind of cheap." Madison swiped again. "Is it close to a refinery? Garbage dump?"

Lincoln chimed in, "How about taking a ride to look at it? We can also Google Map it."

Olivia checked the website and tapped in the address. From what they could tell, there wasn't anything around except a large park and a few other houses. "What about calling Detective Burton and asking him? If anyone knows the area, he surely does."

"Excellent idea, Olivia. Are you sure you do not want to come and work for me?" Madison chuckled.

Olivia rolled her eyes.

"Do you think it's too late to call Burton now?"

Lincoln checked the time. It was almost eight. "I can leave him a voicemail. Maddie, you have his number handy?"

She scrolled through her incoming calls and gave Lincoln the number.

"This is Burton," he answered on the first ring.

"Detective? This is Lincoln Wainwright. Sorry to be bothering you at this hour. First, I want to thank you for keeping Uncle Kirby's legacy alive."

"He was beloved by the community."

"Well, since we most likely won't have an outcome about the water rights for a while, we would like to go ahead and refurbish the place and keep it open for the summer."

Burton became interested. "I think your uncle would be happy to hear that. I know Hannah and Charlie will be."

"I am glad you approve. Which brings me to the next thing." Lincoln paused, then said, "We're thinking about renting a place for the summer. There is a house on Portland Road that we are interested in, but I was hoping we could get your opinion on it."

Burton was surprised. "What's the address?"

Lincoln read it to Burton.

"Nice place. The people who own it live in Colorado now and rent it out for the summer."

"Is there any reason we shouldn't pursue this? The rent seemed more than reasonable, and it made me wonder why."

"They want to cover the property taxes until they know where they will be living permanently. They work for a government contractor and are in Colorado for the next two years."

"Oh, I see. Do you know the agent who is overseeing it? Irene Mariska?"

"Sure do. She's been around here longer than most people. Knows the area like the back of her hand."

"Great. I will give her a call tomorrow to arrange for a walk-through," Lincoln said.

"Sounds good. Let me know if you need any help with anything."

"Thanks. We will try to stay out of your hair."

Burton laughed. "That should be relatively easy."

That's when Lincoln realized what he said to a bald man. "Sorry. No offense."

"None taken." The detective chuckled. "Enjoy the rest of your evening."

"Thanks. You do the same." Lincoln turned to his siter and his wife. "Well, gals, looks like we may have a summer house."

"Yippee!" Madison screeched, sending Mario and Luigi running. "Sorry, guys. Mommy is excited." Then she paused. "What about your nephews?" she asked, looking at Lincoln.

Lincoln gave her a quizzical look. "Nephews?" Then it dawned on him she was talking about her cats. "Let's see what the place looks like, and then we can ask about pets."

"As long as there's a space where they won't be able to get out."

"You could leave them here over the weekend, no?" Lincoln asked.

"But what if I decide I want to work remotely?" Madison asked, doodling on the paper in front of her.

"Let's take this one step at a time," Lincoln urged his impatient sister.

Olivia reached over and touched Madison's hand. "Everything in its own time."

"Yes. I know. But everything is happening so quickly. One minute, we are unaware there is a marina, then there is one, and then there's a dead body, and now we are going to rent a place for the summer. If my calculations are correct, dear math-genius brother, all of this has happened in less than three days."

He mocked her by ticking off the days on his fingers. "Yes, you are correct. But you have always been resilient, and quickly adapt. Why not now?"

"Because I'm not as young as I used to be?" she mocked herself.

"Stop," Olivia urged. "You don't look a day over forty-ish."

"It's the *ish* part," Madison said, pouting.

"You're only forty-eight," Olivia responded.

"Going on forty-nine," she reminded everyone.

"Still not the big five-oh," Lincoln teased.

"Ha, ha. Let us not rush things." Madison leaned her elbow on the table and rested her chin on her fist.

"I am going to call the real estate agent. They usually don't keep normal business hours," Lincoln said. He knew it was past eight, but he also knew agents were always ready to sell or rent. He dialed the number, and it went to voicemail. "Hello, Ms. Mariska, my name is Lincoln Wainwright. My wife, my sister, and I are interested in looking at the rental property on Portland Road. Can you please let me know if it is still available and when it would be convenient to look at it? We are in Manhattan." He left the number, and within minutes, his phone rang.

"Hello?"

"Mr. Wainwright? This is Irene Mariska. You phoned about the place on Portland Road?"

"Yes, hello, Ms. Mariska."

"Please, call me Irene."

"If you call me Lincoln."

"Deal, Lincoln. It's a lovely place. And the rent is quite reasonable."

"Yes, I just got off the phone with Detective Burton, who told me about the property."

"Rob? Good guy. His wife owns a floral shop in town. When is it convenient for you?"

"It will take us over an hour to get there, but . . ."

Irene interrupted him. "Do you know about the ferry?"

"Ferry?" Lincoln asked. He nodded to Olivia, who was already looking it up online.

"Yes. There's a ferry that runs from East Thirty-fifth or Wall Street. Takes forty minutes. I can pick you up at the ferry terminal in town."

"That's very nice of you, Irene."

"No problem. I can give you a little tour of the area if you'd like." Then she paused. "Are you the people who took over Kirby's place?"

"Sort of. He was our uncle," Lincoln added. "We hope to refurbish the place and get it up and running for the summer."

"That would be wonderful. It's a great little hangout place," Irene added.

"So it seems," Lincoln acknowledged her remark.

"Hannah and Charlie make a heck of a fried clam sandwich," Irene gushed. "And wait until crab season. Hannah can whip up a serious crab dip, steamed crabs, you name it. If it's crabby, it's on the menu."

Olivia turned her laptop so Lincoln could see the ferry schedule.

"There is a ferry that gets in at noon. Would that work for you?" he asked Irene.

"Perfect. I'll be wearing a red blazer, driving a white Cadillac SUV."

"Excellent. We will see you tomorrow. Thanks, Irene," Lincoln said.

"Thank you, Lincoln. Looking forward to meeting you, your sister, and your wife."

Lincoln ended the call and turned toward his sister. "You can sneak out of the office for a couple of hours, right?"

Olivia was nodding. She knew Madison's schedule better than Madison did. "According to the ferry schedule, there are several in the afternoon that would get us back into the city between four and five."

"Excellent!" Madison was buoyant.

"I'll look for the agent's number in Connecticut and give her a call tomorrow. I am sure she will be as eager as Irene." Lincoln smiled. "Do you think Giada will join us over the summer?"

"It will depend on which boyfriend she's dating." Olivia chuckled. "She and her roommate usually rent something for a week on Long Beach Island during summer break, but she hasn't mentioned it yet. I'm sure they will come up with something."

"She's really enjoying living in Philly, eh?"

"Don't remind me." Lincoln hung his head. "I know, I know. She is in her twenties now, but she's still Daddy's little girl."

Madison's emotions were always a mess when it came to paternal affection. She adored the way Lincoln cared for his daughter, something she never experienced with her own father. She was grateful that Lincoln's instincts were far greater than what he'd experienced.

It was almost nine when Olivia suggested she and Lincoln head home. "We have another big day ahead." She put her hand on Madison's shoulder and indicated she wanted to speak to her in private. The two women had their own secret language, ever since they were children. Madison led the way into the kitchen and raised an eyebrow.

"Maybe you should let the captain know you are going to be in town," Olivia whispered.

"Oh, stop. I can't do that," Madison said in an equally hushed voice. "What would I even say?"

"Madison, you are never at a loss for words. You'll think of something," Olivia said, smiling.

"Hopefully, he'll be at the seafood festival." Madison couldn't wait to see him again.

"Oh, I think we have to make sure of that!" Olivia winked.

Chapter Fourteen

A Seafaring Adventure, Sorta

It had been a busy week for Madison, Lincoln, and Olivia. Olivia was charged with the duty of scheduling appointments for everyone involved, no easy task given they were about to close the book for the fall issue of the magazine. But she knew all about controlled chaos and kept a whiteboard with markers and an eraser on the wall behind her desk. She got teased about being "old school," but the system worked. She would then send an electronic version to whomever needed to know, but it was much quicker to look at the wall than scroll, swipe, click through a myriad of information. Not only was Olivia an expert in organization, but she was also a bit of a sleuth.

That morning, before Madison got to the office and too enamored by the captain, Olivia wanted to make sure it was clear sailing. *Sometimes the puns were just too easy.* She smiled at herself. It did not take much digging to find out the main details of Captain Viggo Eriksson.

Name: Viggo Lukas Eriksson
Born: 1983 Bergen, Norway
Relocated to Gloucester, MA—1991
U.S. Citizen—Naturalized 1998
Marital status—unmarried, no records of previous
Education: Graduated from Salem University 2005
Degree in Criminology
Joined Coast Guard: 2005
Became Captain in 2013
2006-2021—Stationed in San Diego, New Orleans, Virginia Beach
2022—Transferred to Sandy Hook
Current residence: Gravely Point, Smuggler's Cove

Olivia clicked on Google Maps and located his modest house. She went to "Street View" and saw that the front had stones and several tall grass plants with two Adirondack chairs on the small, front patio. From what she could surmise, the rear of the property was enclosed with a white fence lined with more seagrass. *At least it's neat and well kept. But then again, so is he.* She printed out her short dossier and two photos of the house. Even though she used an incognito window, she deleted her search history from her computer. One cannot be too careful about spying eyes. She folded the sheets of paper and slid them into the pocket of her cardigan. She would share the info with Madison when she got in. As per her usual routine, Olivia fired up the barista-size coffee maker in the kitchen area. If Madison was a snob about anything, it was her morning coffee. That and beer and olive oil.

Olivia's cell beeped. It was Madison letting her know she was on her way up. "Double shot, please." Translated, it meant she wanted a double shot of espresso in her already hair-curling java.

Olivia heard the ding of the elevator and began her special brew. Madison was coming down the hall. Olivia could swear she was singing.

"Aren't we in a fine mood today?" Olivia smiled.

Madison gave her a peck on the cheek. "Yes. Yes, I am. And why not? We are embarking on a new adventure."

Olivia did not want to throw water on Madison's mood, but the last time Madison was this buoyant was when she thought she inherited a fabulous marina just a few short days ago. But Madison was resilient, and Olivia was much more confident about the rental. At least they had seen photos of it and got a good recommendation from the police detective and the real estate agent.

"A newer, new adventure." Olivia gave her a wink. "I have something for you." She slipped her hand into her pocket and pulled out the folded sheet.

"What's this?" Madison asked as she opened the pages. "Oh my. Aren't you the Miss Marple of the fashion industry?" Madison glanced at the information. "Interesting. Have you thought about doing undercover work?"

"Isn't that part of my job description?" Olivia gave her a sly look.

"Indeed, it is. Thank you, darling." Madison returned the sly expression and slipped the investigative work into her bag.

"Maddie, I am very happy you have had a slight change of heart about Smuggler's Cove."

"How could I not? I'm embarrassed to think about the crummy attitude I had."

"Now you can make up for it. Just think, Hannah and Charlie will be able to keep the food truck there, and people will be able to have use of the place, and the amenities."

"Let's not get carried away." Madison took the mug from Olivia and sipped her coffee. She began to walk toward her corner office, then turned her head. "But I was thinking about Hannah and Charlie and the sandwiches. Instead of a drive-thru window, we have a boat-thru window."

"Huh?" Olivia asked. "Is that a thing?"

Madison tossed her jacket on one of the side chairs. "We can make it one." She settled behind her desk. "What if we have boaters phone ahead, and then someone brings the sandwiches to them?"

"Sounds interesting. I suppose it could work logistically. But obviously we must run it past Hannah and Charlie."

"Obviously. I know Lincoln wants to buy a prefab shed, so maybe he can get one that has a pass-through window."

"I'll put that on my list for him." Olivia was always ready with pen and pad.

"What else do we have to do today?" Madison asked.

"Lincoln left a message for the agent in Connecticut, so we are waiting for that call. We must be at the ferry landing by ten forty-five, and then Irene will pick us up when we arrive."

"Do I have any early evening things I need to get back here for?"

"Nope. I took care of today's loose ends."

"You are a miracle worker." Madison was continually impressed at how Olivia managed things with aplomb. That was one reason they became fast friends as children. They always operated as a team. Madison was especially pleased they maintained their relationship all these years. She was not sure what made her happier: her friendship with Olivia or having Olivia as a sister-in-law. Then she thought that both could coexist at the same time.

Madison reached into her tote bag. "Look! I came prepared." She showed Olivia her skimmers.

"Brilliant. And you are looking quite elegantly casual."

"It's part of the job." Madison chuckled. Despite being in

the world of fashion, and a honcho at a leading magazine, Madison preferred casual. Not sloppy, but as Olivia put it, elegantly casual.

"Okay, let's see what my private detective found." She reached into her bag and pulled out the pages. "So far, he qualifies for the job."

"What job?" Olivia asked.

"Summer fling job." Madison chuckled.

"Don't be naughty."

"You mean nautical," Madison teased, and flipped through the pages. "Oh, and we also have visuals." She peered at the photos of Viggo's cottage. "Cute place. I like the seagrass décor."

"It's appropriate," Olivia said, grinning.

"Now all we have to find out is if he has a girlfriend."

"I wasn't getting that vibe from him," Olivia said.

"A girlfriend vibe? Is *that* a thing?" Madison mocked.

"Come on, he was flirting with you."

"True, but that doesn't mean he doesn't have a girlfriend."

"I guess we'll find out when you let him know you are renting a house and you would like some clarification about jetties, wharfs, docks, landings, and all that."

"Let's not get ahead of ourselves." Madison was anxious and nervous. "Plus, he is younger than me. And we know how those relationships worked out in the past. Not great."

"Do not talk yourself out of this, my dear. I know you too well. If you think something might go wrong, you back away."

"I most certainly do not."

"Oh, you most certainly do when it comes to men." Olivia folded her arms.

Olivia was correct in her assertion that when it came to men, Madison was skittish. And who could blame her after Seth? New York was a tough town, especially when it came to people with a limited moral compass, and eager to "make it big," regardless of the cost to others and sometimes to themselves.

"Okay. Okay." Madison took another sip of her coffee. "Let's take a look at the rental again."

Olivia went to her desk and forwarded the link to Madison's email.

A chime signaled it had arrived in Madison's inbox. Madison quickly opened it and began to swipe the photos. "I hope it wasn't photoshopped."

"Oh, please. You go from *yippee* to *uh-oh*."

"It has been that kind of week. But I have a good feeling about this one."

Madison went to her early meeting and informed the staff that she was taking the rest of the day off. Most of them were stunned. Madison rarely took any time for herself. She was always working, and most of her employees assumed her career was her whole life. They weren't that far off the mark. She kept her circle small and didn't like interacting with too many people. It wasn't that she was an introvert or a misanthrope, she was just careful. Besides her coworkers and exceedingly small circle of friends, she mostly kept to herself, her cats, her brother and sister-in-law, and her niece. There were a handful of business associates she would occasionally dine with, and there were the numerous industry galas and events, but Madison was always haunted by her father's indiscretions, and how she reinvented herself. Some people would think it was an admirable feat, but in Madison's way of thinking, she was on a slippery slope of being a fraud.

Olivia would argue that Madison had every right to protect herself from judgment, and the chance of retribution, but Madison often thought she was lying to everyone.

"You are Madison Wainwright. You earned everything you have: your job, your apartment, and most of all, your life. Few people could pick themselves up and meet the challenges of scandal and financial loss. You went from a luxurious lifestyle to humble and modest. You transferred when you were smack in the middle of college and moved out of town. You graduated at the top of your class, you designed a line of clothes, started a blog, and now you are at the top of your game in the world of fashion. Do not sell yourself short."

That was one of the many things Madison loved about her friend. Olivia could be quiet and reserved, but she was keenly observant and could articulate her opinions without alienating people. In Madison's estimation, not only was Olivia the quintessential business associate, but she was also a fierce and loyal friend. Madison would snicker when Olivia would give her the occasional lecture. "You are right. I am spectacular."

Olivia rapped on the doorjamb. "Ready? We must leave in ten minutes to catch the ferry."

Madison was genuinely excited. She put her anxiety on hold. *What's the worst that could happen?* When the only thing that came to mind was the boat capsizing, she reminded herself she was a good swimmer, they had life jackets, and they were close to shoreline. Besides, there was a very handsome Coast Guard captain that might rescue her. Her thoughts were light and breezy. She closed the door to her office and changed into a pair of white capri pants, white sleeveless turtleneck, and a white cardigan—and of course, her skimmers, which had become her favorite shoes—and plopped a trawler cap over her platinum-blond hair.

Olivia gave her the nod. "Time to go. Lincoln is waiting in the lobby."

They headed down William and then to Wall Street and South Street, where the ferry landing was located. Boats of all sizes were coming and going. Announcements for Paulus

Hook, Belford, and Liberty Harbor rang through the air. Helicopters moved up and down, swirling the water below. There was a sign designated for Sea Streak, the boat that would take them to the Highlands, where Irene was going to meet them. Madison was impressed at the size of the boat. "I don't know what I thought we were taking, but this is one big freighter."

Lincoln laughed. "You better get your maritime vocabulary straight. That is not a freighter."

"Ship. Boat. Freighter. Whatever," Madison joked.

Lincoln was happy to see his sister in a much better mood when it came to Smuggler's Cove. He wasn't sure what brought on the change of attitude, but he'd take it. It was going to be a big project, but nothing they couldn't handle, as long as there weren't any more surprises, like a dead body.

It was as if Madison were reading Lincoln's mind. "I wonder if they have any more information about Mr. Farrell."

"I guess we'll find out." Lincoln paid the crew member for their tickets. "Three round-trip tickets, please."

The interior of the boat looked like a 747 jet, with rows and rows of seats, and two aisles that ran between the rows and the booths along the windows. A service bar was in the middle.

"This is much more civilized than I imagined." Madison was used to seeing the small shuttle ferries from Weehawken to the West Side of Midtown that took ten minutes. This boat could accommodate over a hundred passengers and crew and looked extremely comfortable. They found an empty booth on the port side, where they could view the Statue of Liberty as they left the harbor. A few miles south, they would pass under the Verrazzano-Narrows Bridge.

Once they were settled, an announcement was made about safety and life jackets. It went on to advise the passengers that the upper deck was open, and please proceed with caution. Madison was sitting backwards and marveled at the receding city skyline. "How did I not know about this?" She craned her head to get a better look.

"Maybe because you never had the need to use this mode of transportation." Lincoln was also impressed.

"And it only takes forty minutes. Amazing."

Twenty minutes later, they were under the great bridge that connected Staten Island to Brooklyn. A crew member stopped as he passed them. "It's a beautiful day if you want to go aloft. It can be a little breezy, but the view is awesome."

Lincoln chuckled. "I guess we look like tourists, eh?"

"I overheard you guys when you came aboard." He grinned and continued to the bar area.

"What do you think?" Olivia asked. "Shall we be tourists?"

"You guys go ahead. I'm just going to hang out here," Madison said.

Once the boat was past the bridge, a small area of water opened to the sea. They were crossing the harbor and into Sandy Hook Bay. Madison got up from her seat and moved to the other side of the ferry, where she could see the tip of Sandy Hook. Several minutes later, they were passing the Coast Guard Station, and she got a tickle of butterflies. Not from the motion of the boat, but the anticipation of seeing the captain again. If they signed the lease for the house, he was going to be the first person she planned to call. She was rehearsing her story in her head about jetties, wharfs, and piers.

Olivia joined her as the boat continued along the shoreline of the park. Several minutes later, another announcement was made that they were arriving at the first stop, and all passengers were asked to remain in their seats. Madison was almost giddy.

A crew member made an announcement: "We will be arriving at our one and only stop, Highlands. Please remain in your seats until the boat has docked. Thank you and have a nice day."

Madison and Olivia scurried back to their seats, and within a few minutes, the boat was docked. The three were impressed at how easy it was to get to their destination. No tunnels, no traffic.

As they walked down the dock toward the parking lot, they spotted the white Cadillac and a middle-aged woman wearing a red blazer. "That must be her," Lincoln said, and waved.

Irene greeted them with a big "Hello! Welcome to the best-kept secret on the shore. I'm Irene. You must be Lincoln."

"I am." Lincoln smiled and held out his hand. "And this is my sister, Madison, and my wife, Olivia."

"Very nice to meet you all. Such a shame about Kirby. He was a fine man. And how dreadful about that person they found. A treasure hunter, I heard."

Apparently, news traveled extremely fast in the small community.

Irene went on, "This place is steeped in history, from the first Dutch settlers to the fort, the lighthouse, and Marconi's telegraph." She opened the doors for her passengers. "We'll go past some of it."

Irene started the engine and began the short drive to Portland Road. They turned on a street named Water Witch. Irene went on to explain, "It's named after an inn featured in James Fenimore Cooper's *The Water-Witch*."

Madison was taking in the scenery when she spotted a large brick structure with two lighthouses on each side on the top of a hill. "Is that the lighthouse you were referring to?"

"Yes. Built in 1746 by the New Jersey Militia to warn New York of incoming warships. The twin lights were completed in 1828. Marconi set up a kite-shaped receiver that enabled transmission from ships offshore, creating the first wireless means of communications."

"You are an impressive wealth of knowledge," Lincoln said.

"There is also a museum up there. It's quite well done. There you can see one of the bivalve Fresnel lenses—the lens used in lighthouses that produce light that shines far and through fog. And, if you don't have creaky knees like me, you can climb inside one of the towers all the way to the top."

"How high is it?" Madison inquired.

"Sixty-four steps to the observation deck in the north tower, and sixty-five in the south." Irene made a quick turn to a winding driveway. "It's not bad, but my knees get cranky." She parked the car in the best spot to view the terrain.

Everyone got out of the car and exclaimed how spectacular the views were. "They were quite right in their description," Lincoln said.

"It's breathtaking," Madison echoed her brother's sentiments.

Olivia joined in with a "Wow. It is beautiful."

"Come. Wait until you see the rest of the place." She opened the lockbox and then the double doors. "Please." She ushered them inside.

From where they stood, they could see the view from the large windows and patio doors on the lower level. Madison immediately took the short flight down. "This is a great space." An up-to-date, modern kitchen with a large island facing toward a large living area. Sliding doors and windows ran across the back that led to a large patio, partially covered by the balcony above. A tricked-out, outdoor kitchen was on the side surrounded by a slate counter and barstools. The pool was a few yards ahead, and the jacuzzi sat between the pool and the pool house.

Madison was in awe. "This is incredible," she spoke softly, hoping it was not a dream and she would wake herself up.

Irene stepped aside as the three family members stood in silence, taking in the amenities, and of course, the view.

Before anyone could say anything, Madison proclaimed, "We'll take it!"

"You haven't seen the rest of the house," Irene said easily. She knew it was secondary to the living space.

"Right." Madison smiled from ear to ear. She motioned to one of the teak lounge chairs. "I can sleep out here."

"Just so I can tell my boss I showed you everything, come on inside."

Irene led the way back to the kitchen and living area. "There's a laundry room at the far end, and the rest of the utilities are downstairs."

"You mean we must bring our laundry down a flight of stairs? I am out of here," Madison joked.

Irene wasn't accustomed to Madison's dry humor and gulped.

"Kidding." Madison rested her hand on Irene's arm. "I am serious. I mean about taking the place. But, if you insist, we will see the rest."

Irene felt relieved. "Follow me." The four went up the first flight to the level where they entered, then up another short flight to the three bedrooms. They were not particularly large, but big enough for one room to hold twin beds and two dressers, and the other two had queen-size beds. Two of the bedrooms shared a bath that had a long white marble vanity with two undermounted sinks, a separate shower and tub, and a private water closet for the toilet that also opened to the hallway. The master bedroom was equally appointed with a slate vanity, two vessel sinks, a large shower with several shower heads, and a private toilet area.

Each room had sliding doors with screens, which led to a long balcony that ran the entire length of the house.

"Who wouldn't want to live here?" Madison said, as she opened the doors to two large walk-in closets.

Lincoln and Olivia looked at Madison with glee. They, too, fell in love with the house the minute they walked in the door.

Irene remained quiet as they perused the remaining rooms of the house. It was a perfect weekend or vacation home.

Lincoln stepped in. He knew they would have to get a move on if they wanted to refurbish the marina. The sooner they could get a base to begin their operation, the better. The room on the entry-level floor could serve as an office. "Irene? How soon do you think we could move in?"

"The place is yours, but the owners will want an additional month's rent."

"Of course. And a deposit, I assume," Lincoln continued.

"Give me a minute." She excused herself and went outside to make a call.

Madison could not believe how much things had changed in such a few short days. "This is great. We will have so much fun here."

"And also relax," Olivia tossed in.

"Indeed. This is the perfect place for parties, and no parties." Madison's face was pink with delight.

Irene returned with some information. "If you can pay four months upfront, they will waive the deposit. That's a good deal. Normally they want two months' worth. But I told them you were very respectable."

"Thank you, Irene," Lincoln said. "I left my attaché in the car. I will be right back."

Irene ran down all the local summer activities. "Of course, we kick it off with the seafood festival. I hear they are honoring Kirby."

News really did travel fast.

"Yes, and so are we." Madison leaned closer. "Lincoln is going to meet with Charlie in a few days to discuss renovating the marina. Then we are going to rename it."

Irene stiffened. She hoped they were not the usual carpetbaggers or opportunists coming into town, buying up property at a low price, then flipping it for a huge profit.

"We decided it should be called 'Kirby's Marina.' From what we have learned in these few short days, his first name is how people knew him best." She failed to mention how she and her brother wanted nothing to do with the name Taylor, but that was beside the point.

Irene's shoulders immediately relaxed. "That is a fine idea. He would have liked that."

Lincoln returned with a checkbook. "Who should I make this out to?"

Madison shot him a glance as if to ask, *Are you sure?*

He gave her one of their silent sibling signals that he had it covered. Irene gave him the information, and he handed over the check.

"I know you are going to have a wonderful summer here." Irene was genuinely delighted. She could tell this family appreciated the dwelling and its grounds. Too often she would have people looking for a weekend party house, and this certainly fit the bill. But there were always problems, which was why most owners asked for large deposits.

Madison was already dreaming about how wonderful her summer would be, even if the handsome captain was otherwise occupied. Her big challenge was Mario and Luigi, but like everything else in her life, she would figure out a solution.

Madison went down to the lower level and gave it a scrutinizing examination. The laundry room was fitted with cabinets with countertops and connected to a screened-in porch.

Perfect for her boys. Depending on who was at the house, she could shuffle them from the bedroom to the laundry room. She knew they would enjoy basking in the sun on the porch. Madison scampered back to where Lincoln and Olivia were standing in the kitchen.

"Livvy, promise you will make fabulous dinners here."

"Only if Lincoln promises to grill."

"Deal!" He grinned. He could feel the relief rushing through his veins. Things had taken a much better turn, considering what the week had started like. "I want to give Charlie a call to see if he's available this afternoon."

"I can drop you there and then get the keys made," Irene offered.

Lincoln dialed the number Charlie had given him. "Clams on Wheels!" a cheerful voice answered.

"Charlie. It's Lincoln."

"Howdy, my man. What can I do for you?"

"I want to run something by you." Lincoln suddenly realized they were moving at full speed, and he hadn't discussed any of it with Charlie. His buoyancy deflated several notches.

"Sure thing. I'm here all day."

Lincoln looked over at Irene.

"We can go now," she suggested.

"How's ten minutes?" Lincoln asked.

"No problem," Charlie responded.

"Great. See you in a few." Lincoln ended the call. Now he had to convince Charlie to get on board. *Again, another nautical pun.*

The four piled back into Irene's SUV and took the short drive to the marina. Lincoln wasn't the nervous type, but he had a bit of the jitters. He just handed over a check for twenty thousand dollars with the notion they would be renovating the marina. But what if he couldn't get the help he needed? He was about to find out. He squeezed Olivia's hand.

She knew Lincoln was a little anxious, but her instincts told her things were moving the way they should, in the right direction.

It took about five minutes to arrive at the marina. Just as before, a group of people were gathered around the food truck. The crime-scene tape still surrounded the area. Madison shut her eyes and visualized the tape gone, new planks, a new shed, and the new sign. She already had a design for the logo in her head.

Madison was genuinely happy to see so many smiling faces. She guessed they got over their suspicions of the city slickers. People greeted them with big hellos and patted Lincoln on the back.

"What's on yer mind?" Charlie asked through the truck's open window, as he wiped his hands on a towel.

"Can you come outside?" Lincoln asked pleasantly. He didn't want to give Charlie any reason to feel intimidated.

"Go on," Hannah encouraged him, and then waved at Madison. "Hey!"

Madison grinned and gave her a "Hey!" Olivia waved and smiled. Madison indicated she and Olivia should go over and talk to Hannah while the two men sat at the table.

"How ya doin'?" Hannah asked. "Can I get you anything?"

"I'll have one of your tasty sandwiches," Madison eagerly responded. She looked at Olivia, who nodded. "Make that two. Oh, and you should probably make one for Lincoln."

"Comin' right up." Hannah turned and dropped a few handfuls of clams into the hot oil. Then she turned back to the two women. "So, what ya suppose they're talking about?"

Madison knew it wasn't going to be a secret much longer and leaned into the window. "We rented a house for the summer. It's on Portland."

"The Kramer house? Nice."

"Yes. But we have more news." Madison tried to contain her excitement. "Detective Burton told us they are going to be honoring Uncle Kirby at the seafood festival."

"Yessiree. I know Charlie misses him more than he would miss me." Hannah chortled.

"I doubt that. Men usually do not know how to show their appreciation. Something in their DNA."

Hannah let out a huge cackle. "You got that right!"

Madison began to answer Hannah's initial query. "When you told me you were concerned about summer business, Lincoln, Olivia, and I had a meeting. Lincoln wants to refurbish the marina and keep it open this summer."

"Well, golly! That there is good news!" Hannah's smile filled her entire face.

"Lincoln would like Charlie to be a supervisor in the reconstruction and pay him for his time. Lincoln knows how to balance budgets, but he's not the best when it comes to a hammer and nails."

Olivia chuckled. "I think I can use a screwdriver with more precision."

"Do you think Charlie will agree?" Madison was bobbing her heel.

"I don't see why not. It'll be good for everyone."

"We also want to rename it Kirby's."

"Aw, Kirby woulda loved that." Hannah's eyes teared up.

"It is the least we can do." Madison waited as Hannah turned to scoop up the crispy clams and put them on a roll. Then came a dash of tartar sauce.

Hannah handed the sandwiches to Madison, who continued, "This place meant the world to him. It is his legacy, and it is only proper we honor him that way."

Hannah wiped her eyes. "That is one of the nicest things I ever heard anybody say about anybody."

Madison's eyes also welled. She looked at Olivia, who was also blotting her face.

The sound of an outboard motor caught their attention. It was a Coast Guard SPC-SW, a special purpose craft–shallow water patrol boat. Madison almost dropped her sandwich. Her knees got wobbly. Olivia put her hand on Madison's shoulder and smiled at Hannah. "We are very happy to be here and be part of this community."

"Well, we're mighty glad it was you folks who took over the marina. We didn't know what we were in for." Hannah waved at the handsome captain. He grinned and gave her a two-finger salute.

Madison thought she was going to lose her cool. She hadn't expected to see Captain Eriksson, at least not without a plan.

"Hey there, handsome," Hannah greeted him as he approached the food truck.

"You are such a sweet talker." He grinned at her. "And Ms. Wainwright and Mrs. Wainwright, nice to see you."

"It's 'Madison,' Captain." She held her composure and gave him a devilish grin.

"And please call me Olivia."

"Madison. Olivia. Nice to see both of you. What brings you to our corner of the world?"

Madison decided to leave the rental for the last part. "Lincoln is discussing his idea to refurbish the marina with Charlie." She nodded in his direction. "We felt it would be a disservice to the community to have it sit here unattended for the season."

Eriksson was beginning to like this worldly woman. "I am glad to hear it. Kirby's place was kind of a landmark. I'm certain everyone will be willing to pitch in."

"That's what we're hoping for." Madison paused. "When Detective Burton told us they were going to honor Uncle Kirby, we felt compelled to do something in his honor, as well." Madison decided it was time to drop the additional news. "We discovered the ferry service and thought it would be efficient to rent a place for the summer."

"Oh?" Eriksson became more interested in what this woman had to say.

"Yes. We met with Irene Mariska earlier and rented a house on Portland."

"I think you will enjoy the summer here. There are lots of things to do, or you can do nothing at all."

"One thing I am hoping is that you would share your knowledge about wharfs, piers, freighters, and the like." Madison was impressed that she could keep her voice steady.

"I would be happy to. Over dinner? I know some great places in town. That is, if you are available."

"That would be lovely," Madison replied, and hoped she didn't have tartar sauce on her face. *Let him guess how available she is.*

Hannah had a twinkle in her eye when she handed Viggo his clam sandwich.

"I've got to meet Burton. He said they found something in the water near the vehicle belonging to Farrell. Give me a ring next time you plan on coming down." He gave Hannah another two-finger salute. "Glad you will be hanging around," he said, grinning at Madison.

Madison thought her legs were going to buckle.

Hannah hooted, "Well, finally! That boy has been alone since he got here. Glad you're going to have dinner with him. Maybe he'll remember what it's like to have some female companionship." It was obvious Hannah thought highly of the captain, and his personal life.

Madison tried not to blush. "Dinner will be nice."

Olivia was having similar thoughts about Madison and male companionship but was able to keep her mouth shut in front of Hannah. Hannah must have read her mind, because she gave Olivia a wink when Madison wasn't looking. *This is going to be a good team*, Olivia thought to herself.

The three women looked in Lincoln and Charlie's direction. Both men were smiling and nodding. It appeared that things were moving along in a positive direction. They stood and shook hands. Definitely a positive direction.

Lincoln and Charlie walked toward the food truck. Charlie had a grin that stretched across his face. "Hannah, looks like we're gonna be a little busy before the season starts up."

"Oh? Do tell." She gave another wink. This time, it was at both Olivia and Madison.

"Lincoln, his lovely sister, and lovely wife are gonna help put this place back together."

Lincoln interrupted, "Yes, and with the marina expertise of Charlie and Crusty."

Hannah clapped and hooted, "Yeah, man!"

Lincoln continued, "Charlie said that Josh usually works the docks during his summer break, and he would probably come back. He is on spring break now, hence the tuna trip."

Madison's thoughts about ditching the place were long gone. Her mind was filled with what could be ahead.

Irene pulled up and sprang out of the car. She looked like a giant bouncing fire hydrant. She jangled the keys in the air. "It's all yours!" She, too, had a smile as wide as Charlie's on her face.

"Charlie is going to get the permits we need and order the supplies. I am going to arrange for a line of credit at a local home builder supply, rather than a big box store. Charlie has a good relationship with one a few miles from here," Lincoln explained.

"It sounds like you covered a lot of ground in a short amount of time," Olivia remarked.

"This entire week flipped in a short amount of time!" Madison declared. "Including my attitude." Everyone laughed. It had been obvious Madison was not at all pleased with the situation when they first arrived.

Lincoln grinned. He was equally pleased with the outcome. So far. The next hurdle was getting the crime-scene tape removed sooner than later.

They milled around, talking to some of the locals, while Charlie explained what was about to happen. A few *yeehaw*s were expressed, some clapping, and a few more hoots. Again, Madison realized how one decision could change many lives. It wasn't as if she were disconnected, but she lived in a microcosm, as most people do. Madison felt a warmth come over her, and she knew it was not a hot flash.

Lincoln and Charlie arranged to meet on Saturday. Lincoln planned to take the ferry, and Charlie was going to pick him up. By then, Charlie would have applied for the permits and put a materials list together. No doubt, things were moving fast, but they had to. The season was less than eight weeks away. The only thing left was the ugly yellow tape.

Chapter Fifteen

A New Chapter

The ferry ride back to New York went by quickly. Olivia was busy taking notes, and Madison was making lists. Everyone agreed that Lincoln was in charge of the reno, and Madison and Olivia were in charge of the family participation in the seafood festival and getting the house ready. Lincoln's phone rang as they were entering New York Harbor.

"Hello, Lincoln. This is Detective Burton. I have some news for you."

Lincoln couldn't tell by the sound of his voice whether it was good news or bad news. He inhaled. "Hello, Detective. I trust it's good news?"

"In some respects, it is. We were able to track down a few of Farrell's associates. They had concocted a plan that, unfortunately, went awry." He paused. "Farrell parked his car near an area where people can easily launch a small craft. He had a kayak, which we found a short distance from his vehicle. According to his friends, the plan was for Farrell to paddle near the dock, wait until dusk, and then swim to Kirby's.

They are convinced there is a treasure map somewhere and thought it might be in the shed."

"Do you know what happened to him? Aside from him being dead?" Lincoln realized he sounded crass. "Sorry."

"No problem. We got the report from the coroner. Farrell drowned. He got caught in some tow lines, and when the tide came in, he was under the dock and couldn't get out." Burton took a breath. "At least that is what we can surmise. There is no evidence of foul play."

"That is a terrible story." Lincoln did not want to seem coldhearted and resisted asking if they could remove the tape.

"It is, and it could have been avoided. But those are the risks if you are a treasure hunter. Many have been rescued off the coast in search of sunken ships. Anyway, I thought you would like to know that you can remove the tape. The place is yours."

"Thank you, Detective. That is a big relief. We want to get moving on cleaning up the place."

"If you need any local assistance, don't hesitate. Everyone is glad that Kirby's place will be up and running."

"Thanks again. Have a good evening." Lincoln ended the call, lifted his hands, and gave Madison and Olivia high-fives. "We are good to go."

Madison thought for a moment. "How many days has it been since this whole thing started?" She counted on her fingers. "Five? Wow."

The ferry landed at four thirty, just in time for rush-hour traffic. Madison looked up at the FDR Drive. It was bumper-to-bumper cars. "I think I like this ferry thing." She tucked two boat schedules into her tote.

They walked to the parking garage where Lincoln had left his car. He gave Madison a lift to her apartment and then took the West Side Highway home.

Mario and Luigi greeted her. "Kitties! I have lots and lots

of news. How would you like to spend the summer at the shore?"

They looked at her as if to say, *How about feeding us; then we'll talk?* Madison promptly went into the kitchen and put their favorite salmon pâté in their bowls. She went into her bedroom to change into a lightweight tracksuit. Thoughts of wearing jeans, shorts, and summer dresses filled her head. She threw herself on her bed and stared at the ceiling. It brought to mind the afternoon she got the news about her father and threw herself on the hotel bed and stared at the ceiling. She considered Olivia's words. She *had* come a long way from that dark day. Now she didn't care who knew. She thought about springing it on her boss and staff, but decided she could still keep it under wraps. There was much to do, and there was no reason to add confusion to the mix. Someday. Just not today.

Madison was excited to speak to Olivia without her brother listening in. She rolled over and dialed Livvy's cell. "Got a minute?"

"You know I do," Olivia replied. "Dinner with the handsome captain, eh?"

"I thought I was going to pee in my pants!" Madison chortled. "I was not expecting it, for sure."

"I'm not going to say, 'I told you so' but I told you so!" Olivia burst out laughing. "I liked your response. You were agreeable to dinner but veiled your relationship status."

"What is there to veil?" Madison chuckled. "Absolutely nothing."

"Not yet," Olivia teased.

"You know what I always say?"

Olivia responded. "Yes. 'Let's not get ahead of ourselves.'"

"Correct." Madison could not erase the glow and smile on her face. "But it surely gives me something to look forward to."

"So? When?"

"I was considering I would wait until we bring some of our things into the house. Makes much more sense."

"Yes, you have a point." Madison could hear Lincoln's voice in the background. "Why is he interrupting our phone call?" Madison joked.

"What's up, honey?" Madison could hear Olivia ask Lincoln.

"Just got off the phone with Irene. She said the owners told her we can move in any time we want. We don't have to wait a month."

Olivia turned her attention back to her conversation with Madison. "Did you hear that? We can move in sooner."

Madison sat up like a rocket ready to take off. "Really? That's great! Let's go with Lincoln on Saturday. Give the place the once-around."

Olivia conveyed Madison's thoughts. Madison could hear Lincoln's response. "Sounds like a plan!"

Olivia put the call on speaker. "Should we drive?" Madison asked.

"Charlie and I should take a couple of hours. Is there anything in particular you want to do?" Lincoln asked.

"No. The ferry is fine. If we are only going to be there for two or three hours, there is no sense spending four hours on the road when the boat takes forty minutes."

"I agree. We can deal with driving when we have a few things packed," Olivia chimed in.

"Sounds good, my sister." Madison was all atwitter. "See you in the morning." She realized it was Thursday night. One more day in the office, and then the weekend was upon them. In less than a week, her life changed course, but this time was much more exciting. Funny how one family member can disrupt or improve the life of others. Madison looked up at the ceiling again. "Thank you, Uncle Kirby."

Madison was in a courageous mood. She scrolled through her phone and found Viggo Eriksson's number and hit the green button. Two rings.

"Ms. Wainwright?" Viggo answered.

"Captain, you must call me Madison."

He chuckled. "And you must call me Viggo."

"I believe we can agree on that," Madison added.

"To what do I owe the pleasure?" he asked.

"The Kramers offered to let us have use of the house beginning next month."

"As in two weeks." It was more of a statement than a question.

"Yes. The three of us are going down on Saturday. Linc is meeting with Charlie, and Livvy and I are going to check the house—get a feel of the place."

"Excellent idea. I think you are going to like it there. The view at night is spectacular."

"I can only imagine. It is quite spectacular during the day."

"There is something ethereal about viewing the city at night from a peaceful, quiet place," Viggo added. "It's kind of hard to describe."

"I hadn't thought about that perspective. I suppose I have become impervious to the noise. That is not necessarily a plus. One night I was staying at a hotel, and the next day, everyone kept asking me where I was during the fire alarm. 'What fire alarm?' I asked, then realized I had slept right through it. Not a good thing."

"Most definitely not a good thing. Glad you are here to tell about it." Viggo chuckled.

She pulled up another dose of courage. "I wanted to take you up on your offer to tutor me in maritime lingo."

"I would be happy to. Did you have a particular date in mind?"

Madison froze on the word *date*; then she regrouped. She

double-checked her planner, even though she would change whatever plans she had, if any. "Two weeks from Saturday?"

"That works for me. Any particular time you care to dine?"

"Not really. I shall leave all of those decisions up to you." Now there was a big step for Madison Wainwright: putting someone else in charge. And it felt good.

"Let's touch base the beginning of that week."

"Will do. Have a good night," Madison signed off.

"You as well, Madison Wainwright." After he hung up, he turned to Diogo. "Well, pal, looks like your old man has a date."

Diogo *woof*ed his approval, lay down, and put his snout on his front paws. Being Viggo's only love and center of attention was a lot of responsibility.

Madison couldn't believe what she had done. She quickly called Olivia again. "We have a date."

"Who? You? The captain?" Olivia could hardly wait to hear the details.

"You will be quite proud of me, dear Olivia. I phoned him."

"Shut. Up. You did not."

"I did too!"

"I am beyond impressed. What made you do it?"

"The ceiling," Madison answered.

"The ceiling?"

"Yes. I was lying on my bed, staring at the ceiling, and remembered the time I was in the hotel waiting to meet Lincoln so we could get our clothes and say farewell to Sutton Place. You recently reminded me of how far I've come. I thought, 'What's the worst thing that can happen? He mentions a girlfriend?' If he did, then I could put any fantasies away and move on."

"It sounds like a date to me," Olivia said with confidence.

"I have the same feeling. It was an easy conversation. Date material." Madison giggled.

"I am proud of you, my dear. You get a good night's sleep and have wonderful dreams."

"I just might do that," Madison said, smiling, and ended the call.

But in spite of her efforts, Madison could not fall asleep. Her thoughts were on overdrive, and she tossed and turned for hours, drifting off and then waking up. It had been a roller-coaster kind of week, from marina to horrible marina, to dead body, to a handsome Coast Guard Captain, to marina owners, and now, summer renters, in New Jersey of all places.

Madison's routine had become boring. There are just so many galas one can attend before they begin to blur together. With her white wardrobe, she looked the same from one gala to the next. This was a refreshing change of pace and change of wardrobe.

By five thirty, she decided there was no point in waiting for her alarm to go off. Mario and Luigi had moved to the foot of the bed. With all of Madison's flipping from side to side, the two cats decided the edge was a safer bet. They stretched and yawned and slowly followed Madison into the kitchen.

"I know, guys. It's way too early for any of us, but here we are."

She pushed the button on her coffee maker, opened a can of cat food, and switched on the small television in the kitchen area. Nothing major in the news, thank goodness. The past several years were fraught with lots of natural disasters, wars, epidemics, and a whole lot of political monkey business. She was glad things had slowed to a dull roar.

She finished her coffee and said, "Okay, kids, I am going to get dressed and go to work. See if anything blew up in my absence yesterday." Mario and Luigi looked up from their bowls, licked their lips, and continued to finish their breakfast.

Madison was behind her desk by seven o'clock. There were a few messages on her desk. *Art director needs to see you as soon as you get in.* "This can't be good," she muttered, dialed his extension, and left a voicemail. *This better not interrupt my weekend plans.* She snickered. Since when did she have weekend plans? Since yesterday. She grinned.

An hour later, the art director sashayed into Madison's office. "Dearie, we have a problem with Vanessa."

Madison suppressed a groan. Models were always a problem. "And what is Vanessa's issue?"

"She changed her mind about a few photos in the article."

Madison took a deep breath. "She signed off on them, and the book went to press yesterday."

"She said she was aware of that, but she also said you could pull it until she made up her mind."

Madison let out a big laugh. "That would be a big N.O. in capital letters."

"I figured you would say that, but she harassed me all afternoon yesterday." He eyed her carefully. "Speaking of yesterday, you never take an afternoon off. Everything okay?"

"Victor, you are absolutely correct on both fronts. Yes, I said 'no,' and yes, I took the afternoon off. I shall be taking more afternoons off beginning next month."

Victor slid into one of the club chairs. "Do tell, darling." He folded his arms and crossed his legs.

"Lincoln, Olivia, and I are renting a summer house."

"Wonderful! Sag Harbor? East Hampton?"

"Neither. It is a little hamlet called Smuggler's Cove on the Navesink."

"I don't think I ever heard of it." Victor batted his eyelashes.

"Probably not. It is on the Jersey Shore." Madison waited for a reaction.

Victor winced. "Really?"

"It is not what you think or have seen on MTV. It is quite lovely. Miles from amusement parks, boardwalks, and weekend rowdiness."

"Well, that's a shame," he said. "The rowdiness, I mean."

Madison began to explain. "Lincoln and I inherited a marina from our Uncle Kirby. It is in dire need of repair. We originally considered selling it right off the bat, but then decided to renovate it before the summer. A lot of people depend on it for their livelihoods, and we, in good conscience, could not let it sit idle for a season."

Victor's face beamed. "This sounds exciting. Will you invite me?"

"Only if you promise not to be rowdy." Madison chuckled. "Now get out of my office. I have a temperamental model to speak to."

"Oh, please, let me listen," he said with a puppy-dog expression.

"As long as you promise to be quiet."

Victor mimed turning a key in a lock in front of his lips.

Madison looked through her contacts list and dialed Vanessa's number. "Good morning, gorgeous," Madison said, rolling her eyes at Victor. "I understand you are having second thoughts about the photos you approved." Madison listened. "Vanessa, we have been through this before. You signed off on them, and the book went to press. There is nothing either of us can do now." Madison noted the words from the other end of the call. She shook her head. "Of course you can complain to your agent. If you want to cancel all future jobs, I can ask our lawyer to draw up the paperwork." She winked at Victor. Madison nodded. "I thought so." She paused. "Yes, we will give you a few more days to review them the next time you do a shoot for us. 'Bye."

Madison looked at Victor. "And that, my dear boy, is how it is done."

"You are a miracle worker. Actually, you could have worked a miracle by pulling the book."

"Nuh-uh. We accommodated her once. The photos were outstanding, she had ample time to review them, and she approved them. Besides, I cannot allow prima donnas to run this magazine."

"Let me rephrase that. You fixed a situation."

"Yes, and an unreasonable one. Keeping people on their toes and sticking to the script is part of my job, although sometimes I think that is all I do." She let out a sigh of resignation.

"Enough of her. Tell me more about this summer rental," Victor prodded, and Madison described it as best she could without sounding capricious.

"We are going there on Saturday to do some inventory, and Lincoln will be working with one of the local residents. He and his wife own a food truck."

"Food truck? You are getting down and dirty."

Madison chuckled. "You should have seen me when my Jimmy Choos got caught in one of the planks. Broke both heels and did a face-plant. I was a slimy, bait-covered mess."

"Oh, I would have paid to see that," Victor howled.

"You tell anyone, and I will have to kill you." Madison laughed. "Now get out of my office. Please." She shooed him away.

"Okay, but I will hound you for an invitation."

"Get out, Victor." Madison grinned at him. He left her office laughing.

Madison crumpled the message and tossed it into the trash can. She was unusually calm. Had the conversation with Vanessa happened earlier in the week, she would have been ruffled. It was definitely a new chapter.

Chapter Sixteen

Making Preparations

Madison thought she would get a good night's sleep, considering she hadn't the night before. Unfortunately, and much to Mario and Luigi's dismay, Madison was all over the bed. At three a.m., she decided a hot shower might help. She didn't know why she had the jitters. Her date with Viggo wasn't for another two weeks. She convinced herself she had been in overdrive, and the adrenaline was having its way with her. By four thirty, she was sound asleep.

The buzzer at her door jolted her upright. It was nine o'clock. Her brother and Olivia would be waiting. She bounded out of bed and looked at her cats. "Why of all days did you not wake me?" They yawned in response.

"Coming!" Madison called out. Even though Olivia and Lincoln had keys, Madison always put the safety chain on, so they were not able to get into her apartment. "Coming!" She was breathless when she got to the door.

"Did I wake you?" Olivia asked her.

"Yes, you did." Madison stepped aside for Olivia to enter.

"Last night and the night before, I could not sleep. I took a shower in the middle of the night and finally fell asleep around four."

"Well, shake a leg, sister. We have a ferry to catch."

"I'll be right with you." Madison dashed into her bedroom and pulled on a pair of jeans, a wide-striped turtleneck, and her new pair of navy-blue skimmers.

"Well look at you, all nautical," Olivia teased.

"I could get used to dressing like this every day."

"Ha. I doubt that," Olivia balked.

"I am serious. Remember that conversation we had last week?" She tied a cashmere scarf around her neck. "The one about my disguise?"

"Yes, and you still haven't answered my question."

"Now I am. I told you it can be exhausting keeping up this fashion façade. I am going to make a much bigger effort at taking time for myself. I have spent too many weekends at the office, wearing my white uniform."

"What do you plan to do?"

"If it is totally necessary for me to go to work, I will wear whatever pleases me. What do you think about that?" She blew kisses at her kitties, grabbed her tote, and locked the door behind her. "Before I forget, here is a check for the rental."

Olivia blinked. "Lincoln phoned the bank yesterday and asked for an equity loan, and we have enough to cover the check for now."

"Please, just take this. We can square up once all the finances are secured."

Lincoln was waiting in a taxi for the two of them.

When they got into the car, Lincoln tapped his watch. "You look like you just got out of bed."

Olivia chuckled. "She did."

Madison dug into her bag and pulled out a mirror. She fussed with her hair until she was satisfied that she was a bit more presentable. She turned to Olivia. "Better?"

"Yes. You could use a little blush."

Madison dug further. "No such luck," she muttered, but she used a timeless hack and dabbed a little lipstick on her cheeks and smoothed it into her skin. "Passable?"

"Yes, you pass," Lincoln teased.

The taxi got on the West Side Highway, where they met a major traffic jam. "Oh no!" Madison groaned. "What if we miss the ferry?"

Lincoln laughed at his sister. "I never thought you would be so excited to get to Smuggler's Cove."

"Shut it, baby brother." Madison hated being in a situation where she had no control.

The cars moved slowly as they passed the Staten Island Ferry terminal. They were a block away from Pier Eleven and could see the ferry at the dock. The taxi pulled next to the curb, and they scrambled out as a horn sounded the one-minute warning. The same crew member from the other day was standing at the gate and recognized them. He called out to the boat captain, "We gotta a couple of runners!" He waved for them to move faster, and they certainly did.

All of them were out of breath as they puffed up the gangway. They thanked the young man with gulps of gratitude as the boat pulled away from the dock. They wobbled toward a booth and flopped into the seats. "People do this every day?" Madison asked a rhetorical question.

"Thousands," Olivia reminded her.

"I could use a bottle of water," Madison announced.

"I suppose you want me to get it for you?" Lincoln asked sardonically.

"Of course," Madison said, grinning.

Other passing boats were causing wakes in the harbor. Lincoln hadn't yet found his sea legs and used the seats to help steer himself to the bar area.

Olivia elbowed Madison. "Such a rookie."

The forty-minute ride blew by quickly, and soon they were

docking in the Highlands. Lincoln recognized Charlie's truck, and then wondered where everyone was going to fit. It hadn't occurred to him to ask Charlie about the seating capacity. As soon as Charlie spotted the three of them, he immediately solved the problem. "Hey! Welcome back! I'll take the girls over to the house and come round and fetch you. Won't take but a couple minutes." Charlie may speak and walk slower than what they were used to, but he was as sharp as a tack.

As they passed Huddy Park, Charlie mentioned that it was the main area where the seafood festival would take place. He went on to explain that it was named after a revolutionary war hero, Joshua Huddy, murdered in 1782, at the hands of Captain Richard Lippincott, a British Loyalist. At the time, it was not unusual for the Patriots to render retaliation by executing a Loyalist of similar status. So Washington wrote a letter to General Moses Hazen, commander of Lancaster Prison Camp, ordering that a British officer of equal rank be hanged. Hazen left the matter to chance and required thirteen prisoners to draw from a hat. The word *unfortunate* was printed on the paper pulled by Charles Asgill, a nineteen-year-old heir to an English fortune. Asgill's mother began a fervent letter writing campaign that landed in the hands of the French Foreign Minister, who intervened by approaching Congress. It was decided that hanging Asgill would create unnecessary and irrevocable tension in the delicate balance of peace between America and England. Lippincott was never held accountable and moved to Canada, and Huddy became a Revolutionary War hero.

Madison listened with interest. "There truly is a lot of history here."

"Yes indeedy," Charlie answered. "You oughta get yourselves up to the Twin Lights one day."

"Irene gave us a little background on the lighthouses," Olivia said. "I would like to take my daughter there. She is a

European History teacher, but I am certain she would find it interesting."

Charlie proceeded up the road that climbed into the hills. "Here we are. Anything you need?" he asked.

"I think we are fine. Thank you," Madison answered, and dangled the new set of keys. "See you later. And, Charlie, keep a keen eye on my brother. He likes to shop for tools as much as I like to shop for clothes."

Olivia laughed. "Except he doesn't know how to use any of them!"

Charlie was still laughing as he drove off to fetch Lincoln.

Before they entered the house, Madison took a long look at the view. "You did a great job finding this."

"It wasn't that hard. I'm happy it was available."

"To quote Charlie, 'yes indeedy.'" The women linked arms, walked to the double doors, and flung them open. "I know I am going to enjoy this."

Olivia suggested they start with the kitchen. Floor-to-ceiling cabinets flanked one wall. The two women began opening them and taking notes. The inside panels of the doors had lists of inventories. "This makes it easy to keep track of everything," Olivia noted.

There were place settings for eight people, a full set of pots, several frying pans, baking dishes, and drawers filled with utensils. Another cabinet housed three different styles of wineglasses, champagne glasses, highballs, tumblers, and martini glasses. Madison turned to Olivia. "I like the way these people think."

"You mean *drink*." Olivia chortled.

There was a cabinet just for spices, and another for the multitude of appliances. "It seems as if these people like to cook," Olivia noted.

"We should make a list of dry goods we might need. Flour, sugar, pepper, spices." Madison snapped her fingers. "You can teach Hannah how to make bacalaitos! She can add fried cod to the menu."

"As you say, let's not get carried away." Olivia knew Madison was enthralled, but there was a lot to do before anyone started cooking for the masses.

"Okay, but you have to promise me you will make mofongo." Madison hesitated. "I wonder if you can get plantains nearby."

"We are not out on the prairie. I am sure there is a Whole Foods or ShopRite within driving distance. Which makes me think we should buy all the necessities, like soaps, laundry detergent, fabric softener, and household cleaners locally. It will probably be cheaper than buying it in the city."

"Excellent point. I'll ask Irene where we should shop."

An hour later, they decided to take a short break and sit on the patio. It was breezy but pleasant. "I think we should plant an herb garden." Madison pointed to an area on the side of the outdoor kitchen.

"Look at you, getting all domesticated," Olivia kidded.

"And I just might plant some geraniums, too." She clasped her fingers behind her head and rested it on the back of the lounge chair. "This is like being on vacation."

"I don't know why we never thought about renting a summer house. I know you would go out to the Hamptons for a long weekend, but this place is ours, at least for the next four months."

Madison's thoughts ran to something more permanent. But that would have to wait. Wait to see if they liked the area. Wait to see if she could balance her work and play time. Wait to see if she enjoyed the company of the local people—one in particular.

"Shall we inspect the bathrooms?" Olivia asked.

"I suppose we should. I am going to check with Linc and see how far along they are." She dialed his cell.

"Everything okay?" he asked.

"Yes. Why?"

"You. Olivia. Alone. Together," he ticked off the usual joke.

"Ha, ha. So far, we've managed to stay out of trouble. And you?"

"Yes, Charlie has been keeping a close eye on what I'm piling in the cart. They're giving us a twenty-thousand-dollar line of credit. That should cover the first round of materials. The home equity loan should be in our account in two weeks, so we're covered."

"Excellent. You do good work," Madison teased. "What about Nana and Pop's?"

"Working on that. The tenants were happy to accommodate us and took the free rent." He paused. "I gave them a full month." He knew his sister would approve. She wanted to get that show on the road as quickly as possible.

"Good. And the real estate agent?"

"I have to meet her sometime next week. She's going to speak with the tenants to arrange for a walk-through and get their schedules in order to make it as convenient as possible."

"Fabulous." Madison felt a surge of elation. "When do you think you and Charlie will be back?"

"We are wrapping it up now." He said to Charlie, "When will we be back at the house?"

"Twenty minutes."

Madison heard Charlie's voice in the background. "Okay. Good. We are finished for now. Can you text me Irene's phone number? I want to ask her about where we can shop."

"Shopping? Already?" Lincoln teased.

"Food. Supplies. Duh." Madison clicked her tongue.

Lincoln laughed. "See you in a few."

The women did a final once-around. Madison added kitty litter, litter pan, liners, and toys to her list. "They are going to love basking in the sun." Madison noticed a patch of warm rays flooding into a corner of the screened porch.

"I want to come back as one of your cats in my next life," Olivia joked.

"Me too," Madison added.

A short time later, Lincoln and Charlie pulled into the driveway. It was obvious they had become fast friends. Lincoln quickly rattled off what was going to be delivered and when. "Crusty is going to work with Charlie, and Josh will work the dock."

"Josh? I thought he was on a fishing boat."

"There was a strong storm further out, and they decided to head back. They didn't want to pull an *Andrea Gail*."

"Who?" Olivia asked.

"*The Perfect Storm*," Lincoln answered.

"Wasn't that a movie with George Clooney and Mark Wahlberg? What does that have to do with it?" Olivia prodded.

"The movie was based on a true story."

"I guess I missed that part." Olivia snickered.

"I think you fell asleep in the middle of it."

"It was a dreadful story. Can you blame me?"

Lincoln kissed his wife on the forehead. "No."

"Hey, you two, wrap it up. We have to get back to the city so we can shop, and I don't want to miss the ferry," Madison prodded.

Charlie had to make two trips again to get them back to the ferry, but he didn't seem to mind.

"Thanks for everything, Charlie. We could not do this without you," Lincoln said sincerely.

"Glad to help. Kirby would be proud." Charlie wiped a tear from the corner of his eye and pretended it was a speck of dirt.

On the ferry ride back, Madison asked, "What did you offer to pay Charlie?"

"At first, he refused to take any money from me. I told him that was unacceptable, and I would pay him thirty-five dollars an hour."

"Is that enough?" Madison had no idea what construction foremen got.

"He said it was more than enough, so I didn't argue with him."

"And Crusty?" Madison had to resist giggling every time she spoke or heard his name.

"He's happy with twenty, and Josh will get fifteen, plus whatever tips customers give him."

"Look at you, the entrepreneur!" She gave a little clap of applause.

"I am going to have to come down here every weekend to check on the job." Lincoln did not appear to be bothered by that idea.

"You might need a chaperone," Olivia said, smirking.

"I think two chaperones," Madison added.

"I wouldn't have it any other way." Lincoln smiled.

Chapter Seventeen

The Start of Something

The following weekend, Lincoln took an early ferry to the Highlands. He was anxious and excited to see how much had been done. Charlie picked him up and began to rattle off everything that had transpired.

"Got the dumpster and started ripping up the bad planks. I think you might want to consider replacing all of 'em." He tooted his horn and waved at someone walking their dog. "I know it ain't in the budget, but it will look a heck of a lot better."

"What kind of money are you talking about?" Lincoln was prepared for "extras"; just how much was the big question. He hoped he could answer affirmatively.

"Prob'ly another two grand."

Lincoln breathed a sigh of relief. He had set aside five thousand for unforeseen expenses. "We can do that. I want the place to look good."

"With the new shed, and new planks, it's gonna look brand-spankin' new." He pulled his truck next to Hannah's.

When Lincoln saw the new materials, he realized Charlie was right. Not that he had any doubts, but the contrast between the old, splintered planks and the new ones was considerable. "Good call, Charlie."

Charlie walked Lincoln around the job site and explained the process, what was going where, and the timeline. "If we keep getting good weather, the piers should be done in two weeks. The shed is coming down tomorrow. I got a couple of guys who are going to break it down and toss the pieces into the dumpster."

Lincoln stopped. "I better take a look inside and see if there is anything worth salvaging."

"I already got the gear out—traps, lines, rakes, and all."

"What about the maps?"

"I figure you'd want to check 'em out. See if there was anything you or your sister may wanna keep. Ya know, a keepsake sorta thing."

Lincoln thought Madison might want to use them to decorate the walls of the new shed. She had a knack for repurposing things. "Thanks. I'll take a look."

Crusty appeared out of nowhere, something he was prone to do. "Howdy, boss!" He gave a huge wave.

"Howdy, Crusty. I see you've been hard at work." Lincoln noticed the pile of old wood in the dumpster.

"We're gonna take down the shed, but Charlie here said to wait for you."

"Yes. I appreciate it." Lincoln walked down the dock, which led to the shack. He began to unpin the maps from the fishing line when he noticed something wedged between the wallboards. He took one of the fishing hooks and pried it out. Another map. A very old one. He set it on the crooked table and began to unfold it. It appeared to be a rudimentary drawing of a river bend with markings of trees. He separated it from the others and put it in his back pocket. He'd take a closer look when he got back to Madison's. He rolled the other maps and tied them with a fishing line.

As he went through the remaining items, he realized there

was more that should get a second look. He called over to Charlie. "Do you have a box I can put all this stuff in?"

"Nothin' that don't smell like fish," Charlie scoffed.

Lincoln spotted Hannah waddling toward him with a trash bag. "This here is clean."

"Thanks, Hannah. You always seem to have what everyone needs."

"I try to be prepared for any eventuality."

Lincoln then realized Hannah was more than a nice person who made an awesome clam sandwich. She too was sharp and a lot smarter than she made known. It reminded Lincoln of when he was at Hackley and another student was from Louisiana. He made the mistake of thinking the student was not as smart as the rest of them because he had a drawl. That was the last time Lincoln prejudged someone. Or so he thought. Preconceived notions sometimes lay dormant in our heads. He thought about Madison's original biased views about Smuggler's Cove and recognized how easily it could happen. He made a mental note to watch himself for those tendencies and correct them.

Lincoln proceeded to collect anything that could be deemed personal. "Hey, Charlie? Could you swing by the house before I catch the ferry? I'd rather leave this bag here than drag it to the city just to end up bringing it back."

"Sure thing, boss," Charlie echoed Crusty's salutation.

Boss. Lincoln snickered. He could not recall ever being referred to as *boss. Sir. Professor.* An occasional *Dude.* Never *boss.* "It's my sister that's the boss. At least we pretend she is," he said, and laughed.

The men sat at the picnic table to review the next steps. Much to Lincoln's surprise, Charlie opened a laptop. *See, another misconception?* He silently admonished himself.

"If y'all can send me that spreadsheet, it would make things easier. I'd be able to send you an update via email at the end of each day."

"You should have said something sooner," Lincoln remarked.

"I didn't want you to think I was being too pushy and all, getting into your private papers."

"Heck, no! It was foolish of me not to ask." Lincoln shook his head. He reached into his portfolio and opened his laptop. "What's your email address?"

"Charliesgotclams at gmail-dot-com. We figured it was better than Charlie's got crabs!" he hooted.

Lincoln burst out laughing. "Excellent point." He typed it in and sent Charlie the Excel spreadsheet.

"This is how I keep track of Hannah's business. She's not keen on computers. Says they suck the brains outta people."

"I can understand her point. Question: do you engage in social media?"

"Nah. If anything sucks the brains outta you, it's all of them platforms and apps."

"Madison likes to say that her idea of an app is something you eat before dinner." Lincoln chuckled.

"Ha! Can't say I disagree." Charlie laughed.

They finally wrapped up their business for the day and headed to the house, where Lincoln left the bag of memorabilia. "I think Madison is coming down next weekend."

"I think she's gonna really like it here."

"I think you are right," Lincoln replied.

Charlie brought him back to the ferry landing, and Lincoln boarded the boat. He asked a crew member how long a ten-trip booklet would last.

"Ten trips," was the answer.

"Sorry. I should have asked, does the book expire?"

"Ha! Yeah. But not for a couple months. It says on the back."

"Thanks." Lincoln decided it would make sense if each of them had a book and purchased three. It would save a little money and time, especially if they were "runners" again. He ordered scotch and soda, settled into a booth, and stared at the passing scenery. It was a very civilized means of transportation.

When they reached the Verrazzano-Narrows Bridge, he called Madison to see if she was going to be home. He wanted to show her the map.

"Ooh. Do you think it might be the mysterious treasure map?" Madison said with excitement.

"Don't get too excited. We can take a look at it together." He checked his watch. "I should be at your place within the hour. Is Livvy there?"

"Olivia is on her way. I will order food. Greek?"

"Works for me. See ya."

Olivia, Lincoln, and the food delivery arrived at the same time. Madison brought out dishes, napkins, and flatware, while Olivia put the food in serving platters and bowls. It was one of the house rules. Even if you have food delivered, you eat it in real dishes. Lunch in plastic containers was as uncouth as Madison would allow.

Lincoln filled them in on the progress and how surprised he was about Charlie's level of technology.

Madison chastened him, "I know I have done the same thing. We have truly underestimated those fine people."

"I couldn't agree with you more," Lincoln replied.

"I've been thinking about this and the recent discussions about nature verses nurture."

"My money is on Mom as far as our values are concerned. And let's not forget about Jackson."

"I would rather forget about him altogether." Madison frowned.

"What I am trying to say is, perhaps we got some preconceived ideas from him. He was always touting how we are better than other people. Richer. Smarter. It had to have an impact in some way," Lincoln noted.

"You make a good point. For him, it was about more—but not necessarily more tolerance, more patience, more compassion," Madison stated.

"I will take kindness over refinement. Just think about those stuffy neighbors we had on Sutton place," Lincoln contemplated.

"Their refinement was a mask for their narrow-mindedness," Olivia chimed in. "I could see it in their eyes when I would visit. I didn't look like any of them."

"You are far too beautiful to be a tight-lipped grump." Lincoln put his arm around Olivia and gave her a kiss.

"All these years, you never said anything," Madison scowled.

"I didn't have to. You didn't treat me any differently. Neither did your mother. And that was all that mattered."

"What about me?" Lincoln pulled back.

"I love you, too." She returned the kiss on the cheek.

"Okay. What's next?" Olivia asked, knowing she would be in charge of making most of the arrangements.

"We are going to need a car down there," Lincoln said, as he polished off the last piece of spanakopita.

"Should we rent one for the summer? We are going to need an SUV. Food. Supplies. Beach gear," Madison said.

"I'll look into it," Olivia offered.

"I probably have several thousand credit-card points. See if we can use them. I know I am not planning on going anywhere any time soon. Because she is the senior fashion editor, I already told Liz she will be going to Milan and Paris this fall."

"She must be thrilled. But aren't you going to miss it?" Lincoln asked.

"Not one day of it. She is young and ambitious. Let her get pursued by models, writers, stylists, and designers."

Lincoln looked at his sister with surprise. "Are you sure you are okay?"

"Could not be better." Madison smiled with a devilish grin.

After dinner, they cleared the table and sat in the living room for a nightcap.

Madison poured everyone a glass of port and asked, "So what about that map?"

"I completely forgot," Lincoln said, and reached into the back pocket of his jeans. He carefully unfolded it and laid it on the coffee table.

"It looks like a kid's drawing," Olivia said, squinting.

"Certainly not official," Madison added.

Olivia took out her laptop and opened a maps site. She typed in *Smuggler's Cove on the Navesink*. "Wow. Check it out." She turned the laptop so Lincoln and Madison could see it.

"They look similar, except is a rudimentary version," Olivia added.

Lincoln traced the line from Smuggler's Cove to the Rahway River. Madison quickly looked up Captain William Kidd. "It says that he was a privateer but was eventually considered a pirate and was hanged for murder in London." She continued to read. "Legend says that he buried his treasure somewhere along the riverbanks of the Rahway, across from Arthur Kill in Staten Island or along the shores of Long Island."

"Do you supposed this was the map Mr. Farrell was looking for?" Olivia asked.

"According to Detective Burton, when he questioned Farrell's associates, they made reference to a map."

"Wow. And this could be the cause of Farrell's demise," Madison said thoughtfully.

"Could very well be, but I am sure there are dozens of legends about a secret treasure map, Captain Kidd, and his band of privateers or pirates, depending on who you ask."

"We should have it framed and put it in the new shed," Madison suggested.

"I had a feeling you might say something like that. There are a bunch of maps at the house. The ones that were hanging on the fishing line. I figured you would want to take a look and repurpose them."

"Ah, you know me well, my brother." She patted him on the back.

"I'll take this to the framer next week," Olivia offered. Lincoln folded it and handed it to her.

"Floating plexiglass," Madison said. "No frame."

"Got it," Olivia replied.

It was after eight, and they decided to call it a day. Madison trusted she would finally get a good night's sleep. But to be sure, she took a long hot shower and popped two ashwagandha gummies into her mouth, a native and ancient remedy for relaxation. By the time she dried her short bob, she was yawning and ready for bed.

The following weekend, Irene met them at the ferry. She dropped Lincoln at the marina and then took Madison and Olivia to a car-rental agency, where a red Jeep Grand Cherokee was waiting. Irene handed Olivia a list of stores and their locations.

"I made sure there was GPS in the vehicle," Olivia said.

"There's a Target about twenty minutes from here. And if you haven't been to a Total Wine, you are in for a treat. It's Disney for grown-ups," Irene cackled. "Then you can hit Uncle Giuseppe's afterwards. That, too, is an amusement park for foodies."

Madison gave Irene a hug. "You have been so helpful. As soon as we are settled, we will have you over for dinner. On the patio, of course."

"That would be swell." Irene had taken a liking to these city slickers. They were very down-to-earth, all things considered. She, too, had done a little digging about their background. Unbeknownst to Lincoln, Madison, and Olivia, everyone in town knew about their background, and their climb from drama and humiliation.

Madison and Olivia spent two hours shopping for towels, linens, toiletries, and household cleaners. The next stop was the liquor store. When they entered, they stopped in their tracks. "Irene was not kidding. And the place is beautifully appointed with the wood shelves. Rows and rows of them." Madison looked around in awe.

"It reminds me of a bookstore, but with booze," Olivia stated.

"This is amazing! Where have I been all this time?"

"Working." Olivia elbowed her, grabbed a shopping cart, and began to peruse the aisles. A middle-aged gentleman wearing a vest and a headset greeted them.

"Welcome to Total Wine. Is this your first visit?"

"How could you tell?" Madison flashed a big smile.

The man chuckled. "The expression on your face. I've seen it before."

"I'm that obvious, eh?" She continued to smile.

"I'm afraid so, Miss. What can I help you with today?"

Olivia gave the man a list of wines, beer, and alcohol.

"Having a party?"

"Eventually. We are stocking up for our summer rental," Madison answered.

"Whereabouts?"

"Smuggler's Cove," Madison answered.

"Nice little town. Be sure you make it to the seafood festival. Best one along the shore."

"We will. They're honoring my uncle this year. He passed away, but he was a local icon." Madison was surprised at how she spoke about her uncle with such authority. And rightly so. She was beginning to understand and appreciate his value to his friends and the community.

It took about an hour for them to fill their cart, and the gentleman helped them load the car. "Where are you off to now?"

"Uncle Giuseppe's," Olivia answered.

"You gals are going to have a ball in there. They play some of my favorite music, too. Frank Sinatra, Dean Martin. Old school." He grinned. "Nice meeting you ladies. Enjoy the rest of your day. Keep in mind, we deliver."

"Thanks. You've been a great help."

Olivia was behind the wheel as Madison turned to look at their packages. "Do you think we can fit anything else in here?"

"I am sure we will do our best!" Olivia grinned, typed in the address, and exited the parking lot.

When they arrived at Uncle Giuseppe's, they had a similar reaction as they had at Total Wine. To one side was a long case filled with prepared food, from chicken marsala to zucchini muffins, eggplant rollatini to stuffed mushrooms. Dozens upon dozens of olives lined the shelves on the opposite side. "I had no idea there were that many types of olives!" Madison declared.

Olivia knew her friend might go overboard purchasing the food. "Let's get only what we need this weekend, as far as produce and meat."

Madison sighed. "You're right. I'll try not to get carried away." She wheeled the cart toward the back of the store. "But we must get a ball of that fresh mozzarella." She watched as a man behind a glass window swirled the cheese in water and then into a ball. Olivia tapped her shoulder. Behind the next window were people making fresh pasta. Across the aisle was someone making fresh pizza, and in front were a dozen baskets of freshly baked bread including focaccia, ciabatta, ciriola, and pane Pugliese.

"Oh, my goodness. I am going to be in a carbohydrate coma," Madison sighed.

They carefully chose a few items for dinner and breakfast, although it was difficult to leave without purchasing several pounds of cheese.

By three o'clock, they were back at the house and putting their supplies in place. "By the way, we never discussed sleeping arrangements," Madison said. "You and Lincoln will have the master bedroom. I hope you already knew that."

Olivia smiled. "I did not make any assumptions."

"Well, there's no need for a discussion. It's yours. Case closed!" Madison declared.

By the time they were finished, Charlie and Lincoln pulled into the driveway. "Hey there! How was your day?" Lincoln gave Olivia an affectionate kiss.

"Very productive," Olivia answered. "We found two fabulous places." Olivia described their experience at the two stores. Olivia knew Lincoln would not be up for playing grill master that night, so they bought some of the prepared food. All they had to do was heat it up, toss a salad, and plate some mozzarella with tomatoes and fresh basil to start.

"Charlie, would you like to have dinner with us?" Madison asked.

"Aw, thanks. I appreciate it, but Saturday nights are for me and Hannah. Unless there is some kind of special thing goin' on."

"Next time, we will invite both of you," Madison offered.

"That's mighty nice of you, but we don't want to intrude," Charlie said modestly.

"Not an intrusion at all," Lincoln voiced his opinion. "Once we get settled, we will have you and Hannah and Crusty over."

"That would be nice. I know Hannah's gotten fond of all of you."

"Likewise," Madison replied. And she meant it. She was finding a lot to like in this little town.

Chapter Eighteen

To Date or Not to Date

Two weeks moved quickly. Closing the book for the Holiday Preview that was to come out in September had taken up much of Madison and Olivia's time. And with the preparations for the summer rental, the renovations, and the festival, there hardly seemed to be enough hours in the day. Madison comforted herself knowing that things would slow down in a matter of days. Speaking of days, it was only two days until her date with Captain Eriksson. She had hardly any time to get nervous about it, but when she saw the day marked with a big star on her daily planner, she realized she hadn't given it enough thought. Now she was in ultra-overdrive. What was she going to wear? The white wardrobe was not going to fly anymore. At least not at the marina. Maybe a pair of white capri pants, but the "Good Humor Ice Cream Man" look was over. She wondered if she should call Viggo and ask him what the dress code was, if there was any at all.

They had only spoken briefly at the beginning of the week, when they decided on a time. He was going to pick her up at six thirty. In his "clean and organized" pickup truck. He apologized profusely for not having a "proper vehicle," but he had originally purchased it for when he was working on his house. Since the renovations had been completed, he hadn't given much thought to his mode of transportation. He usually rode his bike to work, unless the weather was wet and windy. Madison assured him a ride in a pickup truck was acceptable, and she would wear a disguise. He chuckled at her sense of humor. With that in mind, Madison searched a costume store for a pair of black-rimmed glasses with a big nose and mustache. That would be a true test of *his* sense of humor, and would certainly break the ice, if there were any to be broken.

She decided to phone and ask him what to wear. It was time she got over her insecurities and put on her big-girl pants, white or otherwise.

He answered on the second ring. "Ms. Wainwright." He couldn't resist calling her by her proper name. "To what do I owe the pleasure?"

"Captain Eriksson." Madison grinned. "I was wondering if you could advise me as to the attire required for dinner on Saturday."

"According to my information, you are the fashion expert."

"That might be true, but I want to dress appropriately. I take it, it's not a gala, so I can ditch the sequins and high heels."

He laughed out loud. "You would be correct. I was planning on One Willow. They have their dining deck open now, and the weather forecast is mild."

"I am familiar with the place. Olivia and I had lunch there on our first visit."

"And I was hoping to take you somewhere special."

Madison stopped herself from saying *Anywhere with you*

would be special. Instead, she replied, "The setting is beautiful, the food was excellent, and I am happy to return."

"Great. Chef Nick always has something interesting on the menu."

"I am looking forward to it. See you at six thirty." She ended the call before the conversation would continue to awkward silence.

She called out to Olivia, "Wardrobe check."

Olivia trotted into Madison's office with a pad and pen. "Which edition?"

"Mine. Saturday night." Madison was blushing.

"How about white silk pants and that gorgeous turquoise tunic that you've never worn?"

Madison snapped her fingers. "You are right! I must have bought that two years ago, and it's been hanging in my closet waiting for an opportunity."

"I think that might have been *you* waiting for the opportunity."

"Very funny. But you know what I mean. That will be perfect. And shoes?"

"You have those beautiful Dolce Vita silver ballerina flats."

"Perfect! What would I do without you?"

"Run buck naked?" Olivia chuckled.

"Not so fast, my friend." Madison gave her a devilish grin.

"Aren't we being cheeky?" Olivia returned the expression.

"Back to work." Madison playfully shooed Olivia from her office.

Later that evening, Madison decided it was time to tell her brother about her dinner plans with Viggo. It had been excruciating to keep it from him, but she wanted to be absolutely certain that it was going to happen before she subjected herself to his ribbing.

"Linc, I have something to tell you," Madison began her confession.

"About your date? Or that you ate a loaf of bread when you were at the house last week?"

"Date?" Madison asked with suspicion.

"Maddie. Madison Wainwright. Have you not learned you cannot keep a secret from your brother?"

"But how?" Madison was at a loss for words.

"Your mood, for one thing, and the star on the wall calendar in your kitchen pantry."

"That could mean anything," Madison said with confidence.

"Yes, but it means only one thing, considering you will be in Smuggler's Cove on Saturday."

"Okay, okay, you got me."

"You could have said something."

"I suppose, but I wasn't sure if it was really going to happen."

"Why?"

"Because of my crummy track record."

"For someone who is always harping about looking ahead and not behind, you are such a hypocrite."

"I never said that *I* should do what I say." Madison laughed.

"You got me there. Well, I hope you will have a good time."

"That makes two of us."

"Make that four of us."

"Four?"

"You, me, Livvy, and Viggo. We are all going to have to suffer the consequences if you don't have a good time."

"And this is why I did not mention it." Madison would have stuck her tongue out if she were in the same room with him.

"Seriously, I really hope you have fun. You deserve it,

Maddie. You have been working hard and have had a spate of ne'er-do-wells. It is time for you to enjoy the company of a man, who, in my humble opinion, appears to be a decent gent."

"Thank you. I appreciate your input. Besides, Hannah is a big fan of his, too."

"Hannah, eh? You told her before you told your own brother?" Lincoln feigned being insulted.

"It's a girl thing." Madison chuckled. "I have to go. Mario and Luigi are giving me the stink eye. Time for dinner."

"One more thing. I plan to drive down on Saturday morning. Going to leave around seven thirty. Do you want a ride? Or, if you want me to bring anything down there for you, let me know."

"Seven thirty is a tad early for me, but yes, a suitcase of clothes would be swell. I'll leave it with my doorman."

"You got it. See you on Saturday."

"Love you!" Madison said as she signed off.

It was almost eleven, and she was still wide awake. She decided to use the time to pack the clothes she wanted Lincoln to take to the house. It took about an hour, and by then, she was ready for bed. As she pulled the covers over her shoulder, she whispered, "One more night to go."

Mario and Luigi curled up against her and began to purr.

As she drifted off to sleep, she made plans for the rest of the summer. If all went well, she would work remotely three days a week and go into the office on Monday and Tuesday. There was no reason why it wasn't a possibility. They managed during the pandemic; they could manage now.

Friday morning arrived, and Madison was relieved she had slept well. Finally. She glanced over at the open suitcase on the floor and blinked several times. "What are you guys doing?" Mario and Luigi had made a very nice, comfortable bed for themselves on her neatly folded clothing. "Not this weekend, kids, but I am making plans so we can spend most of the summer at the house. Is that alright with you?" Mario yawned and rolled over, signaling it was time for Madison to rub his belly. "And what about you, Luigi? No belly rubs or no summer house?" Luigi stretched and then flopped over. "A-ha. You also want to be in the fresh air?" She scrunched their faces and gave them kisses on the head.

"Marvin will be looking in on you guys this weekend, so you be nice to him." Mario and Luigi were very mellow cats unless there was a sudden loud noise. But most people are bothered by that, as well.

Madison went to her closet and slid past one piece of white clothing, then the next. "This is getting boring." She decided on a pair of white jeans, and a white crewneck sweater with white Mary Janes. "I wonder what people would say if I showed up in a pair of regular jeans and an orange sweater?" She chuckled to herself. "Maybe next week."

She went through her usual morning routine of fixing her first cup of coffee, feeding the cats, showering, and getting dressed.

Olivia greeted her in the office with a cup of coffee. "Ready?"

"As I will ever be. Hey, did you know that Lincoln knew about my date?"

"No, but he was tossing questions at me like, how you were getting on with Captain Eriksson, and why were you in such a great mood lately."

"Why does everyone keep asking me why I am in a great mood lately? Have I been in a not-so-great mood?"

"Perhaps it would be better to say you've been bubbly lately. Effervescent."

"Aren't I always?" Madison pouted.

"Not like this. You're actually quite serious most of the time."

"Huh." Madison pondered. Is that how people saw her?

Had she been going through life looking like she lacked joy? *Did* she lack joy in her life? Madison didn't want to think about it too much, afraid the answer would make her sad, like she had wasted so much of her life.

She shook herself out of her thoughts. "What do we have to do today?" she asked Olivia.

"Planning meeting."

"Ugh. On a Friday?"

"Yes, the publisher wants to put everything on the board so he can take his summer vacation." Olivia rolled her eyes. The publisher got all the credit, made the most money, and was barely visible.

"We, too, shall have our summer soirees," Madison promised.

She called a few members of her staff to come into her office. "We need to put something on the board for next spring's edition."

There were a few groans. Everyone knew it was almost impossible to predict what was going to be in fashion a year from now, which meant they would have to create what would be in fashion.

"Anyone have any ideas?"

"Melon," Victor said. "Cantaloupe. This spring, it was robin's-egg blue. Time to go to the other side of the color spectrum."

"And this is why I love you, Victor. I think that is a fabulous idea," Madison noted.

"What about watermelon?" someone asked.

"Yes! It can be an entire melon theme! I like it!" Madison was energized. "Now we just have to convince the fashion houses to make that their color palate."

"Liz, that will be your task. Start the rumor mill. Leak that Prada is considering mango, and then tell Dior the same thing." Madison grinned. "And everyone will think it is their idea."

Victor clapped. "Genius."

"Meeting is now adjourned. We can figure out the rest next month. Olivia, let Wagner know that we are on it, and he can enjoy his six weeks in Ibiza, or whatever exotic island he is going to be lounging on."

Madison checked her watch, the same Cartier she had been wearing since she graduated from Hackley. The strap was replaced twice, but it still kept perfect time. She noted the meeting took less than a half hour. A record. She already had ideas as to layout and color combos. Madison was known for mixed-media layouts, and she busied herself with giant color swatch books and fabrics. Before she knew it, it was time to go home.

She said her goodnights to Olivia and the few remaining staff. "Have a good weekend, everyone. See you tomorrow, Liv. Are you driving down with Linc or taking the ferry? I'll be on the eleven-something."

"Eleven thirty," Olivia said. "Yes. Me too. Meet you on the dock."

"Cool. See you manana."

"Sleep well. If you can." Olivia winked.

Madison was all atwitter on the ferry ride to Highlands. Olivia kept putting her hand on Madison's bouncing knee. "Easy, girl. You'll create a wake."

"Listen to you and your nautical lingo." Madison grinned.

"You should think about getting used to it." Olivia raised her eyebrows.

"Please stop. I am nervous enough without you and my brother needling me."

"You told Lincoln?" Olivia was surprised. "I thought you were going to wait until Viggo picked you up."

"That was my original thought, but I figured Lincoln would want to know what we were going to do about dinner, etcetera."

"True."

"Which means the two of you will have the house to yourselves. Make a cozy fire in the firepit? A little moonlight?"

"Sounds like a date," Olivia said.

"Aren't Saturday nights known for them?"

"Not recently," Olivia said, smirking. "For either of us."

"If all goes well tonight, perhaps we can change this rut we have gotten ourselves into."

"Good idea. There will be a lot to explore, or simply relax under the stars," Olivia romanticized.

"I do not want to get . . ."

"Ahead of ourselves. One of your famous mottos. You are a contradiction," Olivia noted.

"How so?"

"You are always looking ahead, yet when it comes to certain things, you always say, 'Let's not get ahead of ourselves.'"

"That doesn't mean I'm not looking ahead. I simply do not want to count on anything until I am absolutely sure."

"You are so full of baloney. You are one of the most courageous people I know. You take chances. Big ones, except for romantic situations."

"And that is because I have failed miserably at it, and I am treading carefully. That is not to say I do not have romantic notions about what *could* be. I believe it is called Creative Visualization. Or in my case, cautiously optimistic."

"That's a step in the right direction," Olivia responded.

When they arrived at the landing, Lincoln was waiting for them. The plan was for him to drive them to the house and then go back and work with Charlie and the gang.

"How are things going?" Madison asked.

"Quite well. So far, everything is moving at a good clip. The dock should be finished by next weekend; then the shed is being delivered. I have Josh cleaning up the skiffs."

"I have something to show you when we get to the house."

Madison and Olivia had been secretly designing a new logo that said *Kirby's Marina*, with a clamshell dotting the *i* and a crab claw as the bottom of the *y*. It was quirky enough and appropriate. When they got to the house, she rolled the paper open.

There it was, with the name in bright red on a white background, with clams and crabs as a border. "This is great!" Lincoln shouted. "When did you have time to do it?"

"Let's just say I had a few sleepless nights." Madison turned to her partner behind the scenes. "Glad you like it, because Olivia and I have been working on this together. Livvy ordered a wooden sign, T-shirts, caps, and overalls. They should be arriving mid-week."

"I am totally impressed." Lincoln stared at the new artwork. "And merchandise, too?"

"Go big or go home." Madison chuckled. "I think it's important to have a cohesive appearance, even if people are not used to it."

"This is great. I am certain everyone is going to appreciate it, especially Crusty. I think he has three T-shirts to his name."

"Now he'll have a Kirby's wardrobe," Olivia said. "Hey, what about Crocs?"

"Great idea!" Madison said with great enthusiasm. "We probably don't have time to get them with logos, but let's get a bunch of pairs in red."

"Not hot pink?" Olivia teased. "I'll see if Target has them tomorrow."

Lincoln was in a fine mood. "I do not want to jinx it, so I will not say anything."

"Jinx? Don't be silly. Mr. Jinx has seen me through every trial and tribulation."

"True. And things are moving along well. There. I said it."

"Good. Now go back to work." Olivia patted him on the

tush. "I am going to pick up some steaks for you to grill later."

"Don't you have a date?" He turned to Madison.

"Yes, and so do you. With your wife."

Lincoln looked a bit perplexed; then it dawned on him. "Oh. Good. Right. We will have the house to ourselves." He rubbed his hands together and raised his eyebrows at Olivia.

"Get. Back. To. Work," Olivia said again.

Most of the afternoon was about putting things away and getting the place organized. At four o'clock, Madison took a look around and surveyed their progress. "I think things are starting to come together," Madison said. "And I'd better start to get *myself* together." She went to the bedroom on the far end of the hallway.

By six she was ready. She went down to the lower level, where Olivia was preparing a salad.

"Well, hello, gorgeous!" Olivia dropped the salad tongs into the bowl. "Let me take a look at you."

Madison did a little twirl. She was grinning from east to west. "I am so glad you suggested this tunic. I feel glamorous but not glitzy. Comfortable but not slack."

"He is going to fall over when he sees you." Olivia nodded with approval.

Lincoln walked in from the patio. "Wow, sis. You look spectacular."

"Thank you." She put her hands in prayer position and bowed slightly. The sound of a truck on the gravel made her stomach flutter. "Yikes," she said in a stage whisper.

A minute later, there was a knock on the door. Madison took a deep breath, slowly climbed the stairs to the main level, and opened the door. She was momentarily speechless. He was wearing a crisp white shirt, steel gray blazer, dark jeans, and loafers, and boy, did he look good.

"You look lovely," Viggo said, staring directly into her eyes.

"And you look rather handsome yourself." She pulled the door open wide. "Please, come in. Lincoln and Olivia are downstairs."

Madison proceeded to the lower level, and Viggo followed. "I've been here once before. This is a great house."

"We were very lucky to find it," Madison said over her shoulder.

Olivia wiped her hands on a towel and handed it to Lincoln to do the same. "Nice to see you, Viggo." Lincoln extended his now clean hand.

"Yes, good to see you," Olivia followed suit.

"Where are you off to?" Lincoln asked.

"One Willow. Have you been there?"

"No, but I hear good things. These two have been, though."

"Yes, I heard. Speaking of which, we should probably get going. Good to see you both," Viggo said.

"If it's not too late, maybe we can have a nightcap later," Lincoln offered.

"Thanks," Viggo replied, without fully committing. "See you later."

Viggo opened the passenger door for Madison and held his hand to give her a lift. She graciously accepted. It was hard these days when it came to chivalry. Some people thought it was dead, and others thought it was still polite. Some women wanted to open their own doors, but if someone was offering, why not? Let them enjoy doing something nice for someone.

Viggo apologized again for the vehicle. "It was either this or riding on the handlebars of my bicycle."

Madison cackled, "That would be some sight! This is fine, really. And it is clean, as you promised."

"Diogo, my dog, likes to take rides. I hope I got all of his hair off the seat."

Madison chuckled. "I have two cats. I don't wear fur unless it's theirs and on my clothes."

"How do you feel about dog hair?"

"I love animals, hair and all."

Viggo was beginning to like this person more than he expected.

Madison shuffled through her purse and bent down. When she lifted her head, she was wearing the goofy glasses and nonchalantly asked, "How long have you lived here?"

Viggo almost went off the road in hysterics. "Didn't see that coming!" His face hurt from laughing.

"Do I amuse you?" Again, she was stoic.

Viggo chuckled. "So far, yes." He also smiled to himself. He was smitten.

When they arrived at the restaurant, Viggo hurried to Madison's side of the truck and helped her out. "Do you need those to read the menu?" he joked.

Madison grinned and removed them. "If I have a problem, you can help."

Viggo could not wipe the smile from his face.

Jason greeted them when they entered the restaurant.

"Viggo, good to see you, my man." Jason patted him on the back. "And, Madison, right?"

"Yes, good memory." They shook hands.

"Nice to see you again. Did you get to the marina you were referring to?"

"Yes. My Uncle Kirby's."

"I heard someone was giving it a makeover."

"Yes, that would be us. We decided to refurbish it and get another season out of it."

"I can tell you, there are a lot of happy people in town. They first heard some highfalutin' folks from up North were taking over, but those rumors got crushed quickly. Glad it's you."

"We are happy to be involved," Madison said modestly.

"Booth or table?" Jason asked.

Viggo looked at Madison. "Which do you prefer?"

"Booth, thank you." She felt it was more intimate, and better for conversation, especially when you are learning about someone for the first time.

Once they were settled and the waiter had taken their drink order, they began to chat. Madison asked him about wharfs, piers, docks, and jetties. He pulled out a small pad and pen from his inside pocket. "I thought you might ask, and decided this would be the best way to describe them."

Madison was charmed by his conscious effort to entertain or enlighten her. To her, it didn't matter. Both were acceptable.

Viggo began to draw what was supposed to be a body of water and then proceeded to draw and explain each term. Madison listened intently, but if you quizzed her later, she would have drawn a blank. She was absorbed. Enchanted.

They each ordered oysters, and the scallop special with polenta and mushrooms. Madison thought the cuisine was as good as many New York restaurants. The wine list was also impressive but not pretentious. For her, it was the best of both worlds.

They chatted about their childhoods, and Madison treaded lightly. As far as her family, she mentioned her parents were "separated" and she spent a lot of time at her grandparents. She wasn't aware that Viggo knew about her father, and he was good enough to steer clear of it. He let her tell him what she wanted to tell him without pressing her for details.

Madison was comfortable with their conversation. She was straightforward with all of it except for her father's sordid past. And it was the past. Done. Over. Everyone had moved on.

Neither Viggo nor Madison was in a hurry, and they decided to share a dessert: a warmed date cake with vanilla gelato. It wasn't until they were halfway through dessert that Madison realized they were dipping their spoons into the same soft mound of sweetness and cream. Anyone would think it was an intimate gesture—unless you were with your girlfriends, and then anything goes. But with a man? On a first date? Was that suggestive or familiar? Madison decided it didn't matter. It felt natural.

They were so engrossed in conversation that they didn't notice they were the last patrons in the restaurant. Viggo finally realized the waitstaff had started to leave. "I think we are keeping these people from going home, or out for fun."

Madison gasped slightly. "How embarrassing."

"Not really. It shows you are enjoying the evening. At least I hope that's the reason we have kept these fine folks past their shift."

"I *am* enjoying this evening." Madison smiled affectionately.

Viggo gave Jason extra cash to spread to the patiently waiting staff, apologized profusely, and said goodnight.

As they walked back to the truck, Madison noticed how clear the sky was, with a sliver of the moon and the city skyline in the background. "Glorious night."

"It is. Have you spent any nights here yet?"

"No. This is my first."

"Wait until you get a look at the view from the house. It is spectacular."

"I'm looking forward to it." Madison sighed. *Should she invite him in for a nightcap? Tea? Coffee?* She decided to decide when they got to the house. If Olivia and Lincoln were still up, she might invite him in or not. She allowed the next few minutes to float by as she enjoyed her feelings of elation.

When they arrived at the house, Madison noticed the lights were still on and decided to invite Viggo in. It was safer that way. Not that she didn't trust *him*. She didn't trust herself, feeling clumsy and awkward. Madison couldn't remember the last time she was with a man and felt the way she felt that night—all goofy and giddy.

Viggo agreed to join her for an evening cup of tea. Olivia and Lincoln were sitting on the patio in front of the firepit. The air was cool enough to warrant the warmth, but not cold enough to shiver. A cashmere throw made it quite comfy.

"This looks inviting." Madison said, "And the view! Wow. This is spectacular."

Lincoln sat up. "Hey. Join us."

"I shall put on a pot of tea. Be right back." Madison went into the kitchen, and Viggo pulled two chaise lounges closer to where Lincoln and Olivia were reclining.

"How was dinner?" Olivia asked with a sleepy yawn.

"Delightful. Madison is quite an interesting woman."

"Yes, she is," Lincoln said. "I am sure you, too, have interesting things to tell."

"Me? Not really."

"I doubt that, but I am not going to pry," Olivia said with a smile, before excusing herself to give Madison a hand, but really to get the skinny from her sister-in-law.

Olivia sidled up to Madison, who was arranging herbal tea bags on a tray with cups, saucers, cream, sugar, and lemon. "And?"

"And it was wonderful. Such an interesting man. Kind. Accomplished. Modest. Loves animals."

"So far, so good." Olivia leaned against the counter.

"Yes. I would like to see him again, but I don't want to seem pushy. You know, as in how I can be pushy, according to my brother."

"Tell him you had a wonderful time. See how he reacts. If he says he would like to do it again, tell him you'll cook dinner. If he says nothing, then let it go."

"Good advice."

"That's what you pay me for." Olivia gave her a wink.

Madison and Olivia brought the teapot and accessories out to the patio. Madison set the tray on a large cocktail table, and everyone fixed their own. An hour later, Lincoln and Olivia said their goodnights, and Viggo acknowledged it was time for him to go, as well.

Madison walked him to his truck. "Thank you for an exceptional evening, and the tutorial on jetties, wharfs, piers, and docks."

"Thank you for joining me, and you are a very good student."

Madison didn't wait for any encouragement. Might as well jump. "I would like to see you again. Perhaps dinner on the patio?"

"I would like that very much," Viggo said. He gently lifted her wrist and kissed the back of her hand.

Madison thought she might faint. "I'll be here every weekend preparing for the opening. Good night." She turned and walked into the house without looking back, but she knew he was watching her glide effortlessly to the door.

Madison was up early the next morning. She brought her coffee to the patio and wrapped herself in a throw. She recounted every minute of the evening before, from when he knocked on the door to the kiss on the back of her hand. If she had to give it a grade, it would be an A+. Now if only she could keep herself from second-guessing herself. How long should she wait to invite him to dinner? One week? Two weeks? She would seek counsel from her brother. Yes, her brother. She wanted a man's opinion. Not that Olivia's didn't matter, but Madison didn't want to make any stupid mistakes.

She gazed out at the crystal-clear water in the distance and noticed kitesurfers gliding on the bay. For her, it was too early and too chilly for such a sport, but she enjoyed watching the colorful sails drift and bob. She could get used to mornings like this. Relaxed. Quiet.

The silence was broken by Olivia making her way outside.

"Good morning! And how are you this lovely day?"

"I could not be better." Madison shielded her eyes from the morning sun.

"The two of you seemed to hit if off rather well."

"I think it was the funny glasses."

"That had to be a great icebreaker."

"It was. I thought he was going to drive off the road." Madison chuckled.

"So? What's next?"

"I suggested coming here for dinner."

"Oh, goody. When?" Olivia was thrilled with the prospect of Madison having a companion.

Madison shrugged. "Eh, you know my slogan."

"Oh, baloney."

"I think I am going to ask my brother for advice."

"Seriously? You are going to ask Lincoln? That ought to throw him."

"Throw who?" Lincoln's voice came up from behind.

"You, dear brother."

"What do you have up your fashionable sleeve now?"

"I need some advice."

"Wait. Hold on. You are asking me for advice? This must be serious."

"It is. I am getting too old to keep making man-mistakes. Here's the situation. Viggo and I had a wonderful time last night. I think I speak for both of us. I suggested I would cook dinner for him."

"Now that's a laugh. You don't know how to cook!" Lincoln cackled.

"Aside from the obvious, how long should I wait to invite him?"

"Wait a week, and then invite him for the following week."

"Should I text him a thank-you?"

"Of course, but an invitation doesn't have to be included. Give it a little space. Keep some of the mystery."

Olivia nodded in agreement.

Lincoln added, "Another idea is to have a small dinner party and invite him. We can include Irene, her husband, Hannah, Charlie, Crusty, Detective Burton and his wife Nancy, and the mayor and her wife."

"Done!" Madison sat up. "See, I knew you were good for something." She grinned.

"Glad to be of service." Lincoln sat in one of the lounge chairs and looked out at the view. "I could get used to this."

"I just said the same thing a few minutes ago." Madison's thoughts were clicking. If this summer went well, maybe she would approach the owners to buy it. *Let's not get ahead of ourselves.*

They spent the next hour discussing the calendar of events. A ribbon-cutting ceremony in the morning would kick off the festival. Two days of seafood, music, crafts, and then the award ceremony. Madison and Lincoln would say a few words and accept the plaque, which would eventually hang in the community center.

Madison sent off a quick thank-you text to Viggo and mentioned a dinner party. "Details to come."

He responded with, "My pleasure. Affirmative."

Now she had to round up the rest of the invitees and find a caterer. She didn't want to saddle Olivia with cooking, and Lincoln would be tired from working all day. She phoned Irene, who was thrilled to be of service again and gave Madison information about Dearborn Farms and Market. She made an appointment with the catering department for later that morning. The next thing on the agenda was to find a date on the calendar. Time was passing quickly. Olivia suggested the weekend after Mother's Day. That would give them four weeks to plan, and it wouldn't interfere with a holiday and the festival.

Madison worked up an evite and sent a text to everyone:

Please Join Us
for
Dinner on the Patio
May 18th
Half past six
29 Portland Road
The Wainwright Family

Chapter Nineteen

Parties and Festivals

In less than twenty-four hours, everyone had RSVPed except for Viggo. Madison sat at her desk. She was deflated. Maybe he was out of town? Maybe he had plans? Then later that evening, he phoned instead. He apologized for not getting back to her sooner, but he was having trouble with his phone. He asked if there was anything he could bring. Madison hadn't planned to bring Mario and Luigi until after the opening, so she suggested he bring Diogo. "Does he have good table manners?"

Viggo laughed. "Better than mine."

"Perfect. If you'd like, he is certainly welcome."

"Thank you. I'll check to see if he's available."

"Is he vegan or have any food allergies?" she asked coyly.

"None that I am aware of," Viggo said, as if he had been asked that question many times before.

Madison appreciated Viggo's sense of humor, and apparently, he appreciated hers. There was an easiness between the two of them that she found refreshing.

They ended the call with "talk soon." Yes, it was *very* easy. Her shoulders finally relaxed. Madison hadn't realized how uptight she was before the phone call. She stretched her neck and looked down at Mario and Luigi, patiently waiting for their dinner. She explained about the dinner party and how she was concerned about whether or not Viggo would attend. The cats stared and blinked. Madison could have sworn Mario looked up at the clock. Had he been wearing a watch, he would have tapped it with one of his paws. "Okay. Okay. You guys are so pushy." Then she laughed at herself. "Do you think Viggo talks to his dog the way I talk to you?"

Mario gave her a *get busy* look, and then rubbed his head against her leg.

The weekends that followed were jam-packed with meetings. Lincoln was meeting with the suppliers and his crew, and Madison and Olivia were meeting with the festival committee. Madison was very aware that the local townsfolk were still a little leery of them, and she held her tongue as much as possible. When she wanted to present an idea, she would use her tried-and-true technique and ask their opinion first. She won most of the time. For example, getting local radio stations to promote the event as a public service announcement due to the money raised for families of victims. It had never occurred to any of them to try that tactic, and it worked. They even got one of the stations to agree to broadcast live from the festival.

They hadn't made any other friends aside from their little group, but that was fine with Madison. Her only agenda was to honor her uncle and have a special dedication and ribbon-cutting ceremony. To that extent, she got no pushback.

The weekend of the dinner party had arrived, and the house was buzzing. Even though it was a small party of twelve, Madison wanted it to be exceptional. She especially wanted to impress Viggo with her hostess talents.

A few days before the party, Madison combed through her wardrobe in her apartment to find the perfect outfit. With all the commotion, comings and goings, and planning, she hadn't given it much thought. The only dinner-party attire she had was white. She picked a white silk pantsuit. It was elegant enough, yet simple enough for the occasion. She took a few days off from work and arrived at the house on Wednesday, just in case anything needed emergency attention. But thanks to Olivia and Irene, everything was going according to plan.

On the morning of the party, the skies were threatening to rain. Madison paced the floor of the kitchen area. "What's Plan B?" she asked Olivia.

"The same as Plan A. I ordered tents to put under the balcony, so we can still be seated outside."

Madison hugged her sister-in-law. "You are amazing."

"I learned from one of the best." Olivia returned the hug.

The caterers arrived around four and began to set up the bar and the long dinner table, complete with linens. They hung string lights along the underside of the upper balcony, set the table with several floral arrangements of white peonies, and scattered tea lights in front of each place setting.

When Madison stepped outside, she was awestruck. "It's gorgeous, like a fairy wonderland."

"And when it gets dark, the city lights will be a fabulous backdrop," Olivia added.

Before she went upstairs to get ready, she chose the music for the evening: bossa nova and soft samba. Madison crossed her fingers and hoped everything would go according to plan. Or better.

By six o'clock, everyone in the house was ready. Lincoln wore a light blue shirt, blazer, and jeans. Olivia had a colorful maxi dress, and Madison floated down the stairs on her white cloud. It was a handsome trio.

The first guests to arrive were Irene and her husband Alan. Lincoln escorted them to the bar, and a server mixed their drinks. Madison didn't want any of them to have to work. It was important to spend quality time with their guests. That was one thing she learned from her mother. Two servers were also on board, leaving the three of them to mix and mingle. It was their first social interaction, and they wanted their guests to feel appreciated. Without them, none of it would have been possible.

Hannah and Charlie were next, along with Crusty. Madison was touched by the effort Crusty made to look respectable. He had gone to the Goodwill store and found a dinner jacket from who knows when, but the brocade collar screamed 1960. Hannah wore a light-blue pantsuit, and Charlie was donned in a plaid jacket.

Burton and his wife were nicely attired, as well. Madison got the impression that everyone was treating the evening with the same regard. It was special.

Viggo was the last to arrive. When Madison opened the door, a very large dog wearing a bowtie had a bouquet of peonies in his mouth. Madison's heart melted. She bent over and thanked the dog. "Aw. This is so sweet. Diogo, it is very nice to meet you." She held out her hand, and he gave her his paw. She gently took the flowers, and without missing a beat, she kissed Viggo on the cheek. It felt good. Easy. Natural. His navy-blue blazer accentuated his deep eyes, as they gazed upon Madison.

"You look beautiful."

"So do you." She turned to Diogo. "As do you. Please come in!" She stood aside as the two well-dressed males entered.

The dinner menu was a choice of pepper-crusted steak or charred tuna. Sides included string beans almondine, twice-baked potatoes or rice, and roasted carrots. A salad of mixed greens and beets was served first.

Crusty sat with his mouth agape. He had never experienced such special treatment. When the servers poured the wine, he cleared his throat. "If nobody minds, I'd like to say something."

It came as a surprise, and Lincoln encouraged him.

"I want to thank our host and hostesses for this special dinner. When Kirby passed, rest his soul, none of us had no idea what was gonna happen. Me, Charlie, and Hannah worried for months. Then when you all arrived, we got even more worried." A few chuckles went around the table. "But when we seen how much you went out of your way to make the place better, we were thrilled. So, I want to offer my thanks for saving the Taylor Marina, for all our sakes."

Charlie stood up next. "I can ditto Crusty. You are some of the finest folks we ever met. But then again, you were related to Kirby."

Hannah raised her glass. "Here's to a ton of clam sandwiches!"

Lincoln was next. "On behalf of my sister, my wife, and myself, our appreciation runs deep. We could never have done any of this without you."

Madison chimed in. "Thank you for your kindness. It has meant the world to us."

Glasses clinked, and the air was filled with laughter.

Dinner and wine continued to be served for the next two hours. When it came time for dessert, Madison asked Viggo if he would give her a hand. He was happy to accommodate her. They went into the craft room, and Viggo carried out a large box. He set it on a table where Lincoln was standing.

Madison opened the box. "I would like to present everyone with our official Kirby's Marina merchandise." Hoots and applause went around the table as Madison handed everyone a cap, T-shirt, and overalls.

"Now you can get rid of that Grateful Dead T-shirt," Hannah teased Crusty.

"Not in your life. That thing's gotta be worth some money."

"Not after you've been wearing it," Charlie joked.

The evening began to wind down, with everyone satisfied and happy. Madison, Olivia, and Lincoln walked their guests out while Viggo and Diogo lingered.

The staff made haste clearing the table and removing any remains of a fine dinner party.

"Care for a nightcap?" Lincoln asked.

"I would love one," Madison replied. "Viggo, what can we get for you?"

"Brandy?"

"Coming right up." Lincoln went into the kitchen and squared up with the staff. He poured everyone a snifter, and they returned to the patio with Diogo in tow.

They sat in silence for several minutes, soaking up the atmosphere. Viggo was the first to speak. "You are wonderful hosts. This was an exceptional evening. I am certain everyone will be talking about it for weeks to come." He raised his glass.

"Thank you. I am very happy we were able to do it, and that you and Diogo were able to attend." After a few minutes, Lincoln gave Olivia a look that said, *Let's leave these two alone.* They got up and bid everyone a good night.

Again, silence. But it was a comfortable silence. Viggo took Madison's hand. "You've been a bright light in my otherwise boring life." Diogo *woof*ed in agreement. "I hope we can see each other again. Maybe without a crowd?"

"I would love that."

More silence, and then a heavy sigh from Madison.

"I should let you get some sleep. You have had one very busy day." Viggo got up from his seat.

"I suppose you're right." Madison slipped her arm through the crook of his elbow as they walked up to the front door. "I am really happy you came tonight."

"Me too." He pecked her on the cheek and opened the truck door for Diogo. "Sweet dreams." He smiled at the stunning woman in the doorway.

She watched him pull out of the driveway. "Sweet dreams, for sure."

The miles of traffic heading to the beaches signaled the official start of the summer. It was Thursday, and people were coming in droves. Burton and his crew had their hands full rerouting vehicles around the town square. As much as the people in town enjoyed the revenue from the festival, it was fraught with logistical nightmares. Food trucks, amusement rides, vendors, and the like, had to drop off their booths and wares, and then move their vehicles down to a parking lot assigned to them. Viggo was already contemplating the number of calls he was going to receive regarding bozos on the waterways. He made sure his shift was covered so he could attend the ribbon-cutting ceremony Friday morning, and the award on Saturday night. He would have to be in and out, but such was the nature of his job. He'd take an hour for each event and then go back to work. He knew Madison wouldn't mind him showing up in his uniform. Even though they hadn't seen each other in a few weeks, they kept in touch over the phone, checking in every few days, updating each other on the impending activities.

Madison knew Viggo would be less available during the season, but she planned to spend more time at the house, making herself flexible to his schedule. She supposed she was being presumptuous, but she had a good feeling about it. For a change.

Over a hundred people showed up for the ribbon cutting, including an officially dressed Captain Eriksson. Madison, Lincoln, and Olivia were stunned at the size of the crowd. The mayor, town council, and Detective Burton stood together on one side. Hannah, Charlie, and Crusty stood on the other, proudly wearing their Kirby merch.

The mayor said a few words of praise and then handed the microphone to Lincoln.

"When we first heard of Uncle Kirby's passing and leaving his legacy in our hands, we weren't sure what to do. Neither my sister nor I know a darn thing about marinas. Charlie can attest to that." He paused for the chuckles. "Most people would have balked at taking on a challenge like this, but not Charlie or Crusty, or any of the fine folks who lent a hand. To all of you, you have our deepest appreciation."

Madison was next. "I shall never forget my first visit here. I was wearing the most inappropriate outfit. My high heels—yes, I was wearing them—got caught in between the planks, and I made the most ungraceful face-plant on to the dock." More chuckles. "As you can imagine, I was covered in bait and a few clamshells. But thanks to Hannah, she rescued me with some fresh clothes so I could go home and not smell like a bucket of chum." Again, chuckles. "Thank you, Hannah, for your kindness, and thanks to all of you for making this day possible." Madison's eyes began to well up with tears. She took a deep breath. "As most of you may have guessed, we changed the name, and we now dub thee, Kirby's Marina." She and Lincoln took the giant scissors and cut the ribbon that was fastened between two pilings. Applause and cheers filled the air. Lincoln took the microphone. "I believe there is a festival you should be attending." More cheers, and the crowd began to disperse.

Viggo made his way over to where they were standing. He shook Lincoln's hand and kissed Madison on the cheek. "Congratulations."

Madison spotted Hannah wiping tears from her face and giving Madison a thumbs-up.

The following night was the award ceremony, which was

met with the same enthusiasm and applause. Madison was proud of what they were able to accomplish, and again welled up with tears. She spotted Detective Burton approaching her. He had a serious look on his face.

"I have some bad news," he addressed the three of them.

"What is it?" Madison asked with great concern.

"The shed was robbed," Burton announced.

"Robbed?" Lincoln looked incredulous. "What on earth could they take?"

"The map," Burton replied.

Epilogue

When people heard of the burglary, they knew it had to be Farrell's bunch. The trick was trying to prove it, and then trying to retrieve the map. Madison, Lincoln, and Olivia promised themselves that they would do all they could to get it back. Even if it meant spending more time at Smuggler's Cove. *Especially* if it meant spending more time at Smuggler's Cove.

Look for the new novel in Fern Michaels's #1 bestselling
The Sisterhood series . . .

Code Blue

The Sisterhood: a group of women from all walks of life, bound by friendship and years of adventure. Armed with vast resources, top-notch expertise, and a loyal network of allies around the globe, the Sisterhood will not rest until every wrong is made right.

Theresa Gallagher has never met her Aunt Dottie, though she remembers her mother's stories about the wild sister who left home at seventeen and moved out west. When a letter arrives from one of Dottie's neighbors telling Theresa that her aunt is now incapacitated and in a nursing home, Theresa decides to fly out to Arizona to see her. After all, family is family.

The staff at the Sunnydale Care Facility seem pleasant and efficient, but Theresa finds it strange that she's only permitted to "observe" her elderly aunt from a viewing room. It's the first of several red flags that lead Theresa to start asking questions. Is it just coincidence that as soon as she does, her car is almost run off the road?

Theresa contacts her attorney friend, Lizzy Fox, who just happens to be connected to a group of women uniquely poised to get answers. Soon the Sisterhood is on the case, uncovering evidence suggesting that behind Sunnydale's compassionate image hides a greedy, cruel enterprise. At Sunnydale centers all over the country, seniors are mistreated, duped, and drained of their savings. And with powerful political figures at the helm, staying one step ahead of legislation and investigation, it seems like the perfect scam.

But no one is beyond justice—not when the Sisterhood's extraordinary women are involved, making wrongs right as only they can . . .

Look for the new novel in Fern Michaels's #1 bestselling The Sisterhood series . . .

Code Blue

The Sisterhood: a group of women from all walks of life, bound by friendship and years of adventure. Armed with vast resources, top-notch expertise, and a loyal network of allies around the globe, the Sisterhood will not rest until every wrong is made right.

Theresa Gallagher has never met her Aunt Dottie, though she remembers her mother's stories about the wild sister who left home at seventeen and moved out west. When a letter arrives from one of Dottie's neighbors telling Theresa that her aunt is now incapacitated and in a nursing home, Theresa decides to fly out to Arizona to see her. After all, family is family.

The staff at the Sunnydale Care Facility seem pleasant and efficient, but Theresa finds it strange that she's only permitted to "observe" her elderly aunt from a viewing room. It's the first of several red flags that lead Theresa to start asking questions. Is it just coincidence that as soon as she does, her car is almost run off the road?

Theresa contacts her attorney friend, Lizzy Fox, who just happens to be connected to a group of women uniquely poised to get answers. Soon the Sisterhood is on the case, uncovering evidence suggesting that behind Sunnydale's compassionate image hides a greedy, cruel enterprise. At Sunnydale centers all over the country, seniors are mistreated, duped, and drained of their savings. And with powerful political figures at the helm, staying one step ahead of legislation and investigation, it seems like the perfect scam.

But no one is beyond justice—not when the Sisterhood's extraordinary women are involved, making wrongs right as only they can . . .